To my grandmother Rosalie Arcuri,
who believed cooking with love could fix anything

Murder with Cherry Tarts

KAREN ROSE SMITH

KENSINGTON BOOKS
KENSINGTON PUBLISHING CORP.

www.kensingtonbooks.com

KENSINGTON BOOKS are published by

Kensington Publishing Corp.
119 West 40th Street
New York, NY 10018

All Kensington titles, imprints, and distributed lines are
available at special quantity discounts for bulk purchases for
sales promotion, premiums, fund-raising, educational, or
institutional use.

Special book excerpts or customized printings can also be
created to fit specific needs. For details, write or phone the
office of the Kensington Sales Manager: Attn.: Sales Department. Kensington Publishing Corp., 119 West 40th Street,
New York, NY 10018. Phone: 1-800-221-2647.

Kensington and the K logo Reg. U.S. Pat. & TM Off.

First Printing: December 2019
ISBN-13: 978-1-4967-2392-5
ISBN-10: 1-4967-2392-9

ISBN-13: 978-1-4967-2393-2 (eBook)
ISBN-10: 1-4967-2393-7 (eBook)

10 9 8 7 6 5 4 3 2 1

Printed in the United States of America

MURDER WITH CHERRY TARTS

Daisy heard panic in Keith's voice.

"Tell me exactly what happened," Jonas said.

"I don't know where to start. I went to the carriage maker and bought a wheel and lanterns. I made a quick trip to the drugstore and then drove to Pirated Treasures. I didn't call because I was doing okay on time. The thing was—when I got there, a patrol cop was outside. He wouldn't let me go in and I was worried about Otis, that maybe he'd had a stroke or something. So I asked. I guess that was my big mistake. The patrol cop asked what doings I had with Otis. So I told him about the wagon wheel and the lanterns in my van. He told me to wait there and he'd be right back. I should have known something more than a stroke was going on."

"I don't understand," Jonas said calmly. "Was something wrong with Otis?"

"Not Otis. Barry. He was dead! It wasn't long until Detective Willet came outside with a look on his face that said I was in trouble."

"I don't understand," Jonas repeated. "You hadn't even gone inside the store."

"Not today. I'd given my name to the patrol cop and apparently he asked Otis about me. Willet said that Otis told him that I had threatened Barry with a marble rolling pin a few days before. Barry and I had argued about a deal that had included the rolling pin."

"What does a rolling pin have to do with it?" Daisy asked.

"Someone killed Barry Storm with that rolling pin. The back of the store is a mess. The body was gone. But, Daisy, your cherry tarts were even mixed in with everything. . . ."

Books by Karen Rose Smith

Caprice De Luca Mysteries

STAGED TO DEATH

DEADLY DÉCOR

GILT BY ASSOCIATION

DRAPE EXPECTATIONS

SILENCE OF THE LAMPS

SHADES OF WRATH

SLAY BELLS RING

CUT TO THE CHAISE

Daisy's Tea Garden Mysteries

MURDER WITH LEMON TEA CAKES

MURDER WITH CINNAMON SCONES

MURDER WITH CUCUMBER SANDWICHES

MURDER WITH CHERRY TARTS

Published by Kensington Publishing Corporation

ACKNOWLEDGMENTS

I would like to thank Officer Greg Berry,
my law enforcement consultant,
who so patiently answers
all my questions.
His input is invaluable.

Chapter One

Daisy Swanson kept a keen eye on Karina Post as her server crossed to the sales counter at the end of their workday. Her twenty-something server with her purple hair and green neon clogs had given Daisy concern over the past couple of weeks. Daisy went by the philosophy that she should mind her own business . . . except when she shouldn't. The mother of two teenage daughters, she couldn't help but feel motherly toward her younger staff.

The aroma of sugar, cinnamon, and chocolate still rode on the cool currents from the air conditioner as Karina smiled at Daisy and approached the sales counter at Daisy's Tea Garden. She was usually a self-possessed young woman with plenty of confidence and sometimes even brashness.

Now, however, Karina kept her eyes lowered as she asked Daisy, "Is it okay if I take some of the baked goods still left in the case?"

Daisy noticed the bag Karina was carrying and recognized the size. In it, there was probably a quart container of soup.

"Sure you can," Daisy said. "I don't want them to go

to waste. The cherry tarts are fine, but some of the white-chocolate blondies have been in the case since morning. They might be a little stale. It seemed everyone wanted cherry tarts today."

"It's the special for the month of July, so that's probably why," Karina suggested, still not meeting Daisy's gaze.

"Has your mom been working extra hours at her shop?" Karina's mom owned a leather shop in town, Totes and Belts. In the summer, particularly in July, tourists provided most of the business for the stores in town. Busloads could arrive unexpectedly and wipe out a store's inventory.

"No, she has a good manager who's doing really well. I think she still wants me to go there and work full time instead of working here. And I'm grateful to her. After all, she took us back in when Quinn was born. But we're around each other enough as it is. I can't imagine working for Mom too."

Not that Daisy wanted Karina to leave, but she wished the best for her server and her three-year-old daughter. "Maybe you could move into that manager spot some day if you worked at Totes and Belts."

"That's possible, but I'd rather go to nursing school. I'm thinking about starting when Quinn is older, maybe after she goes into first or second grade."

Karina was a single mom. Daisy didn't know the whole story, but from rumors in Willow Creek's gossip mill, she'd gleaned that Karina had run away and lived on the streets before Quinn was born.

From things Karina had said, Daisy knew her mother Maris was a fine cook and she baked treats for Quinn. But for the past few weeks, Karina had been asking for the day-old baked goods and buying quarts of soup if Daisy's kitchen manager Tessa didn't have any remaining in the pot at the end of the day.

"Will Iris be in tomorrow, or do you need me to cover her shift again?" Karina asked.

Daisy's aunt Iris, co-owner of the tea garden, had caught a summer cold. She knew better than to be around customers or their tea and food.

"I spoke to her a little bit ago, and she feels she's ready to come in tomorrow. Her sniffles are gone and so is her cough. But—I told her to come in for a morning shift. Can you come in for the afternoon?"

"Sure. I always like picking up extra hours."

Karina *sounded* fine. She acted as if nothing fazed her. But that didn't mean her bravado wasn't hiding something. Daisy took one more stab at coaxing information from her. "I hope you and Quinn and Maris enjoy the cherry tarts and soup."

Karina glanced away from Daisy and into the case. "Quinn tells me every day now that she's a big girl since she turned three and doesn't need her booster seat."

That was a non sequitur if Daisy ever heard one, and Karina had easily sidestepped her question. It was time to give up . . . for now. "They grow up too fast, that's for sure. I can't believe Violet's going to have a baby of her own come November." *And the wedding will be in a few weeks*, Daisy added to herself. The past months had been a bit crazy.

After Daisy packed up the baked goods and Karina left, she began taking the rest of their inventory from the case. Cora Sue, another one of her servers, who had been sweeping the floor while she and Karina were talking, asked Daisy, "Do you need help?"

Cora Sue worked full time at Daisy's Tea Garden.

Her bottle-red hair pulled high on her head in a topknot was as bouncy and bubbly as she was.

"Sure," Daisy answered, eager to drive home.

After the two of them finished emptying the case, Cora Sue said, "I saw you talking to Karina."

"I was," Daisy responded.

"I heard her ask Tessa for the bottom of the soup pot again."

Daisy decided to be forthright with Cora Sue. "I'm a little worried about her. She's been taking end-of-the-day baked goods home for a while now, but she won't say why."

"That's not the only thing she's being secretive about," Cora Sue murmured.

Studying her server, Daisy wasn't sure whether she should become involved or not. A question or two wouldn't hurt. "Do you think she's in trouble of some kind?"

"I really don't know. My car was on the fritz last week, so I walked to work. It's good exercise, only about a half mile. The shorter route takes me up Sage Street, which I know isn't the best section of town, even though the town council is trying to rehab it. But I *have* taken kickboxing lessons, so I wasn't too concerned. The thing was . . . I spotted Karina twice last week at the lower end of Sage Street. The part the town council wants to renovate."

"Did she see you?"

"No, she didn't, but I casually brought it up."

Daisy was always interested in clues. After all, she'd helped solve three murders. Clues had led her to the killer in every instance. "What did she tell you?"

"She told me she enjoys looking around the antiques

shop in that neighborhood, Pirated Treasures. It should be called Pirated *Junk*."

A smile twitched up Daisy's lips.

The owner of the shop, Otis Murdock, used to come in for the tea garden's chicken soup. Lately though, his nephew had dropped in to buy it.

Daisy removed the band from her ponytail and let her blond, shoulder-length hair flow free. "I've passed the shop but I've never been inside. You know what they say—one person's junk is another person's treasure."

Cora Sue grimaced. "I saw a broken bust of Benjamin Franklin in there one time. They'd glued it back together. It wasn't pretty."

Daisy laughed. "So you shop in the store even if you don't like it?"

"No, a friend dragged me in there. She says she finds unusual things for her home decor. But mostly what she finds, I wouldn't pick up at a yard sale."

Thinking of Karina again, Daisy sobered. "Do you think Karina really shops in there or she was using it as an excuse?"

"I don't know. If she has to lie about why she's on Sage Street, I have to wonder about her purpose for being there."

Realizing Cora Sue was right, Daisy told herself she should really mind her own business. But then again, what if Karina was in trouble?

That evening, Daisy backed her purple PT Cruiser out of her home garage, made a K-turn, then opened the driver's side door.

Her daughter Jazzi, sixteen now, had obtained her

learner's permit. Daisy dreaded thinking about Jazzi on the roads with all the crazy drivers who passed through Lancaster County, especially in the summer. On top of that, her daughter would also have to learn how to handle driving on the roads with horses and buggies. Sometimes there was a separate lane for the buggies, but most times there wasn't. In an accident between a car and a horse and buggy, the horse and buggy didn't have a chance.

Jazzi's long, straight, black hair blew in the hot breeze as she asked Daisy, "When are you going to let me back it out of the garage?"

Daisy climbed out of the car, glanced at the garage, and then back at Jazzi. "I promise I'll let you do it soon. Maybe tonight we'll head over to Bird-in-Hand. The farmers' market has a huge parking lot and the market will be closed. You can practice backing up there."

Daisy handed her car keys to Jazzi.

Jazzi winked at her. "I'm getting good, Mom. Honest. You don't have to fear for your life when we go driving."

As Jazzi had probably intended, Daisy laughed. "You are *so* reassuring."

"What else are daughters for?"

As if that comment caused Jazzi to think about something more serious, once they were seated in the car, she was quiet.

Daisy guessed that meant Jazzi was thinking about her birth mother again. In the fall of last year, unbeknownst to Daisy, Jazzi had tried to search for her birth mother on the Internet. Daisy had known that time might be coming because she and her deceased husband Ryan had adopted Jazzi. Still, Jazzi's search had been a shock.

Knowing if she didn't support her daughter Jazzi might pull away, Daisy had aided her in finding Portia Smith Harding. They'd enlisted the help of Jonas Groft, a former police detective who now owned Woods, a furniture store just down the street from Daisy's Tea Garden. At first Portia hadn't told her husband about Jazzi. It had been a long-kept secret. Once she *had* told him, he'd felt betrayed and had moved out of their house for a while. That event had made Jazzi feel guilty, *so* guilty it had affected her schoolwork and her friendships enough that Daisy had sought out a counselor for her. Finally, however, in the spring, Colton had moved back in with Portia and their children. Jazzi's relationship with Portia now was tentative because of Colton's attitude, and when Jazzi needed to talk with someone objective, Daisy made an appointment for her. Part of the reason Jazzi felt comfortable with the sessions was because Lancelot, a yellow tabby, accompanied the counselor to the sessions. With a purring feline on her lap, Jazzi felt more comfortable sharing.

"I wanted to ask you something, Mom." Jazzi switched on her turn signal and made a right turn onto the rural road.

"Ask me anything." Daisy hoped that was true. She hoped both of her daughters could trust her that much.

"It's only a few weeks until Vi and Foster's wedding."

"I'm well aware we still have a lot on our to-do list. Vi and Foster have to decide on a cake, and I have to shop for a mother-of-the-bride dress."

"We might have to take Gram shopping too. She

still doesn't approve of Vi and Foster getting married, does she?"

"I think she's accepted the fact that it's going to happen."

Vi's situation with Foster had brought back so many memories. Years ago Daisy's mother had had to accept the fact that Daisy had married when she was eighteen and moved to Florida with her new husband. However, Daisy hadn't gotten pregnant until *after* she married. She and Ryan had wanted a baby with all their hearts. Daisy wasn't sure Vi and Foster were ready for marriage, let alone a baby. Still, Violet had insisted marriage was what she and Foster wanted. They'd been adamant. So Daisy had helped them figure out how they could make it work.

Raising a baby and supporting themselves wasn't going to be easy. Since the floor above her detached garage hadn't been finished when her barn home was renovated, she'd decided to finish it into a small apartment for the couple. That had always been the plan for added income. Or for one of her girls if either decided to live in Willow Creek. She'd told Vi and Foster they could live there rent free for the first year. Foster's dad, a contractor, had overseen the construction. It was finished now except for furniture.

"When Gram sees her great-grandchild, I think she'll be less disapproving," Daisy reassured Jazzi.

Jazzi still hadn't asked Daisy her question, and Daisy suspected that she was working up to it.

"I'm supposed to call Portia tonight."

As Jazzi braked and switched on the turn signal, Daisy said slowly, "Okay," almost afraid of what was coming.

"I'd like to ask Portia and her husband to the wedding.

That would give me a chance to meet Colton and maybe spend a little time with them both."

Mixed feelings wound around Daisy when she thought about the couple coming to the wedding. However, this wasn't really her decision to make. "You know Vi wants to keep the wedding small."

"I know."

"Why don't you run the idea past her," Daisy suggested.

"Portia might just come herself," Jazzi reminded Daisy.

"That's true."

"If she and her husband both come," Jazzi added, "I suppose they could reserve a room at the Covered Bridge Bed and Breakfast or Tumbling Blocks B and B. That could be expensive for them, though."

Jazzi's comment was like a helium balloon that she wanted Daisy to bat back in some way. She thought about the situation. "Vi will be moving into the apartment as soon as she and Foster find time to go shopping with Gavin to buy a mattress."

"I like that dresser they found at the antiques store in Smoketown."

"Apparently Foster has good negotiating skills," Daisy said with a smile. She'd hired Foster Cranshaw as one of her servers back in the fall, never expecting him to become her son-in-law. He'd quickly become a valuable employee with his knowledge of tea and his social media skills that helped promote Daisy's Tea Garden.

After a pause, Jazzi glanced quickly at her mom, then back at the rural road. "Are you saying Portia and Colton could have Vi's room?"

"Actually, they could have the whole upstairs if you slept on the pull-out couch in the living room."

A sly smile crept across Jazzi's lips. "That's a great idea, Mom. But I know you're going to be busy with the wedding and all and might not want to entertain guests."

"That could be *your* job." Daisy was half teasing and half serious.

"What if Colton doesn't like me?"

"What's not to like?" Daisy asked affectionately.

"Mom . . ." Jazzi drew out the word as she always did when she was frustrated with her mother.

"I'm serious, Jazzi. If Portia's husband comes, then he should at least keep a bit of an open mind, don't you think? Why else would he accept the invitation?"

Reassured, Jazzi nodded and concentrated on driving.

Daisy just hoped her logic was correct.

On Friday around noon, Daisy and her aunt Iris exchanged a look at the sales counter and high-fived each other with wide grins. The last of the tour bus visitors had exited the tea garden to catch their ride to their next destination. The onslaught of sightseers was always good for business, but a tea blogger had once knocked the tea garden down a notch for service, writing that they needed more help. Since then, Foster had garnered more hours in preparation for his new job of husband and father, though he was still trying to keep up with his studies at Millersville University. Out of school, Jazzi and Vi were helping too.

Daisy glanced at the almost empty case. "I'll pull more cookies and apple bread from the walk-in."

"See how many cherry tarts are left. We've been running out of them every day," her aunt reminded her.

"Will do. I suppose we'll have to keep making a double batch of them since they're so popular."

Violet, who had come up to the sales counter, heard them talking. Her daughter's medium brown hair was streaked with blond highlights, but she hadn't renewed the practice since she'd learned she was pregnant. Her morning sickness, which had turned into all-day sickness at the beginning of her pregnancy, had gotten better. But today she looked tired. She had dark circles under her eyes and Daisy suspected she wasn't sleeping because of this high-stress time. Last night she'd heard her daughter come downstairs in the middle of the night. The low whistle of the teapot had alerted her. She and Vi had already discussed the fact that all teas weren't safe for a pregnancy. But Daisy's rooibos tea was. The canister where Daisy kept the tea, usually in her pantry, sat on the counter this morning.

Obviously overhearing Daisy's conversation with her aunt, Vi said, "I was hoping we could take cherry tarts home. As soon as she arrived, Karina put three back for herself to take along tonight. Can we do that? Maybe four?"

Karina's food gathering was still a mystery. "Of course, we can." After a pause, Daisy asked Vi, "Has Karina told you why she takes along the baked goods?"

Vi shook her head and tucked her shoulder-length hair more neatly into the net she wore over it today. "No, she doesn't really talk to me like she used to. When she came in today, I thought she looked upset, so I asked her if something was wrong. She insisted it wasn't."

Pushing thoughts of Karina aside for now, Daisy

studied Vi more thoroughly. As she often did, Vi was turning Foster's high school ring around on a finger of her left hand. It was her engagement ring.

"Do you want to leave early?" Daisy asked. "You look tired."

"No, I'm good. I'm saving the money I earn for a crib. Gavin wanted to find us a used one, but I'd like one new thing for the baby."

Daisy could understand that. "Standards on children's furniture change from year to year too, so putting your money into the crib is wise. Maybe you can consider the kind that transforms into a daybed for when the baby is ready for his own bed."

"Or *her* own bed," Vi joked. "I know some moms want to be surprised, but Foster and I can't wait to learn the sex of the baby. Soon, we'll have the ultrasound and then we'll know."

Iris jumped into the conversation now. "Just remember, honey, I want to be your major babysitter."

"You might have to wrestle Gram for that job."

"Guess who would win," Iris returned with a wink.

Daisy's aunt Iris and her mom didn't always see eye to eye. They had very different personalities. Where her aunt was a listener, accepting, and nonjudgmental, Daisy's mom was the opposite. Rose Gallagher liked to share her opinion before anyone asked for it. Daisy had lived under her mom's critical eye all her life, and her aunt Iris had always been her ally. Daisy and her own sister Camellia had very different personalities too. Their mother and Camellia usually stood firm together. As she was growing up, Daisy had often felt like the odd girl out.

Thinking about that again, Daisy realized that conclusion wasn't completely true because her dad had consistently stood in her corner. At least it seemed that way.

Vi snapped her fingers. "Pregnancy hormones are affecting my memory. Tessa wants to know if she should put the rum-raisin rice pudding on the menu for tomorrow. Something about needing more eggs for the weekend from your supplier if you do."

"I'll talk to her. I can ask Rachel Fisher if their farm has any extra eggs. I could stop on my way home and pick them up."

As Vi moved away, Iris said, "Since I'm leaving early, I could stop for them. You have enough to do with getting the apartment ready for Vi and Foster along with wedding plans." Her aunt lowered her voice. "And with tonight's little celebration."

Her aunt was right about her to-do list, including their surprise for Vi and Foster tonight. "I'd appreciate that," she said. "Let me talk to Tessa."

Early that afternoon, on the way to the kitchen, Karina waylaid Daisy outside the office. "Can I speak to you for a minute?"

"Sure. Do you want to go into my office?"

"No, that's not necessary."

Daisy's gaze slid over Karina. Her hair was shorter, so she must have gotten it trimmed, and the purple was brighter. Her neon green clogs peeked out from the hem of her white slacks. Her yellow apron with the daisy logo seemed to complement Karina's personality. She looked like a colorful garden.

Daisy waited, knowing that if Karina didn't want to go into her office, then she didn't have anything serious to discuss.

"I need to leave around four instead of five. Is that okay?"

Even though the tourists from the tour bus had left, the tearoom was still filled with customers. However, when her employees needed time off, Daisy usually complied, knowing they had responsibilities and errands outside the tea garden. "Do you need to pick up Quinn early from day care?"

Karina didn't answer right away. Finally, she responded, "No, but I have an errand to run before I pick her up. This is important, Daisy. Honest, it is."

There was vehemence in Karina's voice, and maybe something else.

"You can leave early today. We can cover for you. Will you be here for your regular shift tomorrow?"

"I'll be here on time and I'll stay for my whole shift," Karina promised.

"Sounds good. Some day when you're not working, you'll have to bring Quinn in for a visit."

"She talks a mile a minute," Karina said with a smile, and checked her watch. "I'd better get back to work. Thanks again, Daisy . . . for understanding."

Daisy watched her server as Karina went into the kitchen. She had the sense that Karina was hiding something. Just what could it be?

Chapter Two

Daisy's servers and staff had all left when she turned over the OPEN sign to CLOSED on the door of Daisy's Tea Garden. After tossing around an idea in her head, she decided to stop in at Woods for a few minutes to talk to Jonas.

She left by the back door of the tea garden, walked through the small parking lot, and down the drive that led to Market Street. A horse clomped past, pulling a courting buggy. She didn't know the young couple riding on the bench seat but she smiled anyway.

On Market Street she glanced back at the tea garden, a pale green Victorian with white trim, gingerbread edging, and a covered porch. It had once housed a bakery. Converting it to a tea garden with an apartment up above—where her kitchen manager Tessa Miller lived—hadn't been too difficult. Daisy and Tessa had been best friends since their school years. They'd attended gifted classes and skipped a grade, supporting each other through good and difficult times.

As Daisy studied the Victorian with the colorful

ceramic pots on the porch that grew geraniums, petunias, lavender, and pineapple sage, a warm feeling enveloped her heart. This was her business—hers and her aunt's. They'd started it with a wish and a hope and a bit of experience. Her aunt had been the tea aficionado, but Daisy had always liked tea, and she brought her dietician's background to the recipes that she created.

She watched as the horse and buggy pulled into a slanted buggy parking spot about a half block up the street. The young man went around to the other side and helped his passenger down. Then he attached his horse to the hitching post. The slanted parking on this part of Market Street was intended specifically for horses and buggies. There was a public parking lot about a block the other way where buses, tourists, and other shoppers parked.

Willow Creek was Daisy's hometown. She'd quit college at Drexel, where she and Ryan had met, and left Willow Creek when she'd married Ryan and moved to Florida. They'd raised their girls there until he'd died. Afterward, she'd taken a year to sort things out. Then over two years ago, she'd returned to her family in Willow Creek. She'd been devastated by her husband's death from pancreatic cancer. That life as she'd known it had been over, but she had their daughters to live for. Coming back to Willow Creek had been good for them too. Here they were a part of roots and traditions.

Daisy turned away from the tea garden and walked down the street. She passed Wisps and Wicks, a candle shop that was also closed now. Betty Furhman, who owned the shop, hand-made candles with beautiful natural scents. As Daisy walked farther down the block, she passed an insurance office, and a store that sold hand-sewn purses and travel bags. Vinegar and Spice, where Arden Botterill let tourists taste flavored vinegars, olive oils, and various spices, tempted her to go in. But she was on a mission.

After she passed a building with offices for an accountant and a lawyer with rentals available on the second and third floors, she stopped in front of Woods. After she pulled open the glass door, she walked inside.

Jonas's store was well arranged. There were huge cubicle shelves lining one side of the store. In each cubicle stood a ladder-back chair, each one in a different color or finish—from yellow to blue to green to walnut and cherry. The furniture in the rest of the store—pine, oak, and aspen—always shone with a glossy finish. Polished and well crafted, any piece would be welcome for a house or an apartment. Passing pedestal and library tables, she admired the armoires and highboys and breathed in the faint smells of furniture polish, stain, and wood.

Jonas was at the counter to the rear of the store on his stool poring over a legal pad. He smiled and stood as she approached.

Jonas Groft was lean, muscled, and over six feet tall. A scar on his cheek and a stern jaw reminded her of his former job as a police detective in Philadelphia. His black hair, parted on the side, attempted to dip over his brow. Silver strands at his temples showed under the fluorescent light. Just as she had, he had come to Willow Creek for a fresh start.

His green eyes grew darker as he met her in the aisle. "This is a surprise. Or did I forget a date?"

"You'd forget one of our dates?" she teased.

"I doubt it." His tone said he wouldn't even entertain the thought.

"I can't stay long," Daisy said. "Aunt Iris, Jazzi, and I are giving a gift to Vi and Foster tonight."

"How is Jazzi?"

Jonas and Jazzi had formed a trust bond when Jonas had helped search for her daughter's birth mother. Not only had he helped, but he'd found Portia. "She's good. She went home with a friend and her mom, who stopped by the tea garden. Her friend's mom is going to drop her off at Iris's in a couple of hours since they live nearby. Then Iris will bring Jazzi home around seven and we can give Vi and Foster a special gift."

He cocked his head and studied her. "Are you having empty nest syndrome already?"

"I'm not sure how empty my nest is going to be with Vi and Foster living above the garage with their baby. Not that I'm complaining, mind you."

"I was about to close up the shop," Jonas said. "Let me turn the sign around and lock up, then we can go sit in the workroom."

There was a park bench in his workroom that they'd had many discussions on. Due to a clash of important issues in their lives, they'd almost stopped dating before Vi had told them she was pregnant. Since then, however, they'd come to a new understanding. Jonas had been supportive and had accepted the fact that their time together was limited.

Five minutes later, they were sitting side by side on the bench in his workshop with bottles of cold water, eating cinnamon scones that she'd brought along.

"Is this going to be your supper?" he joked.

"There will be snacks for our little celebration."

His eyes were caring as he canvased her face. "So tell me what's on your mind."

She wrinkled her nose at him. "What makes you think I have something on my mind?"

"The fact that you came here before going home. Or did you just stop in for a mad, passionate kiss? I can supply that as well as advice."

She bumped his shoulder with her own. "Do I have to choose?"

"Nope, I can handle both." He leaned close and kissed her.

Afterward, Daisy sighed. That kiss was just what she'd needed. Jonas was usually a perceptive man. That perception had probably come from interrogating criminals.

"I think Karina is in trouble or hiding something."

His attention was riveted on her. "What makes you think that?"

She could tell from the timbre of Jonas's voice that he had gone into his detective mode. "Lately, every night she's taken home soup and day-old baked goods. I'm not sure what she's doing with them, but she won't answer any questions. Cora Sue saw her on Sage Street near Pirated Treasures."

Jonas shrugged. "Maybe she's looking for an unusual gift."

"She can't be looking for one every night. Tonight, she asked to leave an hour early. She said she had an errand before she picked up Quinn at day care. But she's acting oddly and won't meet my eyes when I ask her a question. Today she seemed upset about something."

"So you want answers."

"I do. I'd call her mother but I don't want to ring an

alarm for no good reason. I'd rather find out what she's doing on my own."

"Have you thought of a way to do that?"

"Possibly. I might follow her one of these days after her shift."

Jonas was silent for a few beats. His expression was unfathomable when he asked, "Can I advise you that it would be better to keep your mind on Vi's wedding instead of spying on one of your employees?"

She'd expected that kind of suggestion from Jonas, but she also knew he'd support whatever she decided. At least, she hoped he would.

"The wedding plans are under control. There's not too much angst between Jazzi and Portia right now. Jazzi asked me if they could come to the wedding."

"And you said . . ."

"I said she should ask Vi. If Vi doesn't mind, it's okay with me."

"Do you think it's a good idea?"

"If Portia's husband comes, it will give Jazzi and Colton a chance to get to know each other. Good or bad, it has to happen sometime." She picked up her water bottle and took a few swallows. Then she asked, "Are you trying to distract me from my real reason for being here?"

"No, I'm just giving myself time to think it over. Are you sure you want to follow Karina?"

"I am."

"Let me make another suggestion. Why don't you let *me* follow her? Or let me go with you."

Daisy thought about his idea and considered it seriously. "She's *my* employee. But having your company in that part of town *would* be wise. I know the weekend is busy for both of us. But we could do it on Monday after her shift."

Jonas took Daisy's hand and laced his fingers with hers. "All right. For one night, we'll be a team of private detectives. At least you can't get into major trouble if I'm with you."

That remained to be seen.

In her home kitchen, Daisy pulled two trays from the refrigerator. One held cantaloupe wrapped with prosciutto, and the other held cucumber sandwiches with pimento filling on pumpernickel. She wanted to make sure anything to do with Vi and Foster's wedding was festive and happy. So tonight when she and Aunt Iris and Jazzi were presenting them with a honeymoon gift, she'd decided to serve a few hors d'oeuvres and sweets. After she arranged whoopie pies on a tray, she poured glasses of iced tea.

Glancing at the clock and noticing it was almost seven, she went to the hutch positioned in the dining area next to the floor-to-ceiling stone fireplace. She took placemats from a drawer and set them around the table in the dining area.

As she was adding silverware and napkins to each placemat, the front door opened and Aunt Iris called, "Yoo-hoo. We're here."

"In here," Daisy called back.

When Iris, Jazzi, Vi, and Foster came into the kitchen, Iris explained, "We arrived at the same time. How convenient is that?"

Iris was dressed casually in jeans and a paisley print blouse with sneakers on her feet. Jazzi was still wearing her work outfit of a coral-striped, sleeveless blouse and a white skirt.

Daisy glanced at Foster and her older daughter. "I didn't know if you would've grabbed a bite for supper. If you didn't, here's snacking food."

"This all looks great, Mrs. Swanson," Foster said.

Ever since Vi had told them all she was pregnant, Foster had gone from a more informal title of Daisy to Mrs. Swanson again. That's what he'd called her when she'd first hired him. He'd looked at this pregnancy as his fault, believing Daisy and Gavin had blamed him. Daisy certainly didn't, not any more than she blamed Violet. And she'd told him that more than once. However, he was a responsible young man, and he took that responsibility seriously, especially now that he was going to be a dad.

Daisy gestured to the table again. "Have a seat and we'll get started."

After Vi and Foster exchanged a look, Vi asked, "What are we starting? And not that I don't like seeing you, Aunt Iris, but how come you're here?"

Iris didn't take offense. "Why don't we have a snack first, and when you get to the whoopie pies, all will be explained."

Daisy could see that her aunt was having fun with this surprise. Daisy hoped Vi and Foster would remember tonight along with other cherished memories around their wedding.

Jazzi picked up a piece of cantaloupe and prosciutto. "I wish you could all take me driving instead of just Mom."

Foster shot Daisy a quick look as if wondering if she was offended.

But Daisy just laughed. "I think Jazzi wants to learn

more than one style of driving. Sometimes she thinks I'm too cautious. It's Pennsylvania law that only a parent or guardian can take a teenager driving on a learner's permit."

"I know Jonas would take me driving too," Jazzi added.

Vi caught Daisy's attention. "He's not here tonight. Is there a reason?"

Aunt Iris tapped Daisy on the arm, her eyes twinkling. "I think it's time. These young folks are so impatient."

Daisy produced a small box that she'd slipped under her chair before they'd sat down. Wrapped in gold foil paper, it sported a big white bow. Standing, she crossed to Vi and Foster and set the box on the table in front of them. "This is a gift from me, Aunt Iris, and Jazzi. We hope you like it."

Jazzi already had her phone in hand to snap photos.

"An early wedding present?" Foster asked. "You've already done way more than you need to do for us."

"We know you're watching every penny, and this is just something we thought you should have," Iris explained.

Untying the bow, Vi looked puzzled. The box was about as big as a tie box. After she took off the bow, she tore through the foil paper to produce a plain white box.

She leaned toward Foster. "Why don't you open the lid."

After he did, he stared at the contents. Then he removed it and opened up a sheet of paper that had been folded in thirds. Underneath that, he found a brochure. He handed that to Vi and read the note aloud.

"Since you didn't plan a honeymoon so you could save money, Iris, Jazzi, and I thought you should have one anyway. We hope this respite in New Hope, PA, at a bed-and-breakfast gives you much needed time alone before you start your life together. With our love and good wishes . . . Mom, Aunt Iris, and Jazzi."

Suddenly Vi stood, turned from the table, and rushed into the living room. Daisy spotted the tears on her daughter's cheeks before she ran. Foster started to rise to his feet, but Daisy said, "Let me go to her. I promise I'll bring her back in after I find out what's wrong."

Vi was sitting in a corner of the green and cream plaid sofa, her face in her hands. Daisy sat beside her and put her arm around Vi's shoulders. "What's going on?"

Vi just shook her head.

"Are you panicking?" Daisy asked. "If you are, that's natural."

Vi finally looked at Daisy. "Is it?"

"Sure it is. Your life is going to change. On top of that, the future you thought you were going to have has transformed into something else."

When Vi sniffed, Daisy pulled a tissue out of a box on the lower shelf of the coffee table. She handed it to Vi and Vi blew her nose. But there were still tears in her eyes.

"This is more than panic. I'm worried all the time about everything."

"Define 'everything.'"

"My pregnancy mainly. I never know what's coming next. I can read all the books in the world but that doesn't mean I'll be prepared. What if I don't know what to do with the baby? What if I'm *not* a good mother?"

Daisy hugged Violet closer. "Believe me, I understand your worries. You're going through what every new mom goes through. Sure, you're going to make mistakes. We all do. But you're going to do your best, and you have me and Aunt Iris and Gram to give you plenty of advice. We're here for whenever you need us."

Violet blew out a huge breath, pulled her headband from her hair, and then slipped it back in again, pushing her hair away from her face. "I'd like to find a few small businesses that might let me do their book work. I can probably earn more that way than being a server at the tea garden."

In Vi's first year at Lehigh University, she'd taken courses in business management, including bookkeeping. "If you want to do that, I'll be glad to ask around. I'm sure Jonas would be willing to as well."

"You'd do that for me? What if you still need me to serve?"

"Violet, my staff and I handled the tea garden just fine while you were at college. If I need more help, I'll find it. That's not your worry."

Vi sat back against the sofa. "I didn't want Foster to think I was having doubts."

"Honey, one thing you're going to have to learn about marriage is that you've got to share your thoughts. That's a must. If you tell Foster what you're thinking and he helps you figure it out, I believe your panic will diminish."

"Really? This tight feeling in my chest will go away?"

Daisy gave Vi another hug and then leaned away.

"I don't know if it will go away entirely, not until you feel settled and secure in your life. I certainly think it will be better. A woman named Fawn Weaver once said, 'Happily ever after is not a fairy tale. It's a choice.' When you're married, each day is a choice to forgive each other, to be patient with each other, to love each other all over again. Each day might not be easy, but it will be worthwhile. You love Foster, right?"

"With all my heart."

"Tell him that, and tell him what's bothering you. If you can figure out a problem together, it won't seem as difficult."

Violet studied Daisy as if she were doing it for the very first time. She leaned her head against her mother's shoulder as she might have done when she was ten. "Thank you."

Daisy felt tears misting her own eyes. "Any time." This is what it meant to be a mom. By the end of the year, Violet might figure that out.

On Monday, Jonas arrived at the tea garden around four thirty for a glass of iced tea and a cherry tart. This wasn't an unusual habit of Jonas's, so Daisy knew Karina wouldn't think anything of it. Daisy had already cleared her plans with Aunt Iris that she intended to leave early with Jonas. No one needed to know exactly what they were doing.

The mid-July day had skyrocketed into the nineties. As Karina left with her bags of goodies, Daisy signaled to Jonas. After Daisy tapped her aunt's shoulder, she and Jonas exited through the kitchen's back door. Karina was easy to spot ahead of them on Market

Street with her purple hair, lemon-colored slacks, and neon green clogs.

Jonas said, "We can't follow too close."

"We'll lose her," Daisy protested.

"I've tailed people before," he reminded her in a calm voice.

She was sure he had as a detective. In this instance, she should listen to him.

Jonas seemed to count off seconds in his head, then he gave Daisy a little tug. "Come on. We should be able to see if she slips down a side street."

They kept about a half block between themselves and Karina. Traffic was busy but the tourists had pretty much either gone to their bed-and-breakfasts, to restaurants, or home. Daisy could feel the sweat easing down the back of her neck. She didn't know if that came from nervousness or from simply the heat. The humidity had revved up today along with the temperature. Taking a hair clip from her pocket, she gathered her hair onto the top of her head and clipped it into place.

Jonas smiled and flipped the ends of the makeshift bun. "I like your hair up."

"I'll remember that," she teased.

After a few blocks, Karina headed south toward Sage Street. She turned left at a stop sign and Daisy could see the antiques store, Pirated Treasures, up ahead. She clenched Jonas's arm. "Do you think she's going in there?"

"Watch and wait," Jonas answered her enigmatically.

Still about a half block behind her, they spotted Karina pass by Pirated Treasures and head toward a line of tall maples.

"Let's close the distance a bit," Jonas said.

When they did, they saw that Karina had stopped at the door of a blue van. The sight shot an arrow of worry into Daisy's stomach. Not drugs. Not Karina.

Jonas noted, "The van's not new. It's maybe five or six years old. Do you want to let her know you're here? Nothing is changing hands, though I don't see the bag Karina was carrying."

"I don't know any other way to find out what she's up to, and I don't think she'll believe us if we say we were out for a stroll."

Jonas hung his arm around Daisy's shoulders. "Come on. As a couple, we shouldn't be threatening to whoever's in that van. She's just standing there talking . . . and smiling."

Karina wasn't aware of them approaching. She was too busy talking.

As Daisy and Jonas moved closer, Daisy heard coughing. She knew the sound of that cough. It had come from a child. Since she'd raised two daughters through colds, the sound was familiar.

Closing the distance to Karina, Daisy tapped her on the shoulder.

When Karina swung around, Daisy could see the man sitting on the floor of the van, his legs hanging over the running board to the pavement. He looked to be about thirty and he was wearing a T-shirt and jeans. On his lap he held a toddler.

The little girl with blond ringlets was dipping her plastic fork into one of Daisy's cherry tarts!

Chapter Three

Daisy and Jonas just stared at the man with the toddler on his lap. A buzz cut had left his sandy brown hair as stubble. But he was clean shaven.

After Daisy broke eye contact with him, she caught a glimpse inside the van. There was a small mattress with a sheet over it with yellow ducks dancing across it. Next to it lay a single bed mattress with a plaid sheet. She also spotted a large red cooler and a grocery store bag that looked as if it had one of her scones peeking out of the top in a ziplock bag. There were a few toddler toys—an old-fashioned busy box, a pink teddy bear that looked as if it had seen lots of love, and a board puzzle, its pieces strewn across the van floor. She also noticed a travel bag on wheels. The van was clean except for a power-bar wrapper that was squished under the seat belt of a child's car seat.

Daisy's gaze quickly shifted back to the little girl, whose blond ringlets were adorable. She looked clean, except for the cherry glaze around her mouth from the tart. She wore a cute pinafore sundress in deference to the summer weather.

Daisy didn't know what question to ask first. Before

she asked anything, the man with one arm around the toddler extended his hand to her. "Keith Rebert."

She shook his hand, liking the look of affection in his eyes for the toddler.

He also extended his hand to Jonas. It took a beat for Jonas to take it, but he did, introducing himself and Daisy. "I'm Jonas Groft. This is Daisy Swanson. We're friends of Karina."

Keith glanced toward Karina as if to verify that.

From Daisy's perspective, because she knew Jonas, she could see he was sizing up Keith Rebert, and Keith Rebert was sizing him up.

After biting her lip, Karina turned to Daisy and asked, "What are you doing here?"

"I've been worried about you. It's not like you to be secretive. Can you tell us what's going on?"

Keith and Karina exchanged looks. Karina said, "I made a new friend, that's all."

The little girl on Keith's lap coughed again. She'd finished whatever was left of the cherry tart. Keith took the small foil pie plate and fork and leaned close to the little girl. "How about if I skootch you over and you can sit beside me. I want to throw the garbage away."

As Keith tried to assist her to move to the floor of the van, she raised her arms to him. "No, Daddy. Sit on *you.*"

Worrying about the child's cough, Daisy extended her arms. "May I?" she asked Keith.

Again Keith looked toward Karina. Karina said, "Daisy's my boss. She and her aunt own Daisy's Tea Garden. She makes the cherry tarts and scones that Mandy likes so much."

Keith gave Daisy a nod.

Daisy said in a gentle voice, "Mandy, would you like me to hold you?"

Mandy reached her arms up to Daisy and Daisy lifted her, holding her close against her. "Hi there, honey. My name's Daisy."

The little girl pointed to herself. "Me Mandy."

Daisy listened to Mandy's breathing. She didn't seem to have a stuffy nose. She also didn't feel hot, not the hot a fever would bring. Maybe the cough came from allergies.

Straightening the ruffle on Mandy's pinafore, she was touched when the little girl laid her head against Daisy's shoulder.

Placing one hand against the van, Jonas leaned into it. "It looks as if you've been spending time in your van."

The statement hung in the air without Keith responding. Daisy wasn't going to go behind the man's back to Karina to ask her questions.

As Daisy swayed back and forth with Mandy, she said, "It's obvious Karina has been bringing you food. It looks as if you're living in your van. Do you want to tell us what's going on? Maybe we can help."

"Why would I want to tell you anything?" Keith asked, defensive and frowning as he dumped the empty tart pan into a garbage bag behind the front seat.

Jonas's voice was calm. "Are you from Willow Creek?"

Keith kept silent as he turned toward them again.

Trying once more, Daisy assured him, "We *are* from Willow Creek. We have contacts."

"And just what would those contacts do?" the man asked belligerently. "Call Child Protective Services on me? This is my daughter. I didn't kidnap her. She's not old enough to be a runaway." Reaching under the front passenger seat, he pulled out an envelope. Opening it, he withdrew a piece of paper and handed it to Jonas. "That's Mandy's birth certificate."

Jonas nodded to Daisy. "It looks official."

"How would *you* know?" Keith asked. "Are you a cop?" At that he truly looked afraid.

Once again Karina stepped in. "Jonas used to be a detective, but now he owns the furniture store down the street from the tea garden. It's called Woods."

Keith nodded. "I pass it when I take Mandy for walks."

Karina looked hesitant, but she finally said, "Jonas and Daisy are good people, Keith. Maybe they can help."

He studied her. "Did you bring them here?"

Karina shook her head at the same time Daisy said, "No, she didn't. One of my servers saw Karina walking in this area and she was concerned. Karina could be hurt in this part of town. Jonas and I followed her after her shift today." There was no reason to hide anything. If they were honest with this man, maybe he'd be honest with them.

After studying Mandy, still laying her head against Daisy's shoulder, after looking back and forth between Jonas and Daisy, Keith blew out a breath. "I'm not used to trusting anymore. But Karina has been a huge help, and I trust *her*."

"Start at the beginning," Jonas directed.

Although he'd done it before, Keith sized up Jonas again. He must have decided answering was a better idea than not answering. "My wife and I were a two-income family in Media."

"I was a detective in Philadelphia," Jonas said, "so

I know Media well." He turned to Daisy. "It's about fifteen miles outside the city."

"What was your work there?" Daisy asked.

"Lisa, my wife, was a buyer for an antiques store. I was an elevator installer and I made good money. But when Mandy turned two, Lisa was diagnosed with ovarian cancer. She couldn't work and bills mounted up. I missed work to take care of Mandy and I lost my job. I picked up temp work, but after Lisa died I couldn't meet our mortgage payments. I lost the house, and Mandy and I began living in the van."

"Why come to Willow Creek?" Jonas asked.

"I didn't intend to stop in Willow Creek, but when I drove through here, I thought it might be a good place to start over. It's been working out. I almost have enough money saved to at least get a room somewhere."

"You didn't have family to help you out?" Jonas asked.

With a deep exhale of breath, Keith shook his head. "Lisa was an only child. Her parents were killed in a bus accident when they went on an outing with their church group. I was an only child because my dad left before I was born and my mom died from complications from diabetes. I think that's why Lisa and I gravitated toward each other. We met at a local carnival, started talking, and never stopped." Keith's voice choked on his last words.

Jonas's eyes narrowed. "What have you been doing to manage to save money?"

As if he felt he had to face Jonas man to man, Keith climbed out of the van. "I've been using the knowledge I gained from Lisa when I went antiquing with her. She always liked to go antiquing and worked in an antiques store. Now I'm able to care for Mandy and do that at the same time. We go antiquing, and then I sell those antiques to the uncle and nephew who own Pirated Treasures."

"And that's working for you?"

"It has up till now. The uncle, Otis Murdock, is honest but old and almost blind." Keith studied Daisy. "Otis and his nephew, Barry Storm, go to your place for soup and baked goods often."

Daisy knew Otis. He was a kind and talkative older man who hadn't been by the tea garden for a while. His nephew had been coming in to buy his uncle chicken soup and scones. "Are you saying Otis's nephew isn't honest?"

Keith shrugged, obviously reluctant to say more. Finally, he did. "I've seen the nephew pull bills from the cash register and pocket them. He also lowballs anything I bring him, and every dollar counts. If I could find another antiques dealer to buy from me, I would. You said you have contacts. Do you know any other antiques dealers?"

"I can't think of any offhand," Daisy said. "But my aunt might know someone. She's lived in this area all her life. I was born and raised here but got married and lived in Florida for years. I came back over two years ago."

"Can I see some ID from you?" Jonas requested.

Keith stared Jonas in the eyes for about thirty seconds, but then he pulled his wallet from his back pocket and took out his driver's license. He handed it to Jonas.

Jonas said to them all, "I'll be back in a few minutes." He stepped to the rear of the van and took out his phone.

Daisy imagined Jonas was calling one of his contacts to do a quick background check. Then she saw him glance at the license plate on the van. She guessed he was having someone run the plate too.

Instead of delving more into Keith's background, they talked about accommodations available in Willow Creek. Keith admitted, "We've been going to the community pool to get cleaned up and use the outside shower. There's a family bathroom we can use there. The library has one too. On hot days, we spend a lot of time there."

Daisy knew the community pool had a low per-visit charge, and children under five could go swimming for free. You could also buy a summer pass but obviously that wasn't what Keith was doing. And the library . . . As long as they were reading books, no one would question them. Keith had to become resourceful and he apparently was.

Ten minutes later, Jonas came back to the group. He returned Keith's driver's license to him. "I checked and you are who you say you are. No outstanding warrants, though a collection agency is trying to find you for unpaid medical bills."

"I'm not proud of that," Keith admitted. "As soon as I have a place and a job, I'll start sending payments in again."

Jonas's lips tightened and his brow furrowed as his gaze rested on Daisy and Mandy. Since he could read people well, he could probably guess she wished she could take Mandy home with her. She also knew, though, that Jonas wouldn't want a strange man in her house. She wouldn't either.

Jonas slipped his phone into his pocket, then he

turned to Keith. "You and your daughter obviously need help."

"If you're going to recommend I call a state agency, just save your breath."

Jonas seemed to inhale a patient breath, then let it out again. "That wasn't what I was going to recommend. I have a spare room in my town house. Why don't you and Mandy follow me home and you can get a good night's sleep, bathe, and eat wholesome food. In the morning, we'll strategize for the future."

Karina's mouth had rounded in an O. Keith's eyes were wide with surprise. "Are you serious?"

"I don't do background checks lightly. Yes, I'm serious. How does that sound?"

Finding her voice, Karina agreed. "You can trust Jonas, Keith. Honest, you can. He's one of the good guys."

"He certainly is," Daisy added. "There's a way *I* might be able to help. I attend the Willow Creek Community Church. They have a day care. Tomorrow I'll call the church secretary and find out if there's room for Mandy."

"I can't pay for day care yet," Keith protested.

"Reverend Kemp can make exceptions to their usual fees with scholarships. If Mandy's in day care, you might be able to find a more reliable job. If not in Willow Creek, then in Lancaster."

Keith looked down at his sneakers, then seemed to compose himself. "I don't know how to thank you. Throughout this whole situation, there wasn't any help that didn't have dire consequences. This Reverend Kemp. Will he call CPS?"

"I don't see why he would, not if Mandy is well

taken care of, and she seems to be. We'll do everything we can to help you get a fresh start."

The look in Karina's eyes told Daisy that the fresh start could be for her as well as for Keith and Mandy.

Daisy called Jonas on Tuesday morning and found out he and Keith and Mandy had spent a restful night. She told him she'd stop in after work to join Keith in strategizing about living in Willow Creek and to help with supper. She'd also called the church's secretary and Vanna would be checking with Reverend Kemp about a scholarship.

Midmorning, Daisy stood at the sales counter with Cora Sue, glancing over the tearoom to see if anyone needed service.

Cora Sue nudged Daisy's arm.

Daisy recognized Barry Storm, who'd just walked in. He looked to be in his late twenties and wore that scruffy look that was so popular with millennials. He might not have shaved in three days or he might have a special trimmer that simply made his beard look that way. His dishwater blond hair was shaved on one side and long from the part over the other side. She remembered it falling across his eyes when he'd paid her the last time he was in. His garb was usually the same—an oversized T-shirt and torn jeans. Not torn because they were old, but torn because he'd probably bought them that way. She recognized the look from her daughters' jeans in their closets.

She'd never quite been able to get a bead on Barry Storm. He wore a macho, confident facade. But if he was that secure, his hair wouldn't be covering his eyes. She remembered the last time she'd sold him scones.

His eyes had narrowed when he'd looked at her, and she couldn't even begin to guess what he'd been thinking. That look had made her feel a bit creeped out though.

Daisy leaned close to Cora Sue. "That table near the door looks as if they need some service. Can you take care of that? I'll wait on Mr. Storm."

Cora Sue was heading toward the back table when Barry Storm approached the counter. He eyed Daisy. "Morning."

"Good morning, Mr. Storm."

He grinned. "So you remember who I am."

"I try to identify all my customers. It helps with service."

"Yeah, the last time I was here, I wondered why you work as hard as your employees. You own this place, don't you?"

"My aunt and I are partners."

"Then I think at least one of you should be sitting in the office, not having to serve people off the street."

Daisy had never been to Pirated Treasures, and she didn't know the setup there. But after what Cora Sue had told her, she could take a stab at hitting the mark. "You and your uncle are in charge of Pirated Treasures, right?"

"Right," he replied warily.

"Don't you wait on customers?"

Barry shrugged. "That's different. We don't have anybody else working for us."

"I see." She stopped trying to poke around in his business. "What can I get for you today?"

"I'd like a half dozen of those cherry tarts, and two quarts of soup. My uncle likes your chicken noodle and he says he wants to freeze one of them."

"That's a good idea." Daisy pulled on latex gloves and took cherry tarts from the case. "Then he'll have it when he needs it."

"Yeah. Fast food isn't good for him all the time. I told him it's too hot for soup, but you know how those old people get as stubborn as mules."

The way Daisy looked at it, older folks merely knew what they wanted. But she wasn't going to argue. She remembered what Keith had said—that Otis Murdock gave him a fair amount for what he brought him. Barry didn't.

Barry pointed to the shelves on the wall in the spillover tearoom. That was the room they used for scheduled reservations for afternoon tea, which included multiple courses. That room reflected the best qualities of the Victorian with its bay window, window seat, crown molding, and diamond-cut glass. She'd painted the walls in there the palest yellow. The tables were white and the chairs wore seat cushions in blue and green and yellow pinstripes.

"The last time I was in here," Barry commented, "I noticed those teapots for sale. Your servers carry them around too."

"My aunt collects vintage teapots, and I have a few myself."

"I just wanted to let you know over at Pirated Treasures, teapots come into the shop. Have you ever been in?"

"No, I haven't. Are the teapots you carry antiques?"

"Some of them are," he said. "About two months ago, we had a Queen Victoria teapot with roses. Hand-made in Hungary, you know."

Yes, she did know. "How much were you selling it for?"

"That one went for five hundred dollars. But since

I like your cherry tarts so much, if you came in and found something, I'd give you a good deal."

She bet he wouldn't.

"We get those Chinese porcelain teapots, Limoges, and even James Sadler."

"His I could be interested in."

"You should come over to Pirated Treasures. Like I said, I'd give you a good deal."

"Do you have any of Sadler's now?"

"One with roses all over it."

Barry seemed to know his antiques. "I might be interested in that."

"Then stop over some time. Merchandise comes and goes, but I'm sure we'd have something you'd like."

"I'll think about it," Daisy said. She'd boxed his cherry tarts while they were talking and set them on the counter. "I'll get your soup."

"My uncle's soup," he called after her.

She might just have to stop at Pirated Treasures. It wouldn't hurt to look around. After all, she could add a new teapot to the tea garden's collection.

Chapter Four

Daisy had parked practically in front of Pirated Treasures where there was curb parking along the street. As she stepped into the store, she didn't see anyone around. She was curious to check out whether the store handled junk, as Cora Sue had said, or actual antiques as Barry Storm had talked about.

Seconds later, Otis, who might be in his seventies, approached her. He had wispy white hair that curled over his ears. Wrinkles creased his forehead and drew character lines in his cheeks. His chin looked as if it had once been strong, but now the skin on it sagged a bit.

His very blue eyes seemed to target her when she said, "Good evening."

She tried to remember how long ago it had been since Otis had visited the tea garden. He'd stopped coming in about six months ago. Usually wearing a button-down white shirt with the collar open, even on warmer days he paired it with a cardigan. Today his shop was warm as if there wasn't any air-conditioning. She was glad she'd worn a short-sleeved blouse and a skort to work today.

He pointed a finger at her as he came a little closer. "You're Daisy."

She laughed. "What gave me away?"

"It's your voice and that blond hair. If I remember correctly, you have blue eyes to go with it."

If he remembered correctly? Couldn't he see her eye color?

"Where are my manners?" he asked the public in general. He stuck out a hand to her. "I used to buy your scones all the time. I especially liked those cinnamon ones."

"I'm so glad. You haven't been to the tea garden for a while, have you?"

Shaking his head, Otis sighed. "No. I can't drive anymore, and I don't trust walking too far. My nephew buys me a supply of your soup and scones when he stops in for me." Otis leaned a little closer to her and said in an aside, "We both love those cherry tarts of yours."

"Your nephew is one of the reasons I stopped in," Daisy explained. "He noticed the teapots we have at the tea garden and told me you might have antique ones here. Or even some not-so-antique ones."

"We sure do," Otis assured her. "Come on back and I'll show you. Even though I can't see as well as I used to, every night I go around the place to try to check what Barry added or what he sold."

Daisy felt sweat beginning to collect under her hair and neck. Reaching into her pocket, she took out the scrunchie that she'd worn to work and gathered her hair into a ponytail.

In the back of the shop Daisy spotted the shelf holding teapots. Otis reached up and took one down, handing it to her. "That one has flowers all over it, if that's what you're looking for."

Daisy examined it, top and bottom as well as under the lid. It wasn't one she would use. The glaze wasn't sufficient. She handed it back to Otis. "May I see that one?" she asked, pointing to a rose Victorian porcelain teapot and teacup that was a duo.

Otis handed it down to her. "That one comes with a satin-lined gift box," he told her.

The little teapot with its floral design and its unique infinity-symbol shaped handle stood atop the Victorian-design teacup. The cup had been decorated with green leaves that complemented the flowers on top of the teapot and other flowers around its base. As she examined it, she realized it was a two-cup pot that would be perfect for one of her customers who came in for a quick visit. Burton and Burton had manufactured it. She examined the edges, the handles, and the fluted base and could see no markings or chips that shouldn't be there.

"This really is lovely." She looked for a price tag but didn't find one.

A loud male voice came from the doorway beside the shelving unit. Then Daisy heard a second voice, male too, responding. They were argumentative but she couldn't hear exactly what they were saying.

Otis looked a bit embarrassed, so she hurriedly asked, "How much are you asking for this?"

Otis took the teapot and matching cup in hand, then he gave Daisy a crooked smile. "Thirty dollars would do it."

Should she or shouldn't she? The tea garden had recovered nicely after a major blip from a food critic in the spring. Still . . .

Suddenly Barry appeared in the doorway to the back of the shop and focused on his uncle. He gave Daisy a smile, but said to Otis, "Ian wants to ask you about an antique auger. I'll take care of Daisy. I'm the reason she came in in the first place." He winked at her.

If Barry Storm suddenly thought they were good friends because they'd had one prolonged conversation, he thought wrong. She liked his uncle, who now looked troubled. Barry, she wasn't so sure about.

Otis returned the teapot to Daisy. "It was good to see you again."

"You too. The next time I come in, I'll bring you a scone."

That made the old man smile. However, he crossed to the door to the back and disappeared into it.

"So you came for a teapot," Barry said, making conversation.

"I came to look around in general. But, yes, I found this one." Before she had a chance to say what his uncle had told her it would cost, Barry took it from her hands and examined it. "This is one of my new ones. I haven't even had a chance to tag it yet. Are you interested?"

"I might be."

"It's a bargain at fifty dollars. It even comes with a beautiful gift box."

So Barry was going to charge her fifty dollars when his uncle would have charged her thirty. "Your uncle told me it would cost thirty dollars." She wanted to see what Barry would say.

Barry didn't miss a beat. "My uncle's vision is failing and he often doesn't see the worth in what he sells."

"At fifty dollars, I think I'll pass," she told him.

Barry gave her a probing look, but he didn't lower the price. "It might not be here the next time you come in."

"That's possible, but there are many teapots in the world and I can live without this one."

"I understand," he said, looking as if he did. "Maybe next time you come in we'll have something to fit your budget."

"Maybe," she agreed.

"Whether you come in again or not, you'll be seeing me as long as you're making those cherry tarts."

Daisy didn't respond to that, just smiled politely and turned to go. She could feel Barry Storm's eyes on her back as she left.

Tuesday evening with Jonas, Keith, and Mandy didn't produce any real solutions for the dad and his daughter. But Daisy had given Keith leads from her aunt on where he could find antiques.

Wednesday flashed by in a blur. Daisy texted with Jonas morning and afternoon and both Keith and Mandy seemed at home in his town house, remembering what comfort was. In the evening, Daisy, Vi, and Jazzi had gone shopping in Lancaster with Daisy's mom to find her a dress for the wedding. They'd been successful. Daisy hadn't looked for her mother-of-the-bride dress because she'd wanted her mom to have Vi's and Jazzi's complete attention.

Daisy worked on Thursday but left the tea garden early in the afternoon to stop at Jonas's town house. He'd let her in with a wide smile and a wink that meant he'd kiss her when they were alone.

The times she'd visited Jonas's home, nothing had

been lying around—like sneakers, magazines, or books. A sectional sofa in steel gray took up most of the space in the living room along with a wide, navy fabric-covered chair. The coffee table, however, Jonas had made himself. He'd made every piece of wood furniture in his town house.

Other wood pieces included the low walnut coffee table with chunky legs, two side tables in the same design, as well as an entertainment center that was tucked into the wall on the outside of his staircase. The first time Daisy had been here, she'd noticed the lack of photographs, knickknacks, and treasured items. When Jonas had left his life behind in Philadelphia, he'd truly left it behind. It seemed that nothing from the past had come with him.

His kitchen included a dining area with a black mission-style table with two saddle stools and two high-back chairs. Jonas's town house was definitely no fuss, no bother, and manifested very little of his personality, except for the fact that he did like comfort and practicality.

Keith was sitting at the table in one of the high-back chairs, holding Mandy.

"It's a good thing you taught me how to make iced tea," Jonas said with a smile. He told Keith, "I use tea bags and Daisy uses loose tea. We get the same result."

"So he says," Daisy joked. When Mandy coughed, Daisy didn't like the sound of it. She set her purse on the table and pulled out the baby thermometer she'd brought along in case Keith needed it. She asked Keith, "Do you mind if I take her temperature?"

Keith shook his head. "No, not at all. In fact, I was telling Jonas that I should go to the drugstore for cough medicine for toddlers. Last night, she was awake several times coughing. I should have gone yesterday but I got tied up looking for an address in Waynesboro. The farmer there supposedly had antiques to sell. But no one was there when I arrived."

Daisy looked at Jonas. "You babysat?"

He grinned. "I did . . . and I didn't have to call you or Keith even once. Mandy and I watched *Paw Patrol*!"

Seeing Jonas in a new light—that he was comfortable with children—Daisy laughed. Jonas poured tea over ice into three glasses and set them on the table. Mandy already had a sippy cup with water that Keith was encouraging her to drink.

Daisy ran the thermometer over Mandy's forehead. When she checked it, she said to Keith, "She has a low-grade fever. I'll leave the thermometer here and you can check it again later. But if the cough becomes worse and her temperature goes up, you really should take her to urgent care. The secretary at the church's day care called me back today and said Reverend Kemp would like to interview you and Mandy. But Mandy can't attend day care unless she's well."

"I told Keith I'd watch her again if he wants to go to the drugstore," Jonas commented.

Daisy knew Jonas trusted his manager to handle business at Woods when he wanted to work in the shop or take time off.

Keith rested his hand on his daughter's forehead. Then he straightened. "I called a buggy maker who has wagon wheels and lanterns for sale. If I buy them, I can sell them to Pirated Treasures."

From what Keith had said, she believed he was a man who was determined to pay his own way. "I can stay here with Jonas and watch Mandy." She looked at Jonas. "I can text Violet and ask if she can take Jazzi home with her. They'll be together at home until I get there."

"Vi might have plans with Foster," Jonas reminded her.

"Maybe. But I think Violet was going to move some things into the garage apartment. Jazzi can help her with that. I don't want her lifting anything she shouldn't, and Foster doesn't either."

"You said your daughters are teenagers," Keith remembered.

"My youngest is sixteen and learning to drive. Talk about stress. And Violet finished her freshman year of college, but is pregnant and getting married in a few weeks. No stress there, either."

Keith actually laughed. "I can see you're warning me."

Daisy patted Mandy's leg. The three-year-old was dressed in jeans shorts and a cute little white shirt that said DADDY'S GIRL. "That's a cute outfit," Daisy said.

Keith shrugged. "I went to a thrift store before we hit the road. It's amazing what you can buy there for kids for a quarter or fifty cents. And the clothes look like they've never been worn."

"You know, a thrift store is opening soon in Willow Creek. I'm about to go through my closet for donations."

Daisy held her arms out to Mandy. "Will you come to me, sweetie? Your dad has a little business he'd like to take care of."

When Mandy reached out her arms and wrapped them around Daisy's neck, Daisy put her cheek against Mandy's and rocked her.

After studying them for a good long minute, Keith pushed back his chair and stood. "All right. I should only be gone for an hour. I've been trying to coax her to drink. If you can do that, it would be great. I have her favorite kind of cookies over there on the counter. If she misses me or gets cranky, an Animal Cracker might help."

"Cookies always help. So do cherry tarts," Jonas joked.

"Tomorrow I'll make sure to save you some," Daisy assured him.

"After I drive to the buggy maker, I'll stop at the drugstore. I'll call you then to see how Mandy is faring. If you're doing okay, and I get the lanterns and wheels, I'll stop at Pirated Treasures and see if Otis wants them. Is all of that okay with you?"

"That's fine," Jonas said. "Do what you have to do. With the little one to keep us occupied, the time will go quickly."

Ten minutes later, Keith was out the door.

Jonas and Daisy looked at each other and they both smiled. Jonas said, "Why don't I take her for a little while."

Mandy went to him and snuggled into his shoulder.

"We can sit with her on the sofa," Daisy suggested. "If she falls asleep, we'll be right there to watch her. I just hope Otis is the one who buys whatever Keith finds."

Jonas quirked a brow.

As they walked over to the sofa, Daisy told him about her visit there in more detail. "So it seems to me, Otis is the honest one, like Keith said. I just wonder if Barry makes extra money off the antiques that come in. Does he tell Otis? Does he give it to his uncle? Or does he stick it into his pocket?"

On the long part of the sofa, Jonas settled Mandy

beside him. She curled up on her side, her thumb in her mouth.

Daisy sat on the other side of her and brushed the little girl's hair away from her eyes. "We'll probably never find out what Barry does, but I think I'll go back to Pirated Treasures when Otis is there. I *would* like that teapot and cup."

As Mandy napped, Jonas and Daisy played gin rummy. Daisy could tell that Jonas let her win the last game. She was about to call him on it when he said, "It's already four o'clock and Keith hasn't called."

Daisy said, "Maybe something held him up. This time let's play hearts. I'm an expert at that game and I'll win with skill." She was teasing, but Jonas didn't smile. He looked worried.

Mandy finally awakened after a long nap, had energy and wanted to play. Daisy took her temperature again and it was the same.

"Do you suppose Keith went antiquing farther out of town?" Daisy asked.

"Maybe the buggy maker wasn't at home and he had to wait, or maybe Otis wasn't there alone and he had to wait until Barry left."

"What do you think we should do about supper? Mandy's going to need something and so will we."

As Jonas watched Mandy putting a board puzzle together on the coffee table, he shook his head. "Maybe I was wrong about Keith. Maybe helping him won't work out."

"Don't give up too easily. Something unexpected could have happened. Maybe he had car trouble."

"Then why hasn't he called? I'll text him and see if he responds."

Mandy ran over to Daisy with her pink teddy bear stuffed under her arm. "Hung-y."

"You are?" She looked at Jonas.

"I don't have much in the refrigerator after the past two days. I was going to go grocery shopping tonight."

Crossing to the kitchen, Daisy studied what Jonas did have. A loaf of sliced bread sat cocked against the refrigerator. When she opened the fridge, she didn't find much. However, there was sliced cheese in the meat drawer, a head of lettuce, and a few carrots.

"I'd make scrambled eggs," she told him, "but I don't know if Mandy has an egg allergy. Many children do. Do you have a griddle?"

"Every man should have a griddle in his kitchen," Jonas deadpanned.

She smiled, though she didn't feel like smiling. "Good. How do toasted cheese sandwiches sound?"

"Like a real supper. We can have Animal Crackers as a chaser."

"With a bit of salad on the side. I'll shred lettuce and shave the carrots into it. Mandy should be able to eat that."

"I texted Keith. Let's see if he answers."

Joining Daisy in the kitchen, Jonas wrapped his arm around her waist. "You're a sport for doing this. I know it wasn't what you intended."

"I suppose I should text Vi and Jazzi to let them know I'm still here and don't know when I'll be home."

"Wait five minutes. If Keith doesn't answer his text, I'll try to phone him."

After Jonas pulled the griddle from a lower cupboard, he set it on one of the burners. As Daisy buttered slices of bread for the sandwiches and toasted them on the griddle, Jonas went to Mandy. He found a canister of blocks that Keith had brought along and he dumped them onto the coffee table. She squealed with delight.

By the time the sandwiches were finished, Keith still hadn't returned Jonas's text. After finishing the tower with Mandy and letting her crash it down, Jonas picked up his phone. Daisy put the sandwiches on dishes and set them on the table, then she poured milk for Mandy and water for herself and Jonas.

"Come here, Mandy," she said.

Jonas frowned. "Keith has a burner phone so he doesn't have to have a contract. I suppose it's possible he ran out of minutes."

Daisy cut Mandy's cheese sandwich in sections so she could handle and chew it more easily. She didn't want the little girl to stuff too big a piece into her mouth. She pointed to the lettuce and carrots that she'd put in a smaller dish with a dab of ranch dressing on top. "Can you eat a little bit of that first while your sandwich cools off?"

Mandy nodded, but instead of using the fork Daisy had put at her place, she used her fingers to pick up a bit of lettuce and carrot and poke it into her mouth. Daisy watched her carefully as Mandy chewed, swallowed, and smiled. She didn't seem to have a sore throat or a runny nose but, every once in a while, she still coughed.

Daisy was beginning to think Jonas's call to Keith had been in vain. Maybe Jonas had been right and they'd both been wrong about Keith. Karina too.

Daisy scanned Jonas's face—the scar down the side of his cheek, his five o'clock shadow that made him look sexy and dangerous, the way he was concentrating on picking up Mandy's blocks. He cared about many things and he seemed to care about children.

Mandy pointed to Daisy's sandwich. "Gettin' cold."

Daisy imagined Keith had said that to Mandy many times over. Winking at the little girl, Daisy picked up half of her sandwich and started to eat. Jonas's sandwich was the one that was going to get cold.

Suddenly Jonas's expression changed as his phone buzzed. Picking it up, he went on alert and motioned for Daisy to come over to the sofa. But before she could stand, he must have realized she was helping Mandy with her supper, so he hurried over to her.

"I'm putting it on speaker," he told Keith, and pointed to Daisy's ear. He obviously wanted her to listen.

Keith was saying, "I'm still at the police station. The detective is peppering me with questions. When my phone buzzed, he said he'd give me a break. Right. A break."

Daisy heard panic in Keith's voice.

"Tell me exactly what happened," Jonas said.

"I don't know where to start. I went to the buggy maker and bought a wheel and lanterns. I made a quick trip to the drugstore and then drove to Pirated Treasures. I didn't call because I was doing okay on time. The thing was—when I got there, a patrol cop was outside. He wouldn't let me go in and I was worried about Otis, that maybe he'd had a stroke or something. So I asked. I guess that was my big mistake. The patrol cop asked what doings I had with Otis. So I told him about the wagon wheel and the lanterns in my van. He told me to wait there and he'd be right back. I should have known something more than a stroke was going on."

"I don't understand," Jonas said calmly. "Was something wrong with Otis?"

"Not Otis. Barry. He was dead! It wasn't long until Detective Willet came outside with a look on his face that said I was in trouble."

"I don't understand," Jonas repeated. "You hadn't even gone inside the store."

"Not today. I'd given my name to the patrol cop and apparently he asked Otis about me. Willet said that Otis told him that I had threatened Barry with a marble rolling pin a few days before. Barry and I had argued about a deal that had included the rolling pin."

"What does a rolling pin have to do with it?" Daisy asked.

"Someone killed Barry Storm with that rolling pin. The back of the store is a mess. The body was gone. But, Daisy, your cherry tarts were even mixed in with everything."

"They let you see the crime scene?" Jonas inquired, shocked.

"Maybe Willet thought if I saw it, I'd blurt something out. I'd confess. I don't know. I told him I hadn't seen either Otis or Barry today. Uh-oh, he just came back in. What should I do? I don't know how to handle this. Willet just keeps asking me the same questions over and over again."

"He's trying to trip you up. The best thing to do would be to stop talking to him."

"Stop? He'll put me in jail. What will happen to Mandy?"

"No, he won't put you in jail. Not yet. Not without evidence. I'm going to call a lawyer I know—Marshall Thompson—and see if he can drive to the station to be with you. Do *not* say another word. Just tell them your lawyer is on the way."

"But I don't know if he is."

"They don't have to know that. I'll make sure Marshall, or somebody he knows, will be there to get you out. In the meantime, tell him that you want to wait for your lawyer. Once you say the word 'lawyer,' Zeke Willet will have to stop questioning you."

"How do you know his name?"

"He and I were once detectives on the same police force in Philadelphia. It's a long story."

"He's glaring at me."

"Just do what I said. Marshall Thompson is the lawyer's name," he repeated.

"Tell me one thing," Keith said. "Is Mandy all right?"

"Right now she's eating a toasted cheese sandwich. We'll make sure she's all right, Keith. Once Marshall gets there, he'll get you out quickly. When you return to my place, we'll talk about all of this."

When Keith said, "Thank you," his voice trembled.

Jonas ended the call and quickly found Marshall's number in his contacts. "If Marshall's home, I can fill him in on his drive to the station."

"And if he's not?"

"Then it will just take a little longer for someone to get to Keith."

When Jonas tapped in Marshall's number, Daisy asked him, "Do you think Keith did it?"

Jonas didn't answer, but rather asked *her* a question. "Do you?"

Chapter Five

It was almost seven p.m. when Keith and Marshall Thompson arrived together at Jonas's town house. Daisy was seated on the sofa beside Mandy, who was napping again. She didn't know if that was normal for her or not.

After Keith and Marshall came inside, Marshall put a hand on Keith's shoulder. "Stop worrying," Marshall said. "We gave them pertinent information."

Marshall was a tall man, almost as tall as Jonas at six foot two. His hair was thick and snow white. It was hard to tell his exact age. Always impeccably dressed, today he wore a sage polo shirt and gray slacks. Shined black loafers completed the ensemble.

After a nod to Marshall, Daisy asked Keith, "What are you worried about? Being a suspect?"

Keith lowered himself into the armchair across from Mandy. "Sure, that. But I'm also afraid the police will call Child Protective Services."

"There's no reason for Zeke Willet to do that," Marshall reassured him. "I told him that Jonas will vouch for you. When we spoke, Jonas told me to say you were a friend of his who moved into the area."

Daisy glanced at Jonas, who nodded. "I gave Marshall the rundown when I called him. I told him to tell the detective that Keith was looking for an affordable place to stay while looking for a job. In the meantime, he was staying with me."

"Did they believe you?" Daisy asked.

"No reason not to," Marshall confirmed. He studied Keith again. "I know you've had a rough lot, and it looks as if it might get a little rougher until we get all this straightened out. But for now at least, those questions weren't out of the ordinary. I know you had to repeat many of your answers, and that's why I was there, to make sure you didn't say anything you shouldn't."

Marshall addressed both Jonas and Daisy. "Keith explained about his antiquing expertise that he learned from his wife. He told them he's been selling to Barry and Otis since he moved to Willow Creek. Unfortunately, he already had talked about the argument with Barry before I got there."

Keith shrugged. "I was trying to be straight with that detective. I had taken a wagon wheel to Otis the week before, and he paid me a hundred dollars more than Barry was going to with the new one. All right, I accepted that on the wagon wheel. To me the quality was about the same. Barry thought it wasn't. But then that marble rolling pin . . . I knew that was worth double what Barry told me he'd give me. I just happened to have it in my hand when we were arguing. It's not like I was actually going to hit him with it."

"All of that was too much information," Jonas said with what Daisy considered his discerning detective's eye.

"He wanted the truth, so I gave him the truth,"

Keith insisted defensively. "I also told him Barry Storm cheated lots of people. They'll find that out if they check around."

Daisy wasn't sure that throwing someone else under the bus would work with Zeke Willet. She'd had a bit of an attitude run-in with the new-to-Willow Creek detective not so long ago.

"Detective Willet told me not to leave town," Keith said. "I'm so tempted to pack up Mandy and everything else and just drive away."

Jonas approached Keith and looked him straight in the eye. "I was once a detective. Running will absolutely prove your guilt, nothing else. And just how far do you think you'd get? You have a little girl. What would that do to her?"

Keith rubbed his face up and down with both hands. "I'm not thinking straight."

"You probably need food in your stomach and a few minutes just to breathe," Daisy suggested.

Jonas went to the kitchen and picked up his keys that were hanging on a hook on the wall. "Unfortunately, I don't have much in the way of food here. Sarah Jane's is open until eight. I'll drive over there and pick up a few meat loaf dinners. Marshall, do you want to stay and eat?"

Marshall shook his head. "No, I've got to be going." He studied Keith. "I know you said you can't pay me. This first consultation today was free. But if the police call you again to go in, you call me. We'll figure out something for payment when this is all over."

Keith looked as if he were overcome by emotion and couldn't speak. He simply nodded.

Jonas had just said to Marshall, "I'll walk you out,"

when Mandy awakened and began crying. In the midst of the cry, she coughed.

Not liking the sound of that because it sounded deeper and more congested than before, Daisy picked up the thermometer on the coffee table. After she passed it across Mandy's forehead, she frowned. "It's one hundred now."

Keith rushed over to Mandy, picked her up, and held her on his lap. She stopped crying and turned her cheek into his shirt. "It's okay, baby," he murmured in a gentle voice. Then he looked at Daisy. "I can't afford to take her to urgent care, and I can't keep asking for handouts."

Daisy studied Mandy's face. She was a little flushed, but then children often were after they'd been sleeping. Her temperature could be up because of that too. She knew that when her girls had had fevers, they'd always seemed worse at night. She put her ear to Mandy's chest and listened. The three-year-old was breathing normally, and Daisy couldn't hear wheezing.

"Do you want to know what I would do if she were my little girl?"

"I do. I want to do what's best for her. On the other hand, having a bill collector after me isn't going to help *her*."

"If she'll drink liquids for you, pump them into her."

He pointed to a bag on the counter. "I bought apple juice when I stopped at the drugstore. She likes it and I think she'll drink it. I can dilute it and make sure she drinks water in between."

It seemed he really did know how to care for Mandy. This wasn't a dad with no skills.

"I bought a jar of applesauce too. I'm sure she'll eat that."

Daisy looked at Mandy and asked, "Does anything hurt, honey?"

Mandy shook her head and stuck her thumb into her mouth.

"Watch if she starts pulling on her ears or anything like that. If her temperature doesn't go up, I think she'll be okay until morning. But if she starts wheezing, if her fever goes up, then you need to take her to urgent care. I have a caring family physician. In the morning, I'll call and explain that you've just moved into the area and that you have a little girl who's sick. I'll call you if I can get an appointment."

"I don't know what to say. All of you have been so kind."

Marshall gave Keith and Daisy a wave as he said he'd see them soon. Jonas, however, stopped in his foyer. He admitted to Keith, "Willow Creek and the people here care about each other. It's the reason I stayed. In these times, it's important to help out each other—that's what we are meant to do." He asked Daisy, "Can you stay longer?"

"Yes. I'll call Jazzi and Vi and tell them I'll be home later. If Sarah Jane has mashed potatoes left, be sure to get those so we can feed some to Mandy."

More than once since they'd met Keith and Mandy, Jonas had surprised her. Sometimes she knew detectives pulled away rather than got involved. Apparently, Jonas hadn't been that type of detective. Now, as a private citizen, he believed in helping his neighbor. So did she.

"Can you see if Sarah Jane has gelatin with fruit?

That would be okay with Mandy's cough. It won't make the congestion worse. Dairy products might." Her former career as a dietician—she'd finally finished earning her degree after she'd moved to Florida— had often helped her with her own children.

Mandy's eyes were open and she was staring up at Jonas and Daisy with her cheek still against her dad's chest. Keith looked down at her and touched his chin to her forehead. "I'm surely glad that you and Daisy followed Karina last night. I don't know what I'd have done facing this on my own. I think I'm just getting tired of not having a real life, a life where Mandy and I have roots and a permanent home."

"You have to have hope that tomorrow will be better than today. We're trying to help you make sure it is," Daisy assured him.

Instead of going to the door and leaving, Jonas went over to Daisy and dropped a kiss on her forehead. Then he gently squeezed her arm and left his town house.

Since their almost breakup, they'd been learning more about what each other needed and wanted. When Jonas was quiet, that didn't mean he wasn't thinking about something important. When he was expressionless, that didn't mean he didn't care. He wasn't an open guy with his thoughts and his feelings. But he was trying. They were attempting to understand each other. Maybe, just maybe, they were succeeding.

The following morning, Daisy didn't call Keith, he called her. It was six a.m. when she heard him say, "I'm sorry to be calling so early."

"I'm up. How's Mandy?"

"She's coughing more. Can you make that appointment?"

As soon as the doctor's office opened, Daisy called and explained the situation. The receptionist there, who Daisy knew, conferred with the doctor and came back to the phone. "Bring her in at eleven."

After Daisy thanked the receptionist, she returned her call to Keith. "We have an appointment at eleven. Do you want me to pick you up or—"

Keith cut in. "I just received a phone call from Detective Willet. I have to go down to the station at nine. I might be finished in time but I don't know. Is that a problem?"

"I don't know if Dr. Nadleson will treat Mandy if I take her in alone. But I can try. Can I use your car seat in my vehicle?"

"Yes. All you have to do is attach it to the seat belt. If I'm not here when you pick up Mandy, I'll leave a note for the doctor and drive there as soon as I can."

"Is Marshall meeting you at the station?"

"He is. He said they probably just want to go over the same things I told them yesterday. I don't know if I should tell them I need to meet you at the doctor's to get Mandy seen."

"Ask Marshall what you should do about that. I think Willet will have to let you take an emergency phone call, especially if Marshall's there. So if I have a problem, I can at least let you talk to the doctor."

"I'm so sorry about all the trouble I'm causing you, Daisy."

"I want to show you that Willow Creek is a community you can count on. I'll talk to you soon."

Keith wasn't at the town house when Daisy arrived

but Jonas was. He gave her a big hug and a long kiss when she stepped in the door. He motioned to Mandy, who was curled up on the sofa under an afghan, hugging her teddy bear. "I hate seeing her like this. I hope your doctor can help."

"I've known Zoe Nadleson since I had to see her about strep throat when I was home from college. I'm hoping she'll look at the situation and help no matter what's going on with Keith."

"Is someone covering for you at work?"

"Jazzi and Vi are both working today. Cora Sue can act as their manager. They can cover the tearoom while Iris and Tessa bake. Foster has classes this morning but he'll be in this afternoon."

"I just marvel at your juggling."

She smiled at him. "I'm so glad I'm a marvel."

He chuckled. "I'll put Mandy's seat in your car for you."

A few minutes later Jonas was back. He went over to Mandy where Daisy was watching her carefully. Scooping her up into his arms, he carried her out to Daisy's PT Cruiser.

Daisy drew up in front of the doctor's office building at five minutes to eleven. After climbing out, she opened the back door, released Mandy from her car seat, and took her into her arms. Mandy snuggled her face into Daisy's neck.

Inside Daisy was registering Mandy at the receptionist's window when suddenly the door to the doctor's office burst open and Keith ran in. His face was drawn, his forehead was creased, and he looked pale.

He gave Daisy a half smile and said, "Here. I'll take her."

The receptionist asked for Keith's ID. He managed

to take his wallet from his back pocket and handed it to Daisy. "Can you pull out my license?"

Daisy did and the receptionist made a copy. Keith told her, "I don't have insurance."

Daisy said, "I'm covering the cost today."

Although the receptionist gave Daisy an odd look, she didn't say anything. A few minutes later the LPN from inside the office came out to escort them to an examination room.

A half hour later, Keith carried Mandy down the hall. After they checked out and Daisy paid the bill, they went into the lobby.

"Do you think the antibiotic will do it?" he asked.

"It will help with any secondary infection including bronchitis. Like Zoe said, you caught it in time. Along with acetaminophen, Mandy should feel better in a couple of days. If you want to stop at the pharmacy, I'll drive Mandy back to the town house and meet you there."

Daisy knew Keith was about to thank her again but she just held up her hand. "Jonas told me you cook. He was going to the store this morning to stock up. So how about if you just make us lunch. You can tell us everything you went over with Detective Willet then."

"Depending on what Jonas buys, I'm sure I can cook up something. I'll meet you there in a little while."

Daisy wondered if Zeke Willet had interviewed anyone else or if Keith really was suspect number one.

That afternoon when Daisy returned to the tea garden, Jazzi rushed to her. "How's the little girl?"

"The police wanted to talk to Keith again, but he got to the doctor's in time for the appointment. Dr. Nadleson gave Mandy an antibiotic and Keith is supposed to give her fever medication. He's supposed to force liquids as much as he can."

"Will she be able to go into day care?"

"She can't go into day care if she's sick. So it will probably be a few days. Why?"

Jazzi looked up at her with her big brown eyes that were sparkling, vital, and maybe even content, at least for the time being. "I was thinking. If you don't need me at the tea garden, maybe I could watch her. You know I'm a good babysitter. All the parents I've sat for say so. I'm sure Mr. Rebert wants to try to find work."

Thinking over what Jazzi said, Daisy considered all the babysitting gigs her daughter had had so far this summer. She was right. Parents and kids liked her. And Daisy knew she preferred babysitting over serving customers at the tea garden. "Keith can't pay you."

Jazzi shrugged. "That's okay. It will be good practice for me. I know Vi's going to want me to babysit for her. If Vi's working extra hours to earn as much money as she can, you don't need me here that much, do you?"

Smiling, Daisy thought it might benefit everyone if she gave in. "I'm sure we can manage here for the next few days. If you want to babysit Mandy, I'll talk to Keith and see if he'll trust you to do it. I'm sure he'll want to check in with you often. He's that kind of dad."

"That just means he cares." Jazzi's face grew sober as she lowered her voice and asked, "What happens to Mandy if Mr. Rebert is arrested?"

"I don't even want to think about that. As in other

situations, we'll have to deal with the investigation as it comes."

Jazzi glanced over Daisy's shoulder as the bell above the door rang. "Uh-oh," she said. "Speaking of investigations—"

When Daisy turned around, she saw why Jazzi's tone had gotten worried. Detective Zeke Willet had just walked in.

He didn't even make the pretext of wanting to order anything but headed directly toward Daisy and Jazzi.

Jazzi took a step closer to her, and Daisy knew this was her daughter's sign that she was going to protect and support her. But she didn't want Jazzi involved in whatever was coming. She put her hand on Jazzi's shoulder. "Go back to what you were doing. See if Tessa needs anything in the kitchen. Hopefully this won't take too long with Detective Willet."

After another wary look at him, Jazzi headed toward the kitchen.

Daisy didn't move, and when the detective stood before her, he had his serious face on. "Hello, Mrs. Swanson."

Zeke Willet had short blond hair, a lean physique, and a squared jaw. Apparently, they were back to formal titles. "Hello, Detective Willet. What can I do to help you?"

"I need to interview Karina Post . . . and you."

"Are you taking us down to the station?"

He looked a bit chagrined. "No. I should have made myself clear. I can interview you in your office. I'd like to see Miss Post first, if you don't mind."

Of course, she minded. Having a detective in her

tea garden wasn't good for business. Still, maybe they could do this quickly and get it over with.

Karina was helping to serve afternoon tea in the spillover tearoom. Daisy's tea customers there had made their reservations ahead of time. Nodding to that room, she said, "I'll get Karina."

In the room with the bay window, she touched Karina's arm and tagged Cora Sue. Then she pointed into the green room. "Karina, Detective Willet wants to interview you."

Karina went pale.

"Just tell him the truth—how you met Keith, and whatever else he asks you. Keep your answers short. Don't volunteer any more information than you have to. Got it?"

"Got it," Karina agreed, still pale but squaring her shoulders as if she were going to do battle.

While Karina walked toward the detective and they both headed for Daisy's office, Daisy said to Cora Sue, "I'll help you serve in here until it's my turn. What do we need to do next?"

As Cora Sue filled Daisy in on what course the tea guests were on, and who was drinking what kind of tea, Daisy made mental notes, trying not to think about the detective and what his questions might be.

A half hour later, Karina ran into Daisy as Daisy was taking a new pot of orange pekoe tea, a special grade of black tea, to one of the tables. "He's not happy with me," Karina said. "I did what you told me. He's waiting for you."

Daisy carefully transferred the pot of tea from her hand to Karina's and told her what table needed it. Then she headed for her office, wanting the interview to be over.

Immediately, she could see that the detective looked frustrated. He motioned to the chair in front of her own desk as he sat behind it. Daisy imagined he thought he was in a position of power. That all depended on what he asked.

He didn't beat around the bush. With a piercing glare in his brown eyes, he asked, "Are you obstructing justice by telling Miss Post not to talk to me?"

"I didn't tell her not to talk to you. I told her to tell you the truth and what she knows. I also told her not to volunteer any information that you hadn't asked for. It's advice a lawyer would give her."

He pointed to her. "You are *not* a lawyer."

"I can call Marshall Thompson for Karina and myself if that's what you want me to do. Instead of being adversarial, maybe you could just ask me your questions and I'll answer them."

After studying her for a very long moment, he agreed. "All right, Mrs. Swanson, let's start at the beginning. When did you meet Keith Rebert?"

With the basic facts, Daisy told him essentially what had happened from the night she'd met Keith to taking Mandy to the doctor this morning.

"And you'd do all this for a stranger?" Detective Willet asked.

Daisy wasn't exactly sure where to go with that. On one hand, Jonas had told the police that he and Keith were friends. That was true now.

She answered, "I'd like to think I'd help a friend *or* a stranger."

Before Zeke Willet could ask another question, Daisy's office door opened. At first, she thought it might be her aunt trying to add her moral support.

But it wasn't her aunt. It was Jonas. She was never so glad to see anyone.

Willet's voice was rough. "What are you doing here, Groft? I'm interviewing Mrs. Swanson."

"Her aunt told me you've been in here with her a long time. She has a business to run."

The detective leaned back in the chair and shook his head. "I intend to ask all the questions that I need to ask. I'm getting the feeling that you're all protecting Keith Rebert. That means there's something there to hide."

"There's *nothing* to hide," Daisy protested.

Jonas agreed. "There isn't anything to hide, but we are protecting Keith because we don't want the murder pinned on the wrong man. That happens. Sometimes the police focus on one suspect and don't look anywhere else."

At that Zeke Willet's face turned red and he stood. "I ought to bring charges against the lot of you for obstruction. When I have enough grounds for it, I might."

"Just because you have a beef with me, don't take it out on my friends," Jonas ordered, crossing to Daisy's chair and putting both of his hands on her shoulders.

"My beef with you has nothing to do with this investigation." He pierced Daisy with another glare. "If I come up with more questions, I'll ask you to come down to the station the next time. Then we won't have any interference."

At that threat, Detective Zeke Willet left her office and the tea garden.

Chapter Six

As Daisy and Jonas, Vi, Foster, and Jazzi strolled up the walk to Daisy's childhood family home on Sunday, she thought the landscaping had never looked more beautiful. Her mother had interspersed roses with lavender ever since Daisy had been a little girl. Daisy wondered if that's why she liked lavender so much . . . because it brought back childhood memories.

Daisy hadn't liked sports much, while her sister Cammie had excelled. When her sister would go outside to practice her softball pitch, Daisy would wander around the gardens or sit on the back-porch step, simply taking in all the scents around her. Zinnias from cherry red to yellow to regal purple swayed in the breeze at the corner of the house where they circled a birdbath.

As a child, she'd always used the back-door entrance into the kitchen. As an adult, however, she climbed the few porch steps to the covered front door. It looked as if her dad had repainted the casings on the outdoor lights. She knew he tried to keep up with maintenance so it didn't get ahead of him.

Behind her, Jazzi commented, "The front door's

closed. That means the air-conditioning's on. Thank goodness."

Daisy smiled. Her parents often tried to save costs by opening the windows. But July in Pennsylvania could be sweltering.

"I think I mind the heat more since I'm pregnant," Vi said. "Yesterday, I was hot at the tea garden, but nobody else seemed to be."

Daisy turned to her daughter. "The customers are content because they're not rushing around serving and carrying trays like you are. By the way, I think maybe you should stop carrying trays. Serving is okay. But you could help Tessa and Eva more in the kitchen. I'll make sure we turn the air-conditioning down in there so you're comfortable." Eva Conner, who was nearing her forty-fifth birthday, was their dishwasher and girl Friday. She could easily cover for Vi if necessary.

Daisy had noticed that Vi had worn a loose, short-sleeve, blousy top tonight with shorts. When the breeze had blown against her, Daisy had caught sight of the early baby bump. Her daughter was starting to show her pregnancy. Maternity fashions now weren't what they used to be. Some were clingy and some were shapeless. She really didn't know what direction Vi would go. Daisy was so tempted to take her on a shopping spree, but she knew Vi and Foster had to learn to live on their budget. Certainly, one new outfit for the rehearsal picnic at Gavin's wouldn't be too much.

Daisy rapped slightly on the door and then opened it. They all barreled inside to find relief from the humid heat. Her father was sitting in his recliner. The living room furniture was dated. The sofa had chunky legs and a camel back. The legs on the side tables were chunky too. But all of it was comfortable and that's what mattered to her parents.

Her mom came rushing in from the kitchen. She gave Jazzi, Vi, and Daisy a hug. To Jonas she just nodded. Her mother hadn't really spent that much time around Jonas, but that was Daisy's fault. Maybe she simply didn't want her mother's judgment about the relationship. The thing was—Rose Gallagher gave her opinion anyway. She didn't understand why Jonas had left his life as a detective to own a furniture store and to create some of that furniture himself. She thought he didn't have much ambition. Or maybe the real problem was that Jonas's detective skills gave him perception into other people's personalities and their lives. He was always polite with Rose, calm, and didn't say much. Maybe her mother didn't like him because she couldn't get a rise out of him.

She'd thought about telling her mom about Keith and Mandy. However, after talking to Jonas, they'd decided the best course was not to bring it up.

Her mom nodded to Foster but didn't say anything to him. Her disapproval was again showing. She had tried to do that with Ryan when they'd told her parents they were getting married and moving to Florida. But Daisy had been as determined as Vi. Daisy had felt her dad's and aunt Iris's support. She'd told herself back then, as well as now, that her mom's approval or disapproval didn't matter.

Daisy had brought along a box of cherry tarts as well as a bag of lemon tea cakes. Jonas was carrying them.

Jonas asked her mom, "Should I put dessert in the kitchen on the counter?"

"One thing about my daughter running a tea garden, I don't have to worry about desserts."

After a bit of small talk, they all sat around the table in the dining part of the kitchen. Her father bowed his head for a silent moment before dinner. That was an Amish custom of silent prayer that her family had usually followed.

Her mother had roasted two chickens, steamed fresh green beans, and boiled red-skin potatoes, adding butter and parsley. They'd passed around the platters and filled their dishes when her mom said, "Scuttlebutt has it that you were questioned by Detective Willet about that murder at Pirated Treasures. Is that true?"

Daisy suspected this subject might come up but had hoped it wouldn't. "Mom, it was just a preemptive visit because I knew someone who was involved."

"It wouldn't be wise to stick your nose into it."

Daisy knew she had tensed and she certainly didn't want tonight to be about the murder investigation. That wasn't why they were here. "No, it probably wouldn't be wise."

Jonas squeezed her hand under the table. He said, "Everything is delicious, Mrs. Gallagher. Cooking in all this heat can be wearing."

Daisy could have kissed him right then and there as he changed the course of the conversation.

Her mother responded, "It's not wearing at all when you're doing it for family."

Daisy wasn't sure that her mother was including Jonas in that family remark. Foster, after all, would become her grandson-in-law. And Jonas . . . For the time being her mom didn't exactly consider him Daisy's significant other.

Foster jumped in this time. "Mr. Gallagher, Vi has something she'd like to ask you."

"What's that, honey? Do you need me to help carry furniture into your apartment?"

Vi shook her head. "No, Gramps. I'd like you to do me a much more important favor than that."

He laid his fork down next to his plate. "And what would that be?"

"Will you walk me down the aisle when I get married?"

Daisy watched as her dad's eyes misted, and he seemed to have trouble answering. Finally, he cleared his throat. "I would be honored to walk you down the aisle. Just tell me where you need me and when."

That was a trait of her father's that Daisy loved the most. When he made a promise, he kept it. Glancing at Jonas, she wondered if he was the same type of man as her dad.

On Monday morning, Jonas called Daisy as she was filling the counter case.

"Hi, there," she greeted him. "Are you calling to tell me how much you enjoyed dinner at my mom's last night?"

Jonas chuckled. "It really wasn't that bad once Vi asked your dad if he'd walk her down the aisle. As long as the focus isn't on me or us, that's a good thing," he decided.

"What makes you so perceptive?"

"My investigative skills," he responded, tongue in cheek.

This time she laughed.

"I called to tell you the crime scene has been released. I didn't know if you wanted to know that or not."

Daisy's mind started spinning right away. She remembered the man Barry had been arguing with. His name was Ian. "It's good to know."

"Does that mean you're going to stop in at Pirated Treasures?"

He was beginning to learn her thought patterns. "Do you want to go along?"

There was a pause. "If you think you need me, I will."

And she was beginning to read him too. "That means you'd rather not."

There was a heavy silence before he asked, "What are you going to do if you *do* stop in?"

"Not get into any trouble. I can give Otis my condolences. There are a few other things I'd like to know and sometimes Otis is talkative. Nothing dangerous."

"Where have I heard *that* before?"

The wry tone in his voice told her they both remembered how she'd stepped into danger in the past. "Do you think Zeke Willet will charge us with obstruction?"

"Not unless we interfere with evidence that matters. He has something to prove with his first investigation in Willow Creek. I hear that he's escalating the investigation."

"Who's your contact in the police department?"

"A good detective never reveals his sources."

"I'll remember that if Willet carts us off to jail."

"Daisy, if you need me, call me. I mean it."

Her voice went soft and gentle. "I know you do. I'll

probably drive to Pirated Treasures when I take my lunch break. I'll let you know how it goes."

After she ended the call with Jonas, she was still smiling.

Her lunch break came later than she expected. It was almost two o'clock when Daisy opened the door at Pirated Treasures and walked inside. There weren't any customers in the store. She knew what murder in a shop did for business—nothing good. Just because people wanted to see where a murder happened, it didn't mean they'd buy anything.

She'd expected to see a news van or at least a reporter hanging around. But she couldn't spot anyone except for Otis, who was standing at the counter, looking lost.

Just in case he hadn't heard the bell, she called, "Hello?"

Otis practically shuffled toward her. He looked as if he'd aged at least another five years since she'd seen him last.

"Mrs. Swanson?" he asked.

His hearing must have been compensating for his lack of sight. "Yes, it is. But please call me Daisy. I brought you soup and a few cherry tarts. I know how much you like them. I'm so sorry about Barry."

He took the food from her hands. "Come back to the counter with me. There are two chairs there. We can sit and talk. I have a small refrigerator under the counter that I can put this in."

Behind the sales counter she saw two wooden ladder-back chairs with caned seats. After Otis stuffed the food in the little refrigerator, he motioned to one of the chairs. But then he said, "Maybe you don't want to sit. Did you come to buy something?"

"Maybe a little of both. I'm on my lunch break. I knew you'd probably be missing Barry."

The old man looked down at his scuffed shoes. "He could be a disappointment sometimes, but yes, I do miss him."

"I hope the police didn't question you for too long."

"That detective went after me as if I did it!" he related indignantly.

"Zeke Willet?"

"Yeah. Willet was his name. He acted like he had a bee under his shirt. I told him I found Barry when I opened the store. After all, I wasn't his keeper anymore. Not since he was eighteen."

"I suppose Barry wanted to be independent like most young adults."

"He sure did. He started looking after me more over the past year. I was grateful for that." Otis's words were thick with emotion.

Daisy waited a few seconds. "What will you do now?"

"Hire someone else, I guess. And find someone to do the book work. Barry did all that."

Daisy moved forward on the caned seat. "Do you mind talking about what Detective Willet asked you?"

Otis looked morose when he answered, "I don't mind."

Daisy suspected Otis didn't mind her questions because he needed the company. "Did the detective ask many questions about Keith Rebert?"

Otis rubbed his face with his hand, then let it drop to his lap. "He did. I might have gotten the young fellow in trouble. But I just told them what happened that day when he brought in the rolling pin."

"I understand. And you had to tell them the truth. Do you think Keith would have hit Barry with it?"

"The truth is—I don't know. I can't see so well close up, let alone far away. But I do know he raised it as if he wanted to make a point."

She decided to be truthful with Otis. "I'm trying to help Keith. I don't believe he killed Barry. Did you know he has a little girl?"

Otis nodded. "He brought her in here a couple of times. Cute little thing. I've got to say, it must be hard for him to take care of her all by himself."

"He's trying to make a new life. A friend of mine, Jonas Groft, is trying to help him. So am I."

Otis leaned forward, his chin jutting out. "And you don't think he did it?"

"We don't. But Detective Willet seems to be focusing on him rather than anyone else. So I'm trying to learn a few things."

"Things about Keith?"

She was quick to answer. "No. About Barry and maybe his friends. Do you remember that day that I was here and looked at the teapot?"

"I can't see so well, but my memory's sharp. I remember."

"Barry was arguing with somebody named Ian in the back before he came out to take over for you."

"That's right—Ian Busby. He and Barry went to school together."

"Do you have Ian's address?"

"Sure do. Clovis Platt, the farmer he works for, has lived in these parts for a couple of generations. He lives out on Tumbling Blocks Road."

That road would be difficult to forget. Tumbling

Blocks was the name of a quilt pattern that was popular and recognizable.

Otis went on, "The Platts live in a white house close to the road. It has awful, ugly green shutters. The barns are further back. Ian lives in a cabin on the farm. You can't see it from the road."

As long as she had the man's name and the name of the road, she'd be able to find the farm. As she studied Otis, she realized he not only looked tired but pale too. "Did you eat today?"

Otis shrugged, then shook his head. "I ain't got no appetite."

"You *have* to eat. That's why I brought you the soup."

"I appreciate you bringing that soup by. I used to make chicken soup for Barry, but it wasn't as good as yours."

"Did Barry live with you?"

Otis's gaze looked beyond her as if he was searching for the past. "He did till he was eighteen, then he moved in here above the store. Barry's mom, my sister, had a fondness for drink. She married a no-good who wasn't very kind to her or Barry. She drank to escape. So Barry had a rough time of it. She died from liver failure when Barry was only ten."

"That must have been so tough for him."

"It was, because he was left with his dad. And his dad went to prison for robbing a convenience store. A couple of other warrants caught up with him too."

"Is that when you took Barry in?"

"Yes-sir-ee. He was around twelve, hurt and angry, not knowing where to put any of his energy. But Ian was a good friend to him. They both ran track, so that seemed to turn Barry around."

"Maybe *you* turned him around. Living with you, being cared for, plus having a good friend counts."

Otis sent Daisy a weak smile. "I sure hope so. I promise I'll have soup for supper, but I'll have a cherry tart sooner than that. Did you say you wanted to look at that teapot again that you liked?"

Otis needed to keep his mind on something other than his nephew's murder. After he stood, she followed him to the shelf where the teapot was located. She'd already decided that whatever price he asked, she'd buy the teapot. It was the least she could do for a man who had lost the nephew he'd treated like a son.

After Daisy returned to the tea garden, she counted the minutes until she could drive to the farm that Otis had told her about. Thankfully, Jazzi's plans worked right into hers.

Her daughter arrived around five o'clock and pointed to Vi. "She wants me to go with her to the library. She hopes to find books on child rearing that are up to date. Do you mind?"

"I don't mind. I have an errand I want to run myself. Will Foster be going with you?"

"He has class tonight. He wants to take as many credits as he can *while* he can."

Understanding Foster's desire to earn a degree but to be a good husband and father too, Daisy nodded. "It would be great if he could add credits this summer and at least the first semester."

"I said yes to Vi about going with her because she really seems uptight. Have you noticed?"

"Her life is changing in major ways. In a few weeks, she'll be making a commitment that could direct the rest of her life. Prewedding jitters are called that for a reason."

Jazzi seemed to accept Daisy's reasoning and looked thoughtful as they cleaned up the tea garden, took inventory, and with Tessa decided on the specials for the following day. Then they all went their separate ways. Daisy was glad Jazzi was supporting her sister.

Daisy took her time driving to the farm on Tumbling Blocks Road. The rolling hills, the maple trees, the barns with the Pennsylvania Dutch hex signs always seemed to calm her soul. When she'd lived in Florida with Ryan and the girls, she'd often dreamed of coming back here someday. She'd missed the sights of the fenced-in mules that were used by Amish farmers for plowing and tilling the fields. The roadside stands with fresh produce and baked goods always beckoned to her.

As she neared the Platt farm, it was easy to catch a glimpse of the house with its green shutters. Daisy was truly hoping Ian would be there. He might have been Barry's best friend, but that day she'd heard them fighting. Not that friends didn't fight, but that fight had sounded serious.

She took the road to the left and saw a gravel area where a sedan and a beat-up black pickup were parked. After she pulled in beside the truck, she debated whether she should go to the front door of the house or to the back entrance. As she walked toward the house, she spotted pink coneflowers blooming in the yard along the fence along with black-eyed Susans.

Her debate over which entrance to use was settled when a man in brown overalls, a blue work shirt, and a fisherman's cap came out of the house toward the parking area. As he walked closer, she saw that he might be in his late sixties or early seventies. His chin-length beard was gray and she couldn't see much of his hair under the hat. His eyebrows were almost white.

He had a placid expression as he approached and asked, "Can I help you?"

Daisy didn't hesitate. "Are you Clovis Platt?"

"You found him," the man grumbled.

She smiled, hoping to relieve any awkwardness in meeting a stranger. "I'm Daisy Swanson. I'm looking for Ian Busby. Otis at Pirated Treasures told me he lived here and that he was a good friend of Barry Storm, the man who was murdered recently."

As Clovis frowned, a woman exited the back door and came down the three steps from the porch. She wore jeans and an oversized T-shirt. Her brown hair was laced with gray and pulled back into a stubby ponytail. Her face had as many wrinkles as Clovis's, so Daisy figured she might be around the same age.

Clovis motioned to the woman as she approached. "This is my wife Penelope."

Penelope looked questioningly at her husband.

He explained, "This lady is looking for Ian."

"Just call me Daisy," Daisy suggested.

"Did you tell her what happened?" Penelope asked.

Clovis shook his head.

Penelope's face took on an expression of disappointment that deepened her wrinkles. "Ian just took his stuff in the middle of the night. He didn't say good-bye or anything. Barry visited Ian a lot. We treated those two young men as if they were our own. Now one of them has gone to his Maker and the other skipped out. I just don't understand it."

Was this proof Ian had something to do with Barry's death? Possibly. But Daisy had learned not to jump to conclusions. "Otis, Barry's uncle, is upset over what happened to Barry. I thought Ian might have answers."

"He was a good worker," Clovis assured her. "Ian did anything you asked him without a complaint. Barry was the grumbler. I heard him tell Ian he was working too hard. Young people just don't want to do manual labor anymore. They'd rather sit in front of a computer."

An idea formed in Daisy's mind. "Do you need someone to work on the farm?"

"We do," Penelope said. She touched her husband's shoulder. "I don't want Clovis doing more than he should. He's too old for that, even if he doesn't want to admit it."

"And the cabin. Does that go with the job?" Daisy asked.

Penelope didn't hesitate. "It can, if whoever works for us needs a place to stay."

"I can't pay as much as I should," Clovis admitted, "but staying at the cabin and taking care of upkeep will be free, except for utilities. You want to take a look at it? Then you can spread the word."

When Daisy nodded, Penelope said, "You go back inside and get out of this heat."

Clovis scowled at her. "I've got no problem with the heat."

Penelope eyed him as Daisy's mom often eyed Daisy's dad.

Clovis pushed his hat back on his forehead in sudden surrender. "All right. I'll make sure whatever you've got in the slow cooker is stirred up. Nice to meet you, Mrs. Swanson."

"*Daisy's*," Penelope said as they walked. "That's the name of that tea garden in town, isn't it?"

"Yes, it is. I own it with my aunt."

"With your aunt. That's nice to keep family involved. Clovis is all I've got now. He has heart problems and the doc has him on medicine. But I have to remind him to take it. It would help so much to have someone do the work out here."

They walked down the lane for about a quarter of a mile. Daisy hadn't been able to see the cabin because it was hidden behind blue spruce. Penelope chatted along the way. They both admitted they liked to bake their own bread, and they began comparing recipes.

When they reached the cabin, Penelope took out a key and unlocked the door. Daisy liked the looks of the place. It was built of logs and the roof was shingled. A small porch spread across the front. Two of those white plastic chairs, the kind that big box stores sold, sat beside each other.

Penelope led Daisy inside. Daisy could see the cabin was small. It was basically two rooms and a bath, a tad bigger than Vi and Foster's apartment. The woodstove took up a portion of one wall and there was a tiny galley kitchen. Still, it should work well for Keith and Mandy. She'd stop at Jonas's town house on the way back home and talk to him about it. Maybe for the first time in a while, Keith and Mandy would actually have a home.

Chapter Seven

Later that day after Keith checked out the Platt farm, he returned to Jonas's town house with a huge smile on his face. Daisy had waited at Jonas's to spend time with Jonas and Mandy. When all this started, she'd thought Jonas might be awkward with the little girl, but he wasn't. He had seemed to enjoy his time with her, and Daisy had enjoyed the time with him.

Keith's excitement was obvious as he went to Mandy, picked her up, and swung her around. Daisy thought her cough was a little better, and her fever was down to ninety-nine.

"Are you going to take the job?" Daisy asked with a smile.

"I am," he said, his grin widening. "The cabin will be perfect for me and Mandy. While she's at day care I'll be doing most of the work—fixing fences, mowing, landscaping, feeding livestock, and anything else Clovis and Penelope need done. They seem to be nice people. I talked mostly to Clovis. Apparently the cabin was once a *dawdi haus*—a grandparents' house for Clovis's father. Repairing the main barn is going to take some time, and I'll have to learn how to tend to the cows. But Clovis says he'll show me everything. At least I'll have a real address and a home for Mandy. I'm so grateful to the two of you for helping me. I promise I won't let you down. Since I don't have to spend money on room and board, I'll just have to pay for food, gas, and electric, and I can start paying down bills. Wood for the stove is on the property."

Jonas asked Daisy, "Should I order takeout and you can stay here with us for supper?"

Her daughters knew where she was in case they needed her. It sounded as if Vi might want to have a talk fest with Jazzi. Daisy didn't want to interfere with that. "I'd like to stay for supper." Her gaze connected with Jonas's and a little hum zipped between them. That's the way it always was with him, and she liked the feel of it. "Things are going to get crazy in the next couple of weeks with the wedding."

"We'll survive it," he assured her.

She liked the fact that he'd used the term "we."

Jonas's cell phone buzzed. He grabbed it from the counter and checked the screen. After he did, he frowned. "It's Detective Willet."

Keith had been holding Mandy. Now he set her on the floor near her pile of blocks.

Jonas said to Zeke, "I'll put him on."

Keith looked puzzled. "Why didn't he call on *my* phone?"

When Jonas handed the phone to Keith, he said in a low voice, "I think Zeke just wants to see if you're staying with me. Remember, let *him* do the talking."

After Keith took the phone, Daisy could see his hand was shaking a bit. Calls from detectives could do that. He put the phone on speaker.

"I need to speak with you again, Mr. Rebert, down at the station."

"Can you tell me what you want to talk about?" Keith asked.

"I want to discuss the list of items you sold to Pirated Treasures, especially the antique firkin sugar bucket, the Spiderman comic book, the Civil War powder flask, and there was a military belt and buckle. I'd like you to tell me where you found each thing."

"I can do that," Keith said. "I keep a notebook with the item, date, and prices."

"You do, do you? Isn't that handy? You know I'll be checking on each item, so if there's fake information in there, it's not going to fly."

Keith rolled his eyes. "I wouldn't take the time to write down fake information." His voice sounded on the edge of irritation.

Jonas put his hand on Keith's shoulder as if to calm him. Keith took a deep breath and nodded.

"Ever hear of cooked books, Mr. Rebert? One set for your eyes and another set for somebody else's?"

"All I can tell you, Detective, is that I have a list. Everything on it is verifiable."

"Then our chat will be a short one. See you in the morning around nine a.m."

"Yes, you will," Keith assured him, and ended the call.

"He's trying to get a rise out of you," Jonas said. "You can't let him do it. Are you going to call Marshall?"

"No. I'm just going to go down there and hand him the book."

"He'll try to question you about it," Daisy reminded him.

"If he asks questions, I'll tell him he should talk to

my lawyer. If it gets too serious, I'll call Marshall. I really don't need any extra expenses right now. And before the two of you say anything, I don't want you to cover them either. I was going to fix up the cabin tomorrow for me and Mandy. If it doesn't take too long at the police station, I still can."

"Are you going to use the furniture that's there?" Daisy asked.

"There's a double bed there now. Clovis bought a new mattress when Ian moved in. I'll give Mandy the bedroom and I'll sleep on the couch. For now, I just want to make sure everything's clean before I bring her in."

"I have an extra set of double sheets," Daisy said. "I brought them along from Florida but my daughters both have single beds and I have a queen. I'm sure I have an extra pillow or two too."

Keith looked as if he were about to refuse her offer. Before he could say anything, she warned him, "Don't let your pride stand in the way of making Mandy comfortable. Soap and water don't cost much but bedding is expensive."

Jonas nodded. "Listen to the lady. She's a mom and she knows."

After another moment of hesitation, Keith nodded. "All right, I'll give in this time. But one of these days I'm going to buy you both a very big dinner." He sighed and went over to the sofa where Mandy was playing on the floor. He placed his hand gently on the top of her head and ruffled her hair. "I suppose the detective wants that list to make sure I didn't steal anything."

"Or there's something on that list he's particularly interested in," Jonas said. "You never know. Zeke

Willet can be canny. Watch your step tomorrow, Keith. I mean it."

Daisy could see the worry in Jonas's eyes. She just hoped the detective's request was a straightforward one.

When Jonas came into the tea garden the following day, Daisy had just served Daisy's Blend tea—a decaffeinated green tea infused with raspberry and vanilla—to a table of four. They'd chosen maple walnut scones for their midafternoon treat.

She gave Jonas a bright smile. She'd enjoyed the time she'd spent with him last night, even though they were babysitting for part of it. She was still hesitating to get more serious with him. Her life was changing day by day. After Vi's baby was born, she wasn't sure how much time she could give Jonas. Once before he'd backed off their relationship. The truth was—she was afraid he'd do it again. So it was better just to keep their relationship as a deepening friendship until they were both on an even keel. Maybe their timing was off, maybe not. But she did so enjoy time spent with him. Now she hoped he'd brought news about Keith.

She motioned for him to come to the kitchen with her. He zigzagged with her through and around the tables and went through the doorway that led to her office on the left and the kitchen on the right.

She knew Vi and Pam Dorsey, a temp server, were bussing tables in the two tearooms. Cora Sue and Karina were taking orders. In the kitchen, Tessa was removing a tray of cookies from the oven while Foster mixed a batch of scones at the mixer. Eva was putting dishes away. Today, Jazzi was babysitting Mandy at Jonas's town house.

Stopping beside Eva, Daisy asked, "Could you take care of table five, six, and seven for about ten minutes? I need to consult with Jonas about something."

Eva smiled a sly smile. "Of course, I can cover. Take as long as you need." She gave Daisy a wink.

Daisy knew her staff was rooting for her and Jonas. If only that was all they needed to make a relationship survive.

Jonas had heard what she'd asked Eva, and he stood at the back kitchen door. Daisy followed him outside. Once they'd crossed the paved area used for parking, they walked down the garden path toward the creek.

Jonas encircled her waist with his arm. "Busy day?"

"Several buses this morning. This afternoon I think we mostly just had tourists. They're keeping everyone busy. Not much time for breaks. With Jazzi babysitting today, we're short a pair of hands."

"So it *is* working out to have Vi and Foster on the same shift?"

"Yes. They're all about work. Vi wants those tips and Foster just wants to show her how responsible he is. Jazzi is putting all her money toward a car."

"Keith was grateful she could watch Mandy today."

"I checked in with her at noon and she says they're doing fine. Mandy's fever is gone. In a day or two she'll be able to go into day care."

"That will be a relief for Keith."

"What happened at the police station this morning?"

"Nothing new. Willet did want to go over that list with Keith. Truthfully, I think Zeke wants to show Rappaport and Chief of Police Schultz that he knows what he's doing. But hassling Keith doesn't prove that. I can't find out much because Rappaport isn't on the case, and Zeke won't tell me anything."

"I hope Detective Willet can verify everything on Keith's list."

"If he doesn't try hard enough, I'll help him out."

"Jonas—"

"I know. I know. Don't make anything worse. I won't. But if he says he can't verify one of the items and if I can find the person who sold it to Keith, I will."

Jonas took a deep breath, moved a little away, and took her hand. "Let's just breathe deeply and try to forget about the rest of the world for at least five minutes. Can you hear the babble of the creek?"

She nudged him with her elbow. "Let's try and skip a few stones."

After skipping a few stones and a kiss later, Jonas returned to his shop while Daisy went back into the tea garden. She used the side garden entrance where Iris was serving customers on the patio under the yellow and white striped umbrellas. To her surprise, she found Otis at one of the tables with a younger woman—possibly in her late twenties. Her hair was dark brown with French braids all around her hairline. Daisy walked over to say hello to Otis.

"How are you?" she asked, pulling out a chair and sitting down next to him.

"I'm okay. It's just hard missing Barry and running the store without him. Did you know his funeral is on Thursday?"

"Thank you for telling me," Daisy said sympathetically.

Glancing to his right, Otis explained, "This is

Mariah Goldblum. She's never been here before and I thought she might enjoy your tea and sweet things."

Mariah nodded to Daisy. "I went to school with Ian and Barry."

A small smile turned up the corner of Otis's mouth. "My nephew was sweet on her."

Daisy said, "I've been looking for Ian. I went to the Platt farm but he'd moved out. A friend of mine is going to take over the cabin and the job there. Do you know where Ian is now?"

"He moved out?" Otis asked. "Since when?"

"I'm not exactly sure, but it sounds like it was around the time Barry died. Penelope and Clovis were very disappointed. He didn't say good-bye or give them a forwarding address."

"That doesn't sound like Ian," Otis protested.

If Mariah thought Daisy would forget her question, she was wrong. So Daisy repeated it. "Mariah, do you know where Ian is?"

A worried expression crossed Mariah's face. She gave a small shrug. "I once dated Ian, but after we broke up, Barry and I got close. I haven't been in touch with him, but one of our other friends mentioned he'd moved back in with his parents."

"So you don't know if the police questioned him."

"No, I don't. Like I said, after Ian and I broke up, we haven't been friends. I've been too upset about Barry to think much about Ian."

Daisy thought that was odd. Apparently, Barry and Ian had been in touch, and if Mariah had been close to Barry . . . It seemed all of them would have known something about the other. And now that Barry was dead, wouldn't Ian and Mariah have something to talk about?

However, she'd just met Mariah. Both Mariah and Otis were grieving. She wouldn't push now. At least she had a lead. If Ian was staying with his parents, it wouldn't be hard to find him.

Daisy stood and saw that Otis's glass of iced tea was empty except for the ice. "Would you like more iced tea? I'd be glad to get you another glass, or something else to snack on."

Otis shook his head. "We're good. Mariah and I both had those cherry tarts. I told her they were Barry's favorite and she wanted to taste one. I asked your aunt Iris to put three aside for me, and some chicken soup, so I can take it along. I finished what you brought me."

"I'm glad you enjoyed it. You take care of yourself."

"I will. As soon as I find some help in the store."

After Daisy said good-bye to both Otis and Mariah, she went into the tea garden.

The rest of the afternoon flashed by. Tourists were out in full force. She was thankful for the business and hoped it continued through the fall.

At closing time Daisy said good-bye to most of her staff. Vi stopped by the sales counter and asked, "You're still going to the bakery with Jazzi and Foster and me at six, right?"

"I wouldn't miss it. Do you have any idea what you want in a wedding cake?"

"Not yet," Vi answered. "Mrs. Denton said she'll show us the styles she has to offer as well as the flavors. I just wish—"

"What do you wish?"

Vi shook her head. "Nothing. Did you hear from Keith? Did he get home so we're sure we can go?"

"I received a text from him a short while ago. He

cleaned out the cabin and was pleased with the way Jazzi cared for Mandy."

Karina had been standing nearby as if she were waiting to talk to Daisy. Vi saw Karina and said to her mom, "I'll see you at the bakery. Foster's going to meet us there."

After Vi left by the rear entrance, Karina came up to the counter. No one else was in the tea garden. She asked Daisy, "Can I talk to you?"

"Sure, you can. What's up?"

Karina looked down at her clogs, then her gaze met Daisy's. "I like Keith. I like him a lot. The first time I met him was one day when I went to Pirated Treasures. I'd taken along one of your cherry tarts, and I was eating it on the way. I'd also bought chocolate chip cookies for Quinn." She stopped as if to think about how to tell the rest.

"Mandy and Keith were in Pirated Treasures. You know how kids are. Mandy saw the cherry tart and then she pointed to the bag I was carrying. She was so sweet about it, so I gave her one of the cookies. Keith and I talked a bit. I stayed in the store shopping, but I watched him leave with Mandy. They went to his van. He didn't drive away. The next day I went to Pirated Treasures again just to see if his van was still there. And it was. He had the door open and I stopped and talked with him. That's how we got started. We've talked about so many things, a lot of them serious. My mom doesn't know about Keith, and I'm not sure if I should keep seeing him. What if he's charged with Barry's murder?"

"Once he starts taking Mandy to day care, you might run into him when you pick up Quinn."

"I know. I haven't seen him since the night you guys

followed me there. But I want to. Will he be staying with Jonas?"

Daisy shook her head. "Tomorrow he's moving into a cabin on a farm on the outskirts of town. He's getting room and board free for him and Mandy. He's going to do repairs around the farm, take care of the cows, and that kind of thing. My guess is, he'd probably appreciate a visit from you. But you have to decide whether or not you want the friendship with him. You have to decide whether or not you trust him. If you do, then you'll tell your mom about him."

"I know you're right about telling Mom. Actually, I'd like to arrange a playdate for Mandy and Quinn. How is Mandy now?"

"She should be ready to go to day care in another day or two. If you run into Keith there, that would be a perfect time to see if he'd like a visit from you."

"I have a lot to think about," Karina said. "I've been burnt before . . . badly. I don't want to take the chance that it's going to happen again."

"I understand that. Would you rather be on your own raising Quinn? Could you see someone in your future someday . . . someone who could be a partner?"

"I'm not sure. I guess the only way I'll know is to be around Keith more."

"If you're willing to take a chance, the reward could be sweet. On the other hand, if Keith is charged with murder, that could change everything."

Karina looked troubled as she decided, "I've kept you long enough. All I can do is see what happens next."

Maybe that was the only thing any of them could do.

* * *

The bakery in Lancaster was a wedding couple's dream, especially if they liked cake. Sample cakes stood two, three, and even four tiers tall. One even had three sets of pillars. As Daisy examined the cakes, she realized the designs seemed more simple now than when she had gotten married. On many, the icing was smooth, the decorations sparse, edible flowers trailing from the top tier to the bottom tier. There were specialty cakes, of course, unique for a couple, but they cost much more.

The proprietress of the shop, Gail Denton, showed Vi first one cake, then another, explaining styles and prices. Jazzi and Daisy, wandering across the other side of the room, glanced at Vi and saw her roll her eyes. Did that mean that particular cake was too expensive? Or maybe she didn't know. Foster hadn't arrived to meet them yet.

Iris had promised to give Vi and Foster their wedding cake as her wedding present. But Vi still wanted to be careful how much they spent.

"I have a tasting table set up for you over here," Gail said. She was chic with spiral-curled gray hair, a purple short-sleeved pant suit, and lilac heels. Daisy wondered if she dressed like that every day. Maybe she had nothing to do with the cake baking and decorating. She was simply the proprietor.

Daisy thought about just being a proprietor and not baking or serving. That didn't suit her. She liked getting into the middle of her customers, serving tea and goodies, working in the back with Iris and Tessa and Eva. Foster now too.

Daisy noticed that Vi kept glancing at her watch. She stared across the room at Daisy, and Daisy could see she was unsure what to do next.

Crossing the room, Vi asked, "Should we start the tasting without Foster? I really hate to do that. This is his choice too."

"Did you text him?"

"He said he was on his way, but that was twenty minutes ago."

"Maybe something held him up. Go ahead and text him again."

Vi did and they waited for a response, but one didn't come.

Vi was almost near tears. "I don't understand where he is. This is *important*."

Daisy wrapped her arm around her daughter's shoulders. "Traffic could be jammed up. Maybe his professor wanted to talk to him. Maybe he got a ticket for speeding, and that's what's delaying him. There's no knowing, Vi. Don't start worrying before you have to. Let's start the tasting. Gail has appointments after ours. We can't cause her to be late for them."

Daisy, Jazzi, and Vi moved toward the table and seated themselves in the chairs.

Gail smiled at them. "Now remember, you can mix and match flavors. For instance, if you want a white cake layer, that's fine. But you can also have a strawberry layer."

Vi didn't look as if her attention was on cake tasting as she glanced again at the door.

The three of them had tasted a strawberry cake, a lemon cake, and a spice cake when Foster finally came in. Vi stood and went to him. Their voices were raised so Daisy and the others could hear them clearly.

"Where have you been?" Vi wanted to know.

"I had to stop at home. Ben had something he wanted to give me." Foster looked apologetic.

Daisy knew Foster felt responsible for his younger brother and sister. He'd tried to keep communication open with them both since their mom had died.

"What did he want to give you?" Vi asked.

"It's something for our apartment. He made it in wood shop."

Daisy could tell Foster was trying to keep his voice calm.

"And you had to do that *now*?" Vi asked.

"Ben texted me and was excited and it seemed important to him."

Vi's voice became shriller. "Isn't cake tasting important to *you*? We have a *wedding* to plan."

"Don't I know it."

"What's *that* supposed to mean?"

Daisy didn't believe in interfering with the couple's relationship. However, Jazzi had no compunction not to say what *she* was thinking.

She swiftly rose from her chair and went over to the two of them. "Everyone can hear you. If you want to argue, wait until you get home. Let's taste these cakes or you won't have one for your wedding."

Foster glanced at Daisy and his cheeks reddened. Nudging his rimless glasses higher on his nose, he came across the room to her and Gail. "I'm sorry I'm late."

Gail spoke to him before Daisy could. "This happens. I leave a little time in my schedule just in case of emergencies. So come on now, sit down and try the ones that your mother-in-law-to-be, your wife-to-be, and sister-in-law-to-be already tasted."

In the next few minutes, Foster sat with Vi next to him, but Vi was keeping at least six inches between them. After he tasted the flavors, he asked, "Can't we just do a chocolate and a vanilla layer?"

"Chocolate for a wedding cake?" Vi asked. "I don't think so. Everything about our wedding is pastel. I want things to match."

"And I want the cake to taste good."

It was obvious to Daisy he was feeling perturbed because of their argument.

Gail still didn't look ruffled. She pointed to a cake on display in the corner. It was about nine inches round and had two layers. "Believe it or not, the flavors often come up when deciding on a wedding cake. We have a groom's cake too. Vi can decide what she wants in the main cake and he can decide what he wants in his."

"I don't think we should burden Aunt Iris with the expense of two cakes," Vi said. "As it is, we have more guests coming than we expected. Our list is up to fifty now."

Foster blinked. "Fifty? Since when?"

"Since your father called me and gave me more names."

Foster rolled his eyes and Daisy thought it was time she *did* intervene. "Since we're having the reception at the tea garden, everything doesn't have to be strictly . . . receptional."

Vi and Jazzi looked her way. Vi said, "Can you explain that?"

"Sure. Pick the cake you want and the decorations you want that will go with the wedding." Then she transferred her gaze to Foster. "As far as the chocolate cake goes . . . I'm going to be fashioning tiered plates of other goodies. I can incorporate chocolate petit fours, miniature chocolate muffins, even scoops of chocolate mousse and chocolate tartlets. In other words, I can give you as much chocolate as you want."

The tension lines around Foster's mouth eased, and he even smiled a bit. "That sounds good. I want the men to enjoy all of this as much as the women."

"Foster has a point, Vi," Daisy pointed out. "Sometimes in wedding planning the men get lost in the shuffle. Are you okay with tea garden chocolate desserts along with a cake?" She didn't want to make any decision her daughter might resent. She remembered her mother's hand in her and Ryan's wedding. They'd married in Willow Creek. To keep the peace, Daisy had agreed to food and decorations she hadn't particularly wanted.

Vi looked around the table at all the people who were watching her . . . especially Foster.

"I'm fine with the chocolate," she agreed. "As long as we can have a layer of white and a layer of strawberry on the main cake . . . pretty flowers . . . and maybe some silver or mother of pearl sprinkles." She cast a sideways glance at Foster. "Is that okay with you?"

"The strawberry tastes good," he agreed. "And everybody likes white cake." Foster smiled at Vi and took her hand.

Vi didn't pull her hand away.

Apparently, her daughter and her fiancé had come to a compromise. But something was bothering Vi. Was it just the tension of planning the wedding? Or something deeper?

Chapter Eight

The following evening, Daisy realized she should be working on table centerpieces for Vi and Foster's wedding. But her mind was elsewhere. After the cake tasting, she'd tried to talk to Vi about any worries she had about the wedding. But Vi had insisted that talking about everything made her more anxious. Daisy would like to get to the bottom of Vi's panic, if that's what it was, or it would increase day by day. Feeling at a loss, she didn't know how. If she went behind Vi's back and talked to Foster, Vi would never forgive her.

When Daisy went to her bedroom, she studied the cartons of flameless candles and wicker baskets. She'd intended to attach the candles to the baskets. Jazzi and Vi had gone to a craft store to choose the silk flowers Vi wanted to use in the centerpieces while Foster had class again tonight. Daisy suspected that could be at the bottom of Vi's worries. How could Foster keep up with school classes, work, and be a dad?

Daisy wondered how Keith and Mandy were settling in at the cabin. Reverend Kemp had offered a scholarship to Mandy for day care until January. Then they'd revisit Keith's situation. He was going to take Mandy there tomorrow before his day started at the farm.

Daisy glanced at the cartons again. She really should get started. On the other hand, she wanted to help Keith, and in a tangential way, Karina. There was a way to do that. Mariah had mentioned that Ian was staying with his parents. She could find their address online. There was plenty of daylight left to visit the man who had argued with Barry.

Over her lunch break, she'd stopped in at the library to study yearbooks. Estimating Ian's, Mariah's, and Barry's ages, she'd found a yearbook with their photos. Ian couldn't have changed that much that she wouldn't recognize him. She'd snapped a pic of the yearbook page.

A half hour later, Daisy found herself driving out of Willow Creek. Turning off Market Street onto Hollowback Road, she passed the freshly constructed Willow Creek Little Theater. A multimillion-dollar land developer from Lancaster, Rowan Vaughn, had donated funds for not only the construction of the theater but also for an endowment to keep it going. He was Vanna Huffnagle's brother-in-law and Vanna had told Daisy all about it. Planning would be starting soon for a holiday production.

After continuing down the road, Daisy turned right into a retirement village of sorts. Duplexes were attached to each other in threes and stretched into a few streets of a planned neighborhood. When she pulled into the driveway of number 318 Songbird Lane, she was surprised to see two cars at the double car garage. One was a sedan, a Ford Taurus, but the other was an Audi A3. She knew the car and what it cost because Vi and now Jazzi often scanned new cars online. They enjoyed looking at vehicles as much as fashions, dreaming of the day when they could afford a new one.

Daisy suspected that Ian's parents drove the sedan. Could the Audi be his?

Talking to someone she'd never met had gotten easier since she'd been involved in murder investigations. Or maybe she was just becoming more facile at it. That didn't mean her heart didn't beat fast and her palms didn't get sweaty. She'd worn a pale blue tank and shorts with slip-on tennis shoes. She hoped she didn't seem threatening. On the other hand, sometimes threatening wasn't a bad idea.

She pressed the button for the doorbell and noticed the precision cut of the lawn, the boxwoods along each duplex that were exactly the same size. This was definitely a planned community with maintenance included. She wondered if her mom and dad were thinking about moving to a place like this after they retired. However, she couldn't see her dad letting someone else handle his landscaping. Running a nursery had been his life and he loved it.

She could hear the doorbell ring inside the domicile. If no one answered, she supposed she had no recourse except to leave. Soon, however, she heard footsteps and braced herself for whoever answered the door.

The man who answered the door looked like the yearbook photo even though he appeared sleepy eyed and tousled as if he might have been taking a nap. He was barefoot, wearing khaki shorts and a gray T-shirt. His blond hair was slicked back from his forehead to the crown of his head. The rest of it was longish, dragging over the neckline of his shirt.

"Hi," she said brightly. "Are you Ian Busby?"

He studied her with suspicion. "Who wants to know?"

She extended her hand. "I'm Daisy Swanson. I know Otis Murdoch and I knew Barry."

Ian stared over her shoulder for a few seconds as if he was lost in thought.

She added, "I'm the one who makes those cherry tarts that Otis and Barry liked so much."

Directing his attention back to her, he looked wary again. "Did you bring me cherry tarts?"

"No, but I wanted to talk to you for a few minutes if that's okay."

He crossed his arms over his chest and leaned against the doorframe. "So talk."

"I understand you and Barry were best friends."

"We were."

She could see his body tensed with the words. He added, "I guess you know the police were here."

"So they found you. I wasn't sure if they would after you left the Platt farm so quickly. Penelope and Clovis were really broken up."

Ian had the grace to look embarrassed. "I shouldn't have left like that, I guess. But after Barry was murdered, I just felt . . . adrift. I didn't want any long good-byes. I didn't want Clovis convincing me to stay on. I needed a change."

"So you came back to your parents' house?"

"I don't consider this their house. They sold the place I grew up in so they could move here for their golden years and all that."

From her own parents' discussions with her, Daisy knew the golden years weren't all that they were cracked up to be. "I suppose the police asked if you knew anyone who wanted to harm Barry."

"I don't know anybody who wanted to harm him. And we were this close." Ian crossed his fingers so they intertwined.

"I believe you were close, but apparently somebody wanted him dead. No ideas about that?"

Ian seemed to relax a bit, though his arms were still crossed, a typical defensive stance. "Otis and Barry had all kinds of characters in and out of that store. Some were pretty scraggly. Some wanted something for nothing."

"You mean they didn't want to pay Otis or Barry's prices?"

"Yeah. You know, like when people go to a yard sale. Something's labeled a dollar and they want it for a quarter. People want you to give stuff away. Barry and Otis couldn't do that. They had to make a living."

"I've become friends with Keith Rebert."

"That guy who lived in his van?"

"You knew him?"

Ian shrugged. "He was at Pirated Treasures once or twice when I was there. He sold stuff to Otis and Barry."

"Yes, he did. But he said that Barry cheated him. Do you know anything about that?"

"Keith was the opposite of those people who came in wanting something for nothing. He wanted a lot of money for very little. Barry *never* cheated him."

Daisy could see that Ian would stand up for Barry no matter what. She wasn't going to find out anything more here, at least not specifically integral to the investigation. She nodded to the red Audi in the driveway. "That's once snazzy car."

For the first time since Ian had come to the door, a smile slipped across his lips. "Yeah, sure is. And it's

mine. I let my pop drive it now and then just for fun.
But I sure don't like driving his."

Daisy laughed. "I can see why. You must have saved
for a long time to buy that."

Now Ian looked as if he might have made a mistake telling her the car was his. "Financing it makes
it all easy."

Financing enabled some people to buy cars, but
Daisy also knew that monthly payments on that kind of
car were higher than a man working on a farm could
make. She saw the moment when Ian realized that
she'd figured that out.

He said, "I'm done here. Don't bother coming
back. I'm not going to be here that long."

Daisy wondered exactly what that meant.

On Thursday at Barry's funeral, Daisy walked
beside Jonas up the gravel cemetery path to the grave
site where a green canopy had been set up. She'd been
surprised when Otis had told her there wouldn't be a
service at the funeral home before the actual graveside
service. She wondered if he had planned that because
Barry didn't have many friends.

Jonas had decided to accompany her to the cemetery. "I'm surprised you wanted to come along," she
told him as they headed toward the burial plot.
She spotted Reverend Kemp walking toward the head
of the casket.

Jonas looked around. "I thought you'd like the
company." At the last funeral Daisy had attended, feelings about her husband had cropped up and she'd
talked about them with Jonas.

Ian stood near the head of the casket beside Otis.

But Mariah Goldblum had hung back and was sitting in the second row of chairs. "I wonder why Ian and Mariah aren't together," Daisy said.

"You told me they'd been friends . . . that Ian had dated Mariah before she hooked up with Barry. Maybe that breakup wasn't so pleasant."

A slight morning breeze ruffled the hem of Daisy's pale green short-sleeved dress. "Yeah, but a friend of theirs died. Don't you think that should bring them together?"

Soberly, Jonas pointed out, "Funerals separate more than reunite—maybe because of past arguments, wills, and dealings that never go away."

She and Jonas stood in the second line of observers beside the casket.

Leaning close to Daisy, Jonas kept his voice low. "I'm a prime example. Zeke and I used to be good friends. But when Brenda died and he blamed me, our friendship was gone. That's not so unusual."

More freely now, Jonas spoke of his relationship with his former partner and significant other, another detective who'd been killed in the line of duty. Daisy was glad that he was open with her about Brenda . . . and Zeke. Daisy nudged Jonas's arm and pointed with her chin. When he glanced behind them, he saw Zeke Willet was standing there.

Jonas paid him no mind and nodded to the spray of wildflowers that spread along the top of the casket. "If you notice, Otis picked a simple wooden casket. My guess is that he didn't have the funds for more. Maybe that's why he decided not to have the service at the funeral home."

"That's possible," Daisy said. "But wooden caskets are more eco-friendly."

"That's one way of looking at it," Jonas agreed.

Reverend Kemp had opened his Bible and was about to say a few words when there was suddenly a shout from the maple trees about twenty yards from the grave site.

Jonas's arm swung around Daisy as he nudged her behind him protectively.

Not hearing any gunshots or mayhem, Daisy peeked around Jonas's shoulder. A rough-looking man in a T-shirt and jeans with tattoos up and down both arms hurried toward them. He had a shaved head and a nose that might have been broken a couple of times. As he approached, his brown eyes targeted Otis and so did his pointed finger. "It's *your* fault my son is dead. If he hadn't been working for you, this never would have happened."

"Barry's father?" Daisy whispered into Jonas's ear.

"Apparently out of jail," Jonas muttered. "I wonder for how long."

Although Otis seemed to be mild mannered, now he straightened his shoulders under his plaid, snap-button shirt, and stood straighter than he had when Daisy had seen him at Pirated Treasures. "Glen, you just turn around and go on your way. I don't know who the fool was who let you out of prison, but it was a mistake. You abandoned Barry into a bottle. He was better off without you then, and better off without you now."

Funeral-goers scattered as Glen Storm neared the casket and Otis. "Tell me what happened to my boy," Glen Storm demanded.

Otis shot back, "Maybe *you* know better than I do."

Reverend Kemp stepped between the two men. He

spoke in a low tone to first one and then the other, and the three of them walked over to a nearby tree.

Leaning close to Jonas, Daisy watched the men. As Otis and Glen seemed to calm down, she nudged Jonas's arm again. "I know you and Zeke aren't getting along, but I'm going to drop back and talk to him."

"Are you sure you want to do that?" There was concern in Jonas's voice.

"I won't say anything stupid. I promise."

Jonas sent her a small smile. "You never say anything stupid."

"I'll give you a kiss for that one later," she joked, then turned and strolled over to the tree where Detective Willet stood with his arms crossed. The stance reminded her very much of Ian's when she'd questioned him. But Zeke Willet was closed off for a different reason.

The first thing Zeke said to her was, "I saw Jonas tried to protect you. Don't count on him to do a good job of it."

She wasn't going to rise to the bait. She knew Zeke blamed Jonas for Jonas's partner getting shot and killed. There was a lot of hurt there that needed to be settled, but that wasn't going to happen today. "How is your investigation going in Barry Storm's death?"

Zeke's lips tightened and he kept silent.

"Does that mean you don't have any more suspects?" she prompted.

He didn't answer her about that. "I'm surprised your friend Keith isn't here."

"Keith, Otis, and Barry were business acquaintances. They weren't friends. When I spoke with Keith,

he said he would have come for Otis's sake, but he
didn't want to cause a scene."

Zeke shifted his focus from the three men at the tree
and finally looked at her. "I know Keith is homeless."

"You must have old information. He's not homeless
anymore."

"You mean he's living with Jonas?"

"I mean he has a place of his own for himself and
his daughter, as well as a job to go with it. You can't say
I'm obstructing justice if I give you information you
didn't have." As soon as the words were out of her
mouth, she knew she shouldn't have said it. No, it
hadn't been stupid, but it might have been defiant.

Zeke uncrossed his arms. "Did you have anything to
do with him finding a place to stay and a job?"

"Several people did. Maybe you haven't figured it
out yet, but caring people do live in Willow Creek. Just
give them a chance and you might warm up to some
of them."

Zeke scowled. "You mean like Detective Rappaport has?"

She decided to keep her answer light. "Detective
Rappaport is coming around. He's even starting to
enjoy Pennsylvania Dutch cooking."

Zeke stayed silent for a few seconds. "Detective Rappaport and I are very different."

What would it take to coax this detective to relax
and maybe enjoy life again? "Just because you're different from Detective Rappaport, that doesn't mean
you can't fit in. That doesn't mean you can't make
friends and enjoy Willow Creek for the town it is."

He gave a humorless chuckle. "So now you're a PR
emissary for Willow Creek?"

She would not enter into a sparring match with him. She knew better than to do that. "As a member of the Chamber of Commerce, that's what we do. Have a good day, Detective Willet."

She didn't give him a chance to say anything else but rather returned to Jonas's side and waited for the reverend to bless Barry Storm's soul.

The afternoon was going to be hot with a capital *H*. Daisy had learned from her aunt that customers had sat under the umbrella-topped tables while she'd attended the funeral. But she suspected the clientele would want to sit in the air-conditioning for the rest of the day. The tea garden was serving afternoon tea by appointment today in the yellow tearoom. Reservations were sold out.

In the summer they sometimes served afternoon tea twice, at one o'clock and again at three. That was the case today. The prep in the kitchen was crazy busy. Daisy had created zucchini soup for their first course and a cucumber salad for the second course. Then came the savories—bacon and cheese crostini and an avocado pepperoni spread for mini sandwiches. Daisy had also prepared mini chicken salad sandwiches—a regular favorite—and an egg and olive salad that they spread on whole wheat bread that was crispy with seeds and nuts. The dessert tiered tray was a combination of Tessa's mini-bite cookies, red velvet miniature muffins with a buttercream icing, and apple cinnamon bread. They'd made several batches of iced tea, from peach-infused white tea to strawberry-infused green tea. This morning they'd been hardly able to keep up with the iced tea demands. The hot weather guaranteed big thirsts.

At almost noon, Daisy hurried from overseeing operations in the kitchen to connecting again with her aunt, who was setting up the yellow tearoom. Daisy was about to hurry into the kitchen once more when she caught sight of someone she'd recently met—Penelope Platt. She knew she shouldn't take the time, but she was eager to find out what Penelope and Clovis thought of Keith and Mandy. She was hoping all was going well.

Foster was serving today since he didn't have class. She tapped him on the shoulder. "I'll take care of table seven."

He raised a brow but didn't argue. Instead he assured her, "I'll make sure Iris has everything she needs."

She thought again about talking to Foster about Vi, but she dismissed the idea. She wasn't even his mother-in-law yet and she'd been thinking about interfering. Not good.

Giving Foster a fond smile, she crossed to Penelope's table. Penelope looked up, crumbs from her slice of apple bread dotting the corners of her mouth. She took a swig of her iced tea and set it down. "Hi there, Daisy. Keith has told me so much about this place, I wanted to try it out."

"I'm glad you could stop in."

Penelope's sunny expression soon faded into one of worry. "I just think it's terrible about the rumors going around."

The tea garden was not the only beehive of gossip. In a town the size of Willow Creek, other businesses were gossip centers too—from Sarah Jane's to the convenience store. "What rumors?"

"The rumor is that the police believe Keith murdered Barry. That has to be ridiculous. I've watched Keith with his daughter. There is no way that a man who can be that kind and gentle would murder *anyone*."

"I feel the same way," Daisy admitted. "That's why I wanted to do everything to help him and Mandy."

With a grandmother-like smile, Penelope said, "He took Mandy to day care this morning. I hope that works out for him. He's a good worker and doesn't slack off because of the heat or because he's already put in a full morning."

The explanation for that was clear. "He's grateful to have work."

"He told me about his wife's medical bills. That's such a shame. I wish we could pay him more."

"I'm sure he's just thankful to have the cabin."

"He cleaned it up real nice. We appreciate that."

Daisy had a sudden thought. "Did you ever see Mariah visit Ian at the cabin?"

"Mariah Goldblum? Sure we did. She dated Ian but something happened between them, so then she started dating Barry. Ian told Clovis that was hard for him to watch. I think Ian still loves her. Maybe they'll get back together."

If Ian and Mariah *did* get together again, that could be Ian's motive for murder.

Chapter Nine

The scene with Glen Storm and Otis kept running through Daisy's mind that evening as she lined cupboard shelves in the garage apartment. Had Glen really cared about Barry all those years he'd been in prison? Had he ever tried to contact his son?

Suddenly Daisy heard footsteps on the stairs leading up to the apartment. Foster's father, Gavin, appeared carrying a glider rocker. With sandy brown hair, a square jaw, a longish nose, and his six-foot height, he was a good-looking man. But his face was lined with creases brought on by the tragedy of losing his wife and raising three kids on his own. Daisy could relate.

Seemingly holding the chair without much effort, he asked, "Living room area or bedroom?"

The apartment was tight on space, that was for sure. The bedroom with a bath—sink, commode, and walk-in shower—took up a chunk of it. In consultation with Vi and Foster, the architect had designed a bigger bedroom rather than trying to wall off space for a nursery. Vi and Foster had chosen to use a double bed and essentially keep the baby in their bedroom. They'd use a curtain or screen to separate the crib if necessary. Hopefully by the end of the first year, they'd be able to afford and rent a bigger place somewhere else.

"You should probably put the rocker in the bedroom, don't you think? That will be nice for bedtime for baby. I'll attach the cushions Vi chose for it. They're in the closet. I heard you insisted she buy new ones instead of used ones, and you paid for them."

"They need a few new things to start," Gavin responded, putting down the chair in the bedroom, then returning to the kitchen area once more. "I don't want the baby to be near dust mites from the old stuff."

Daisy chuckled. "You know about dust mites?"

"You'd be surprised what I know."

There was a teasing note in Gavin's voice that Daisy didn't often hear. Turning away from lining the upper cupboards, her gaze met his.

Gavin was in his forties. As a contractor, he spent time outdoors and he had a deep tan.

"Kids take learning to a whole new level," she agreed.

"When I told Vi and Foster I'd help them furnish this place, I guess I thought selecting furniture from a thrift store would punish them for being pregnant or teach them some kind of lesson." Gavin seemed embarrassed as he admitted his reasoning.

"I understand that you wanted them to realize the costs of having a family and bringing up a baby," she said.

"I did and I do." He gave a shrug and pushed his hands into the pockets of his jeans. "But when we went looking for furniture, I found I wanted them to have nice things. I wanted to buy them nice things. Yet I knew they had to realize parents couldn't bail them out of every situation."

"They're going to need our emotional support much more than a new piece of furniture. I believe Vi's already panicking about what kind of mother she's going to be."

"Instead of regretting how they got into this situation, I should be teaching Foster how to be a responsible dad."

"You are! You do it every day."

"And how would you know that?" Gavin asked, his eyes narrowing.

"From what Foster has told me . . . and Ben. You care, Gavin. That's what matters. You know, I've never met your daughter."

"You'll meet Emily at the rehearsal picnic. She acts more adult than a fourteen-year-old, so don't be surprised if she asks precocious questions. She's heard us talk so much about you that she thinks she knows you."

"Uh-oh. I hope you just told her about my cats or something like that."

Gavin chuckled. "She knows about Pepper and Marjoram. She thinks you're pretty great for giving Vi and Foster a place to live. Were you really going to fix this up eventually for a rental property?"

"I was, or for Vi or Jazzi if they wanted to live out here and stay in Willow Creek."

"This worked out great." Gavin turned toward the stairway again. "I'm going to place that old rolltop desk into the office area in the garage." He'd almost reached the stairway when he turned toward her again. "Can I ask you something?"

"That question means I'm probably not going to want to answer."

"True," he agreed. "Are you involved again in another murder investigation?"

Daisy shook her head. "Not really. Jonas and I are trying to help a young man get back on his feet. He has a daughter and they were homeless for a while."

"And he's accused of murder?"

"Not officially, but he's high on the suspect list. He didn't do it."

Gavin's frown cut deeper lines around his mouth. "How can you be so sure?"

"He's not that kind of man." She knew that assessment might seem lame to Gavin, but it was what her instincts told her.

"Daisy, depending on the circumstances, *anybody* could be capable of violence."

She shook her head, her hair slipping over her shoulders. "I think you're wrong."

"And I think sometimes you're naive."

Was Gavin another one of those men who underestimated her because of her blue eyes and blond hair? As she was growing up, attending college, and becoming a dietitian, she'd learned that looks *do* matter to others. In her case it seemed to take precedence over her intelligence. She usually became defensive when that happened.

However, Gavin went on, "When my wife died, I was lost. From what Foster tells me, you were strong when you lost your spouse. I wasn't. I was weak. I turned to alcohol for a while. After the kids went to bed, I'd drink.

When I did, I didn't have control of my emotions. I still remember one night when Foster came home late. I yelled at him like I never had before. That night he made me wake up. He said, 'Dad, I'm late. I didn't die. You're so mad at Mom for dying, I don't think you love her anymore.'"

Gavin rubbed his hand across his jaw and looked as if the memory still haunted him. "This from a teenager. There were times with that anger, especially when I was wielding a hammer, that I didn't know myself."

Daisy took a few steps closer to him. "I'm not naive, Gavin. After all, I *have* helped solve a few murders. I recognize the good and the bad sides of people. And even though you yelled at Foster and maybe damaged a two-by-four now and then with a hammer, I don't believe you could kill someone."

Gavin appeared surprised at her words. Finally he said, "I'm not sure why I told you all that."

"Because you don't want me to get into trouble and bring it home to our kids."

He sent her a crooked grin. "Ah-ha! So you *are* good at detecting motives." Then as if the conversation had gotten way too serious, he changed the course of it. "I hope Foster comes home in time tonight to help me move the sofa up here."

"Vi and Jazzi should be back soon. They went with Aunt Iris to help her find a dress for the wedding."

"Tomorrow night, Foster doesn't have class. I'm trying to convince him to rent a tux for the wedding, or to buy a new suit. I don't even think he has one that fits."

"What about you, father of the groom? Tux or a suit?"

"I'll go with whatever Foster decides, but I vote for the tux." Gavin winked at her before he descended the stairs.

Daisy realized that Gavin, like Jonas, was a complicated man. She was glad he was Foster's dad. She was glad they'd all be family.

Friday evening Jonas flipped burgers and turned kielbasa over at the grill on Daisy's patio. Daisy watched him, which was always a pleasure. He looked good in black shorts and a gray, short-sleeved Henley. He wore dock shoes with no socks, and just the sight of him made Daisy realize with a little thrill up her spine how much she was attracted to him.

Rolling over the kielbasa again with a set of long-handled barbecue tongs, Jonas stepped away from the grill as it flared. "I hope you like your kielbasa charred."

"I do," Jazzi said, "with lots of hot mustard."

Jonas shook his head. "I'm a ketchup guy . . . dill pickles too."

Jazzi wrinkled up her face. "Yuck."

Jonas laughed. "So how's the car fund coming?"

Daisy watched the two of them conversing and decided to stay out of it. Jazzi and Jonas were developing a deeper bond. Her daughter needed a male role model in her life.

"I'm building it up, thanks to my hours at the tea garden. If I find something good and used like Violet did, I might have a car by next summer."

Daisy considered Vi's blue Chevy Malibu. After Vi had decided to go to Lehigh to college, Daisy knew they wouldn't want to depend on carpooling for her to drive to and from school. They had been fortunate. An elderly customer who regularly came into the tea garden with her daughter had revealed she was turning in her keys and her daughter was selling her car. The Malibu was only five years old and in wonderful condition. They'd gotten a bargain. If they could find another vehicle like that one, it was possible that Jazzi *could* have a car by next summer. Did Daisy want her to? That was another question entirely.

Jazzi crossed to the grill with her plate, waiting for her burger and kielbasa.

"Well-done on the burger and the kielbasa," Jonas said.

"You should be a chef," Jazzi joked.

On the way back to the table, she ran her hand over the leafy stems in four patio pots that Daisy had planted with lemon thyme, lemon balm, rosemary, and lavender. The scents mingled and dispersed over the patio. The temperature had dipped to eighty, and as the sun began to set, the sky turned a beautiful orange and purple. Daisy could see Jonas and Jazzi were enjoying conversation that had nothing to do with anything serious. It was nice to have a break from wedding planning and the murder investigation.

Daisy had baked a peanut-butter sheet cake for dessert. She'd have it on hand if Vi and Foster stopped in. Vi had decided to meet Foster and Gavin at the tux rental shop so they could run a few errands afterward.

Dusk descended as they finished squares of cake. Afterward, Daisy began cleaning off the table. They were all going to go inside and play a game of hearts . . . or maybe Cat-Opoly.

Jonas took care of shutting down the grill and washing off the grate with the hose before he took it inside to finish cleaning it in the sink. Daisy and Jazzi followed him in.

The two cats met them with meows. Marjoram was the tortie and a talkative one. She had a split-color face, almost black on one side and golden tan on the other. Her chest was divided into black and tan too. When her golden feline eyes studied Daisy, Daisy asked her, "I suppose you want dessert too?"

Marjoram meowed again. Pepper on the other hand, a tuxedo—a black cat with a white chest— wound about Jonas's legs. Then she pounced on one of his shoes, playing with the leather tie.

He laughed, set the grate on the counter, and stooped to pick up the cat. "One of these days, you're going to trip me."

Jazzi reached to one of the upper cupboards and plucked out a bag of treats. "Come on," she said to the two of them. As she shook the treats in the bag, Marjoram jumped out of Jonas's arms and the two felines followed her to their dishes.

Daisy heard the drop of the treats into the ceramic dishes right before her cell phone played its tuba sound. That tuba tone was the only ringtone she could hear when she was working at the tea garden. Now it sounded loud in the kitchen as she took the phone from its charger on the counter and checked the screen. Vi was calling.

"Hi, Vi. Are you and Foster headed this way?"

"Mom, you've got to come."

Daisy could hear tears in her daughter's voice and it terrified her. "Come where?"

"To Lancaster Hospital. I'm spotting. Mom, I'm spotting."

Taking a bolstering breath, knowing she had to stay calm, Daisy asked, "Are you there now?"

"Yes, we just got here. I called my doctor's service as soon as I realized what was happening. She called me back and said to meet her here. We're at registration and they're going to take me back."

"I'll be there as soon as I can. Hold on to Foster's hand and try not to panic. That will only make everything worse. Do you want me to call you while I'm on my way?"

Vi sounded relieved at the suggestion. "Yes. If I can't talk, it will just go to voice mail."

"All right. I'm grabbing my purse now. I love you, honey."

"I love you too, Mom." Vi's voice was shaking and she hung up with a little sob.

As Daisy went to the island for her purse and stuffed her phone inside, she explained to Jonas and Jazzi what was happening.

"I'm going with you," Jazzi said.

"And I'm driving," Jonas announced. "You're too shaken up to do it. You'll be able to talk to Vi on the phone easier that way. I'll get the SUV while you close up."

Twenty minutes later, they entered the emergency department at the hospital. Jonas's foot had been a trifle heavy on the accelerator. After Daisy explained that she was Vi's mother, she was shown back to the ER cubicle while Jonas and Jazzi stood in the waiting room.

Daisy rushed to her daughter and gave her a hug. Vi looked pale and Daisy didn't know if that was from fear or from what was going on. Foster didn't look much better.

After Daisy leaned away from Vi, her daughter said, "The doctor will be back in shortly. I already had blood drawn but she's going to do an exam and maybe an ultrasound. Can you stay with me?"

Daisy glanced over at Foster.

He came to Vi's side and took her hand. "Do you want me to stay or do you want me to go?"

"Can you wait with Jonas and Jazzi until we find out what's going on? Your dad will probably arrive soon. I'll call you back in here if it's anything serious. I promise."

Foster leaned down to Vi and gave her a gentle kiss. Then he left the cubicle.

Daisy pulled up a chair beside Vi, but she didn't have to ask the question. Vi read her mind. "He's scared out of his wits just like I am. I think it will be easier for him out there, especially when Gavin arrives."

Her daughter was five and a half months pregnant. What would happen if she lost the baby? Daisy took Vi's hand and held on to it.

An hour later, while Vi rested, Daisy went out to the waiting room where Jonas, Jazzi, Gavin, and Foster immediately came toward her. She quickly took a deep breath and then smiled with her relief. "Dr. Geisler has prescribed bed rest for a week. If there's no more spotting after that, Vi can resume her daily activities."

Foster's face finally took on some color. Gavin was

so relieved that he stepped toward Daisy and they hugged. They were family.

When he stepped back, however, he looked embarrassed.

Daisy said to Foster, "You can go on back. I'm sure Vi wants you with her now."

They all sat quietly, engrossed in their thoughts until Foster emerged from the back hallway with Vi in a wheelchair. She had discharge papers in her hand and instructions for the following week.

Daisy crouched down at the wheelchair. "I've been thinking about the next week. Dr. Geisler said you should limit steps too."

"But I wanted to live in the apartment," her daughter complained.

"I know, but you have to do what's best for you and the baby. So this is what I suggest. Why doesn't Foster move into the apartment. You can stay with me and Jazzi for the week. In fact, I'll give you my bedroom. That will make bed rest easier for you. I'll sleep upstairs in your room. Maybe Jazzi and I can share fashion tips."

That brought a smile to Vi's lips. "We'll have to have a conference call so I can be in on the discussions."

Jazzi laughed, and it was good to see her younger daughter was relieved too.

Daisy glanced up at Foster and Gavin. "Does that work for you?"

"That works swell," Foster said. "Dad can help me move in the rest of my stuff and I'll settle in."

After Daisy stood, Foster put his hand on Vi's shoulder. "You're going to do great, and we're going to make sure you do."

Daisy hoped prayers and good wishes would be enough going forward. In a way, she had to be ready for anything. If Vi and Foster's wedding didn't take place as planned . . . she'd have to pick up the pieces.

Foster, Jazzi, and Vi were already standing at the front door when Jonas dropped off Daisy. He'd been quiet on the way home and so had she. "Do you want to come in?"

"I think Vi has had enough excitement. Wait until you get her settled downstairs and bring her whatever she needs. You're going to crash."

She said with a weak smile, "You're probably right."

He leaned across the gear shift and kissed her, but it wasn't as deep or long as usual. After he pulled away, she studied him. She could see he didn't want to have a long conversation and neither did she. Not here . . . not now.

She opened the door, then tapped Jonas's arm. "I'll see you soon."

After he nodded, she left his SUV and went to her front door. Jazzi had already pressed in the security code and gone inside.

Daisy followed Vi and Foster. "Come on, Vi, let me get you settled in my room."

Taking her lead, Jazzi trailed Vi and Foster into Daisy's bedroom. "Tell me what you need and I'll get it from upstairs," Jazzi offered.

Daisy knew Vi and Foster needed private time to talk, so she followed Jazzi out of her bedroom and went to the kitchen to bring out a snack for Vi and Foster.

Marjoram appeared from somewhere and meowed plaintively.

"You want to know what's going on, don't you?"

The tortie meowed again.

"Vi's sad right now. Maybe you can cheer her up." Daisy pointed to her bedroom. "I'm sure she'd appreciate your company."

Making eye contact, Marjoram blinked her golden eyes, gave a short meow, and headed for Daisy's bedroom.

Daisy had pulled the cake pan from the refrigerator when her cell phone, which she'd stuffed into her pocket, played its tuba sound. She thought about letting it go to voice mail, but this late it could be important. When she checked the screen, she saw that Keith was calling.

"Hi, Keith. How are you and Mandy?"

"We're settled in. Mandy seems to like the place, especially since she can play outside."

"How does she like day care?"

"She likes being with the other kids. She and Karina's daughter Quinn have become good friends. I think we're going to set up a playdate for them."

After he paused for a moment, he said, "I just wanted to run something by you. I tried to call Jonas but his phone went to voice mail."

"He might have it turned off. We were at the hospital with my daughter."

"Something serious?"

"We hope not. It was a scare about the baby, but everything seems to have checked out okay. She's on bed rest for a week."

"I'm sorry I'm bothering you."

"No bother. Tell me what you're thinking."

After a brief hesitation, Keith continued, "I'm considering why Detective Willet wanted a list of items I'd sold to Otis and Barry. What if they never turned up in the shop? He could think I'm lying. What if Barry cheated others, and one of those suppliers came after him? Revenge could be a mighty motive."

"How much money are we talking about?"

"Prices varied. A linen Haversack, that's like a pocketbook, was six hundred dollars. I think it was much more, like nine hundred, on an auction site. For quartermaster shoulder straps, Barry paid me nine hundred dollars, and I think they might have been worth double that. He gave me seven hundred for a general's officer's sash, but it was worth so much more."

Daisy almost whistled. No wonder Keith had been able to take care of himself and Mandy, albeit temporarily.

Keith said, "I know what you're thinking. I should be rich, right? I found these things over a two-month period. You'd be surprised the stuff people intend to throw away and don't know what it's worth."

"So you bought the items cheap and sold them to Barry for more, who sold them to his customers for even more yet."

"That's right. It's a matter of supply and demand, and Barry had lots of demand for Civil War memorabilia because of Gettysburg being less than two hours away. I didn't go near there for antiquing because those dealers know exactly what that memorabilia is worth. I couldn't have afforded to buy it. If a supplier was consistently cheated, the amount could add up quickly."

"I want to stay here with Vi tomorrow, but I'm sure she'll get tired of my company by afternoon. If Foster or Jazzi will be here with her, I'd like you to meet me at Pirated Treasures and talk to Otis. Do you think that's possible?"

"I don't see why not. Penelope and Clovis are flexible about my work schedule. As long as I finish my work, they don't care when I do it."

"Great. I'll call you tomorrow when I can get free and see if you can meet me. Deal?"

"That's the easiest deal I've made in a while. Thanks, Daisy. I appreciate it."

"Give Mandy a hug for me."

"I will."

After Daisy ended the call, she wondered if she was doing the right thing getting involved, especially if Vi was on bed rest. On the other hand, her little adventure could give them something to talk about.

Chapter Ten

After Foster left and Jazzi went upstairs, Daisy called Iris and then her mom to fill them in on what had happened. Iris was going to call Pam Dorsey, a temporary employee who was attending college at Franklin and Marshall, to see if she could cover for Daisy. Daisy's mom said she'd stop in as soon as she could.

After the calls, Daisy slipped into the bedroom to talk to Vi. Her daughter wore her raspberry-colored tank and shorts pj's. In Daisy's queen-sized bed, Vi had pulled the sheet up to her waist. Marjoram lay stretched out at her side and Pepper sat in a bread-loaf position on the padded bench at the foot of the bed. As Vi gripped her tablet in her hand and petted Marjoram with the other, tears streaked down her face.

Vi had pushed the sunshine and shadow quilt down to the corner of the bed. After Daisy folded it over and laid it on the chair, she crawled in under the sheet beside her daughter. Her shoulder against Vi's, she tried to imagine what Vi was thinking. There was only one way to know for sure.

"Tell me why you're crying," she said softly.

"I can't even number all the things running through my head right now. I'm scared for the baby most of all."

"I know you are. But the doctor said the baby's fine."

"She can't know that for sure. I've been reading up on all the things that can happen—placental abruption, hemorrhaging, eclampsia. . . ."

"Stop!" Daisy's voice was firm. "You can't do this to yourself and to Foster. You have to think positively."

"What if I have to stay on bed rest longer and we can't have the wedding?"

"Vi, you are my coper. That means in any situation you can figure out what to do. If you have to stay on bed rest, think about the possibilities. No, you couldn't get married in a church, but you could be married while you're in bed. Or you can postpone the wedding."

"I don't *want* to postpone the wedding."

"Because you're sure it's what you want or because you think it's the right thing to do?"

Vi stared at Daisy unblinkingly. "Both. It's what I want to do and it's the right thing to do."

Asking a hard question when Vi was in this upset state was difficult, but it had to be asked. "Are you afraid Foster's marrying you merely because of the baby?"

Averting her gaze, Vi murmured, "He says he's not."

"Do you believe him?"

Vi faced Daisy once more. "I *have* to believe him. I have to trust him or we won't have any kind of marriage."

Daisy took Vi's hand and squeezed it, aware of Foster's high school ring on her daughter's finger. "Then trust and hope and let it all go for tonight. Stress isn't good for you or the baby. Know that we're all here to help you, whatever you decide and whatever happens."

"There's something else I wanted to talk to you about," Vi admitted.

Pepper stood and stretched, then padded across the bed and curled around Vi's foot.

"What's that?"

"If my pregnancy isn't derailed, and we're able to get married like we planned, and everything seems okay—"

Daisy held her breath because she had no idea what was coming next.

"I'd like to have a midwife deliver the baby."

Daisy didn't say anything. If her daughter carried this baby to term, she'd imagined her in a nice sterile hospital room, not in the apartment above the garage with a midwife by her side. Would a midwife even consider delivering the baby when this scare had happened? Daisy knew midwives were gaining in popularity again. A qualified, highly recommended one would do what was best for Vi and her baby. The only way Daisy would support this idea was if the midwife practiced in consultation with an ob-gyn.

Vi went on quickly. "I've been watching this reality series on TV. All the moms have their babies at home with midwives. It's supposed to be good for the baby, Mom. No bright lights or noise. Just mom and dad and family around the baby, bringing him or her into the world. The midwife knows what to do. And if anything looks as if it's not going the right way, she has a backup doctor. I really want to check into it. And ask Dr. Geisler what she thinks."

Her daughters had dragged her into new territory

each day of their lives. "I want you and the baby to be safe. With that being said, I'll reserve judgment until you find out more. If Dr. Geisler approves and if you find somebody in this area who comes highly recommended, and I do mean *highly*, then I'd like to talk to her too. Would you be open to that?"

"I would as long as you don't interview her with a negative attitude. You ask good questions, maybe some I won't think of."

Daisy bumped Vi's shoulder affectionately, noticing Vi's tears had stopped and she seemed more peaceful again. "Now do you think you can sleep or do you have something to do that isn't stressful?"

"I'm putting a playlist together for the reception. All that involves is listening to music." She smiled at her mother and it was a good smile, not a fake one. "Foster said he'd call me after he gets home. He wants to make sure I'm okay. So if you hear me talking, that's who I'm talking to."

"Do you need anything before I go upstairs?"

"No. Jazzi brought me water, a bag of pretzels, and one of your scones."

"If you need anything, text me. Maybe I should sleep on the sofa tonight."

"Mom, we have a week of this. You're going into work tomorrow, aren't you? Jazzi can stay here with me."

"I'm taking off for the morning. Iris texted me. She said Pam will be glad to come in tomorrow and help. She hasn't been getting as many hours since you and Jazzi have been working at the tearoom."

"Will Pam be enough help?"

"If she isn't, Aunt Iris will call Ruth Zook. Her daughters can help too. Priscilla and Louise are good workers. They're going to help with our children's tea next weekend. So I'll be home with you tomorrow morning, then I have an errand to run. But if for any reason you want me to stay home all day, I will."

"Go to bed, Mom. You have as much on your mind as I do." Vi gave her mom a hug.

Daisy kissed her on the cheek. "Sleep well, honey."

Daisy left the door open to the bedroom so the felines could come and go. She also didn't want to feel closed off to Vi even if she was upstairs. As she mounted the stairs, she knew sleep would be hard coming tonight. Vi was right. She probably had as much on her mind as her daughter did.

Early afternoon the next day, Daisy met Keith outside Pirated Treasures. The sign on the door was turned to OPEN. However, Keith hesitated to go in. Instead of reaching for the door handle, he asked Daisy, "How's your daughter?"

"Although she'd rather be doing anything else, she's resting. Her sister is keeping watch over her for now. Jazzi's supposed to call me if anything comes up, or if Violet gets out of bed without a good reason."

The anxiety on Keith's face lessened a little. "I guess that's what sisters are for—to tattle on each other when they see they're getting into trouble."

"Jazzi and Vi have always had each other's backs, but we're in uncharted territory now."

"You mean because of the baby? I remember how Mandy changed my life . . . and Lisa's. After she was born, it was like a shock wave went through me with the realization that I had to care for her twenty-four hours a day, seven days a week for the rest of our lives. I think Lisa was ready for it more than I was. But I soon got on board with the program. With that little face looking up at me and trusting me, I couldn't help but want to do the best for her."

With another glance at the OPEN door sign, he kept their conversation going. "I saw Karina last night. When I picked up Mandy at day care, Karina was there picking up Quinn. So we stopped for takeout and took it back to the cabin."

"A playdate for adults and kids," Daisy teased. Keith seemed to want to talk and she imagined he didn't have many people he could talk to.

"I'm still tentative about future plans because I don't know what's going to happen with the police. But I asked Karina what she wanted to do when Quinn started school."

Daisy and Karina had had this conversation, but she wondered what her server had told Keith. Without prompting, Keith revealed, "She told me she wants to work full time at your tea garden and rent her own place. It's not that she's not grateful to her mom, but she wants to be independent."

"That sounds like Karina."

"The job I have now at the farm will be great for me and Mandy. If I'm still there when she starts school, I can take her in the morning and I can pick her up afterward. Or if I'm tied up, Karina said she'd pick up both kids at day care or school. It feels great to have a backup."

"It will be good for you to have support, and for Karina too. Is that all it's going to be?"

"We're just friends," he insisted, his face reddening a bit.

Daisy could easily understand why Keith didn't want to date Karina or think of her as more than a friend.

His life was still verging on the uncertain. She admired him for not wanting to rush ahead with Karina.

Keith blew out a long breath and nodded to the door. "I'm procrastinating because I don't know what Otis is going to think of me coming here. If he believes I'm guilty, he has the right to throw me out."

"He does," Daisy agreed. "But you're not going to know until we go in. And if you want to still sell to him besides working on the farm, you're going to have to talk to him."

"Why do *you* want to talk to him?"

"I'd like to find out if he knows anything about the police's investigation."

Keith took a steady grip on the door handle and pulled it open.

As usual the shop smelled musty. That mustiness was intensified because it had been closed since the murder.

Otis called from a display area to the left. "Be right with you."

"Otis, it's Daisy, and I've brought somebody with me, Keith Rebert. Is that all right?"

Otis appeared from behind a set of shelves that held lanterns of all shapes, sizes, and ages. He looked disheveled. His hair didn't have its usual part, and it stuck up in the back. He wore a short-sleeved, snap-button shirt that had wrinkles as if he'd worn it yesterday too. Suspenders held up his jeans.

"I understand if you don't want me here," Keith offered quickly. "If you think—"

Otis plucked one of his black suspenders. "Don't go thinking you know what I'm thinking. Just because I told the police you lifted that rolling pin, don't mean

I believe you did it. They were asking questions, so I had to tell them the truth."

Keith's astonishment showed. "You *don't* think I did it?"

"Did you?" Otis retorted.

"No," came out of Keith's mouth firmly and evenly.

"I think you're a fine young man who's in a tight spot. This woman wouldn't be helping you if she thought you had evil in you."

Keith glanced at Daisy and she nodded. "Otis is right. I believe in you, Keith, and there are other people who do too." Daisy addressed Otis. "I'm trying to help Keith. Can you tell me what the police questioned you about besides the rolling pin?"

"They wanted to look at my bookkeeping program. I let them look because I want Barry's murderer caught."

"Did they take your computer along?"

"Nope. They had some evidence guy here. The computer's mine, you see, not Barry's. That had something to do with it."

"Do you know if they found anything?"

"They didn't tell me nothing."

"Do you mind if I have a look at it?"

Otis shrugged. "I don't care. I turned on the dang thing when I came in this morning, but I can't look at that screen very long. It makes my eyes go crazy."

Daisy could only imagine. Even if a person's eyes were a hundred percent, staring at the computer screen could tire them.

Keith had made Daisy a list of the items he had given Detective Willet. As Daisy followed Otis to the back of the store, they went through the doorway to the area where she'd heard Ian and Barry fighting. It was a storeroom of sorts and an old desk sat in one corner, beaten up around the edges. But the computer looked state-of-the-art with at least a twenty-four-inch monitor.

Otis motioned to the desk chair on rollers that sat in front of the old desk.

As Daisy sat in front of the keyboard, she found that the computer program was like the one *she* used for book work.

After a half hour she'd discovered what she wanted to see. She turned to Otis. "Keith has a list of the items he sold you and Barry, but they aren't listed in your inventory."

"Do you think Barry just forgot to put them in?" Otis asked, eyes narrowed as he peered at the monitor.

"I'm not sure about that," Daisy admitted. "Can you tell me if Barry often left the shop to consult with customers."

"He had a few customers who called him. If they couldn't get here, he'd go to their place." After a pensive pause, Otis added, "I know what you're getting at. You think Barry was cheating me."

Daisy sighed, wanting to be honest with Otis but not hurt him. "I don't know what Barry was doing, Otis, but I think he was doing something that got him killed."

"Do you think the police will figure out what that was?"

"I do. I hear Zeke Willet is a good detective." She checked her watch. "I really have to get going and check in at the tea garden. I don't want my staff to think I'm leaving all the responsibility up to them."

When she glanced at Otis, she saw his forlorn look that she and Keith would be leaving.

Keith must have seen it too because he asked the older man, "Is there anything you need me to do while

I'm here? I have a couple of hours before I have to pick up Mandy. I finished my chores at the farm for the time being."

Otis looked relieved. "I need to inventory some stuff that came in. It would be great if you could help me unpack the boxes."

"Sure thing."

Daisy said to Otis, "Do you have anything to eat tonight?"

"I have some food left in the refrigerator. Kind folks from church brought me casseroles."

"Good. I'll stop over tomorrow and bring you more soup, okay?"

"Sounds good." His smile was grateful.

Keith said, "I'm going to walk Daisy out, then I'll come back to help you."

Keith didn't speak until they reached the door. "I'll let you know if I learn anything else from Otis."

"Why don't you and Mandy come over for supper tonight? I'll call Jonas and ask him too. We can discuss everything we know and see if we can come up with a lead. Is there anything Mandy doesn't like?"

Keith shook his head. "She's not picky. When we were living in the van, we had to make do with what we could afford. She's taken a real liking to anything I didn't have to cook, and that includes vegetables and fruits."

"How about something easy like BLTs? I have plenty of tomatoes from the garden and lettuce too. And I'll bring home a sour cream cucumber salad from the tea garden along with dessert."

"That sounds like a feast."

"Hardly," Daisy said with a smile.

"What time would you like us to come over?"

"How about seven? That will give me time to see how Vi's doing and put supper together."

"One of these days I'm going to treat you and your family and Jonas to steaks at one of those steak houses. That's a promise."

Daisy believed Keith would keep it.

When Daisy got home and walked into Vi's, or really *her* own bedroom, Vi was in bed propped up with her laptop sitting on a lap desk and books around her.

Vi said, "Gram was here to visit. She's glad she's going to be a great-grandmother, but I'm not sure she approves of Foster."

"Do you care?" Daisy asked, aware of how her mom's disapproval had affected *her* before her wedding.

"I do. But not enough to change what my heart's telling me."

At that, Daisy smiled. She'd learned to do the same.

With woeful brown eyes Vi gazed at Daisy. "Mom, I need to keep earning money. I want to do what's best for the baby, but I can't just lie here and do nothing. What if I have to do this for more than a week?"

Jazzi looked at her mom and said, "She's really worried about this." Jazzi was sitting on a bedroom chair near the closet.

Daisy sank down onto the bed beside Vi. "So let's brainstorm. You sent out résumés. Did you hear from anyone?"

Vi shook her head. "They won't want to hire me anyway if I have to rest."

"If bed rest is what you and the baby need, then I imagine that's what you'll be doing. But that doesn't mean that your brain has to rest, right? You don't want to add more stress, but that doesn't mean you can't do *something*. The thing is, Vi, even if you can go off bed rest, I'm not sure the tea garden is the best place for you."

"Why not?" Her daughter sounded wounded.

"Because as your pregnancy continues, you're not going to want to lift heavy trays, pans, and teapots. Sure, I can put you on the sales counter, but is that what you really want?"

"I don't really enjoy sales. But I do enjoy talking to the customers. What about hiring me to do your book work?" Vi asked with a smile.

Daisy smiled back. "I can pay you for that. But if you could find a small business in Willow Creek that could use your services, that might work too. One job generates another. You sent résumés to larger businesses in Lancaster. Maybe you can find small businesses right here. If they want someone on site, that wouldn't be too challenging during your pregnancy."

"I *will* ask around. There are so many small businesses in Willow Creek that I'm sure *someone* needs help." Vi turned toward Daisy and gave her a huge hug.

"There's something I wanted to talk to you about too," Jazzi said. "I know you have to start dinner if we're having company."

"It's an easy dinner to fix. You know that. What did you want to talk about?"

"I asked Vi if it's okay if Portia and Colton come to the wedding. She said if there *is* a wedding, she's okay with it. Right, Vi?"

Vi nodded. "Two more guests won't make a difference. Right, Mom?"

Jazzi addressed Daisy again. "I wasn't sure if you were okay with it. I don't want you to feel left out or as if I'm giving Portia and her husband all my attention. But I'd like to get to know Portia's husband. That's if he wants to get to know *me*."

They'd gone over this, and Daisy didn't know what Portia's husband was going to do. But if Jazzi was willing to take a chance, then she was too.

"I'm okay with it. Just remember, though, weddings are emotional, can be noisy, and they don't always bring out the best in people. On the other hand, it's a time for family to be together and make amends."

"It's just like when I first met Portia," Jazzi murmured. "You told me not to expect too much."

"Or too little," Daisy reminded her. "You need to keep an even keel."

"Do you mind if I call her now?"

"I don't mind. Go ahead. Then you and I can work on dinner and it will be done in no time."

As Jazzi left the room, Daisy felt fatigue wash over her. The day had seemed long. She slipped off her shoes and pushed them under the nightstand.

When she wiggled her toes, Vi turned to her laptop. "I think I'll search through the businesses in Willow Creek and make a list."

"That's a good idea."

Vi brought up her search engine but then she stopped. "Mom, what if Colton won't come? What if he never wants to meet Jazzi? What if he wants Portia to forget all about her?"

"Then you and I and Jazzi's counselor will have to help Jazzi deal with that. I can't imagine, though, that a man wouldn't want to meet his wife's daughter, whether he fathered her or not."

"We've never talked about Jazzi's real father. I mean, biological father," Vi automatically corrected.

"I know what you meant. No, we haven't. Jazzi's never told me she has any intention of searching for him. On the other hand, I didn't know about it when she first searched for Portia. She did it in secret for a couple of months."

"What if she wants to, especially if this thing with Portia doesn't work out? She might feel she has that connection to turn to."

"Yes, she might. But I think she has enough to deal with right now. If she tells you she's thinking about it, I would like to know, though."

"Sisters keep secrets for each other," Vi reminded her with a wicked smile.

"Sisters reveal those secrets when it's for their own good. But that's up to you. Loyalty to Jazzi is important."

"Jazzi told me Jonas is coming over tonight. How is that going?"

It was strange really. Her daughters felt as protective about her dating as she felt about them. "Since we never know what's going to happen next, we're just going slow."

"Don't go so slow you stall out," Vi advised her.

"I care about Jonas . . . a lot." She thought about last night at the hospital. He'd seemed quiet on the way home. That wasn't unusual for him, but they hadn't said two words in the car. If something was bothering him, maybe they could talk about it tonight. She wanted to think about a future with Jonas, but she still had to wonder how much *he* wanted a future with *her*.

* * *

Jazzi sliced the zucchini that Daisy had just peeled. "We have enough zucchini left in the garden that we can make three of these casseroles."

Jazzi had just gotten off the phone with Portia. Portia had said she'd ask her husband if he would come to the wedding with her. Daisy knew her daughter would be waiting with her breath held for the answer to that one. In the meantime, maybe she could keep her busy.

Pulling the glass casserole to her on the counter, Daisy began layering it with the sliced zucchini. She'd add cheese and shredded carrots between layers and pour an egg mixture over the whole thing and bake it.

Daisy had just set the oven timer when the doorbell rang. She checked the video monitor on her phone. "It's Jonas." She heard the delight in her voice and wasn't ashamed or embarrassed by it. Could a woman her age really be having teenage feelings? Maybe.

After she opened the door to Jonas, she said, "You don't have to ring the bell."

"Habit, I guess," he said with a shrug. But Daisy knew it wasn't just habit. He didn't feel comfortable enough with her family atmosphere to just walk in. They'd have to work on that.

He'd been holding his hand at his back and now he produced a bouquet of roses.

"They're gorgeous!" she said with surprise. "That color is very mysterious." The roses were a mixture of mauve, lavender, and purple.

As Jonas followed her to the kitchen, he said, "You're getting good at solving mysteries."

In the kitchen, she turned toward him. "Do you want to talk about that now or later?"

"Let's wait until Keith gets here. He might have something to add. You never know."

"I need to find a vase for these," Daisy started, but before she could continue, Jonas took her into his arms and kissed her. It was one of those kisses she'd remember until tomorrow.

When she looked around, she saw that Jazzi had disappeared, probably into the bedroom with Vi. Feeling color in her cheeks, she focused solely on Jonas. "That was a nice greeting."

"I need to do more of that. I'm not just a friend."

She wondered where this was coming from. Jonas had always had a confidence about him that she admired. But now he seemed a bit unsure. Tonight he was dressed in a wine, short-sleeved Henley, white shorts, and boat shoes. When he embraced her, she felt as if she couldn't be anywhere safer.

She wrapped her arms around his neck. "I know you're more than a friend. Maybe I have to show you that."

"We've both got a lot on our plates."

"I know I've been distracted by the wedding, and now by Vi's medical condition."

He shook his head. "That's understandable. I've been distracted too. I'd like to get back on a decent footing with Zeke, but he's so closed off that it's not possible."

"It's hard to lose a friend. You'll have to keep trying."

Jonas pushed Daisy's hair behind her ear. There was a look in his eyes that she hadn't seen there before. She wasn't sure what it was. Longing for more than they had right now?

Suddenly he took a step away and glanced around the kitchen at the supper preparations. Jazzi had already set the table and his focus took that in too. "You're cooking for a big crowd tonight. Who all's coming?"

"Just us and Foster and Keith and Mandy. Did you expect anyone else?" She let a bit of amusement fall into her voice because she didn't know what he was thinking.

"I thought maybe you'd invite Karina and Quinn."

She shook her head. "I'm not playing matchmaker. If Keith and Karina want something to start, they're going to have to do that on their own."

Jonas hesitated a moment and then said, "And I thought maybe you'd invite Gavin."

"Gavin?" Daisy knew she sounded puzzled.

"I thought he might stop in to see how Vi was doing."

"He called this morning, and I gave him an update. He's busy with his life and his other two kids. He'll be here tomorrow when he helps Foster move into the garage apartment."

As Jonas nodded, she saw tension in his shoulders that hadn't been there before. What was he thinking? That she was getting closer to Gavin? Before she had a chance to examine that thought, the doorbell rang again.

Jazzi called, "I'll get it. It's Keith and Mandy. Foster just texted Vi he's going to be a little late but he's on his way."

Before Daisy could ask Jonas another question while she still had the privacy to do so, the timer went off for the zucchini casserole in the oven.

Jonas moved to the counter for the oven mitts. "You open the oven. I'll take out whatever's in there."

Back to normal? Possibly. Or perhaps they'd be having a discussion about Gavin after they put together clues about Barry Storm's murder.

Chapter Eleven

Keith's daughter Mandy sat on Daisy's lap through-out dinner, even though she could have claimed her own chair. When Daisy had asked her if she wanted cheese on her BLT, Mandy had grinned and nodded. She was eating with alacrity the four cubes of the sand-wich that Daisy had cut. There was a tad of mayonnaise on her chin and melted cheese on her upper lip.

Keith shook his head as he leaned over to wipe the mayo from Mandy's chin. "She's a good eater but a messy one."

"As kids should be," Jazzi said with a smile. "She even ate the zucchini casserole with the carrots. When I was her age, I wouldn't have touched it."

Daisy laughed. "You remember that, do you? I have cherry tarts for dessert. Does anyone want a refill on their iced tea or want to have coffee?"

Foster had disappeared into the bedroom to eat his supper with Vi, Pepper, and Marjoram. The cats were sticking close to Vi, watching over her. Now Foster en-tered the kitchen and asked, "Did you say cherry tarts? I'll take two for carryout."

Daisy laughed again. "With or without whipped cream?"

After Foster had returned to the bedroom to have dessert with his fiancée, Daisy asked Jazzi, "Can you sit with Mandy over at the island to have dessert?"

Jazzi glanced from Jonas to Keith to her mom.

"You want to talk about the case. Will you fill me in later?"

Jonas's brows arched. "This really shouldn't become a family affair."

"Sometimes younger minds can think of things older minds can't," Jazzi joked.

He softened his tone. "I'm sure your mom will fill you in if she thinks it's a good idea."

Jazzi stood and took her cherry tart and Mandy's over to the island. Then she held her arms out for the little girl. "Come on, honey. We've been exiled."

All Mandy cared about was that cherry tart with the whipped cream on top. She settled on the stool, took the spoon that Jazzi gave her, and dipped into that white mountain of creaminess.

"Was Otis welcoming today when you stopped at Pirated Treasures?" Jonas asked both Keith and Daisy.

"More welcoming than I ever expected," Keith responded. "He doesn't think I can care for Mandy the way I do and commit murder too. I'm not sure if that's true. A man never knows what he's capable of until he hits bottom."

"Did you hit bottom?" Jonas asked.

"I'd say my bottom came after Lisa died. After I lost the house, there wasn't anything else to do but pick up Mandy and as many of our things as I could and go. I've watched shows on TV about those houses that realtors flip. The whole family's possessions are left behind. That happens because they can't take it with them. They can only take what's most important. For me, Mandy was all I cared about."

"When you hit bottom, though," Jonas said, "did you ever think about going after the bank president or the people who had foreclosed on your house?"

"Never. That would have been futile. I would have ended up in jail and Mandy would have had no one."

Daisy understood what Jonas was getting at. Otis had been right. A man like Keith couldn't care for his daughter the way he did and commit murder. The two things just didn't compute.

"We asked Otis what the police wanted," Daisy explained to Jonas. "He told us they couldn't just take his computer without a subpoena because it was his for his business. Pirated Treasures is in his name and Barry worked for him. Still, he didn't want any trouble and he wanted to figure out why Barry was murdered, so he let them look at the program."

"With his consent they didn't *need* a subpoena," Jonas agreed. "From the scuttlebutt at the station, the police didn't find anything of importance at Barry's residence upstairs. They did question Ian, by the way, but that didn't lead anywhere."

"Since the police wanted to look at Otis's computer, we wanted to take a look at it too," Daisy added. "He uses a bookkeeping program like I do, so it was easy to navigate. We did find something interesting. Remember that list that Keith gave the police?"

"Sure, with the Gettysburg memorabilia on it."

"Right," Keith affirmed. "Nothing from that list was included in the items that Barry had recorded in the bookkeeping program."

"We checked several days after the dates they came in," Daisy said. "There was just no sign of any of them."

Jonas pushed his dish back and crossed his arms on the table in front of him. "From my experience, when items aren't on an inventory sheet, the store owner's keeping two sets of books, or he sells the items he didn't list for cash and doesn't record it. Not as much income to declare that way. It's illegal, of course."

"I don't believe Otis would do that intentionally," Daisy mused.

"I agree," Keith said. "When Otis realized what we'd found, he said he didn't want to think that Barry was cheating him. But the way Barry reneged on deals, and the way he lowballed merchandise that came in, my guess is he was the one who was hiding income."

"Something Barry was involved in got him killed," Jonas pointed out. "It could have been business, or it could have been personal."

Daisy began gathering their plates.

"We haven't talked to Mariah Goldblum yet," Jonas said. "What she has to say could give us a lead."

Could one woman's perspective solve a murder? Either she or Jonas or Keith were going to find that out.

On Monday morning, Daisy arrived at the tea garden early to make something special. Actually, the early hour wasn't to bake as much as to work out her frustration. Kneading bread dough for cinnamon rolls would do that. She should have at least six dozen baked by the time Iris and Tessa came to work.

After she deposited the bread dough in a proofing drawer, she began mixing dough for cherry tarts.

An hour later, Daisy had rolled and cut four trays of cinnamon rolls when Tessa came in the back door. She usually arrived at work about five a.m. She was a little early today. "I saw the motion detection lights go on in the back," she told Daisy. "Then I saw your car."

"I've been away from the tea garden a lot lately, and I wanted to make up that time."

"You're the proprietor. If you want to take off, you can whenever you want to." Twitching her nose, Tessa said, "Boy, they smell good."

After Tessa took her purse to the office and placed it in Daisy's lower desk drawer, she came back to the kitchen, her colorful smock in hues of lime and yellow flowing around her. Today she wore her caramel-colored hair in a braid that was wound around her head. Tessa wore smocks when she baked rather than an apron. She said it was because she always spilled flour all over everything. But Daisy knew she just liked the color of the smocks. The artist in her wanted to be creative.

"I have the list of baked goods to make for today. Do you want me to start on snickerdoodles or something else?"

"We'll probably need more cherry tarts."

"Tarts it is." Crossing to the walk-in, Tessa brought out butter and cream cheese.

Daisy removed the first tray of cherry tarts from the oven and placed them on a cooling rack.

"So why did you really come in early?" Tessa asked.

Since she and Tessa had been friends all the way back to their school days, they confided in each other and didn't keep secrets. Daisy wasn't keeping a secret, but she didn't know if Tessa would want to get involved in the murder investigation. That had happened once before.

"I'm trying to collect information about Barry Storm. I'm wondering what to do next."

"Next, as in you've already done something?" Tessa began scooping flour into a giant measuring cup.

"I've spoken with Keith about his interactions with Barry. Saturday, we talked to Otis. Oh, and I visited Ian, Barry's friend."

Tessa eyed the flour in the measuring cup. "You've been busy."

"Busy, but I don't know exactly what I've learned."

After pouring flour into the mixer bowl, Tessa suggested, "Why don't you run it by me?"

"Are you sure you want to get involved?"

"I'm not involved. I'm just listening."

Daisy knew how that went, but she really could use an objective listener. She told Tessa everything she'd learned in the past few days, but ended it with, "Barry really had it tough. His father went to jail and his mother drank herself to death. That's when Barry went to live with Otis. Otis has been everything to him. That's why I can't imagine Barry cheating him."

"But it all adds up to that." Tessa added orange zest to the flour. "You said Barry Storm's father went to jail. Is he out?"

"Oh, yes. Apparently, he's been out a few months. He showed up at the funeral and blamed Otis for Barry's death."

Tessa scrunched up her nose. "Really? Was that deflection or misdirection? What if Barry's father was the one to blame for his son's death? Who knows what he might have gotten mixed up in while in prison.

That could have spilled over to Barry when his father was released."

"I hadn't thought of that. You *are* a good listener."

"And a good deducer. Sometimes."

"Now I know what I should do next—visit Glen Storm."

Tessa stopped what she was doing and stared at Daisy. "You're not serious."

"I *am* serious. He's out of jail. If I go during the day and stay outside wherever he lives, what can happen? Maybe he really is grieving."

"You can't go alone."

"Yes, I can."

Tessa's tone became cajoling. "If you go after work, I could go with you."

That suggestion worried Daisy for a multitude of reasons. "Tessa, you really have to think about this. Zeke Willet already threatened me with obstruction of justice charges."

"That has nothing to do with me. I'm just going along with you to pay our condolences."

Daisy's hands stilled as she considered Tessa's offer. "I have a date with Jonas tonight. We're going to meet Aunt Iris and Russ Windom at Sarah Jane's Diner around seven."

Tessa was already washing her hands. "Let me see if I can find out where this man lives."

Before Daisy could stop her, she took out her phone. "What's his first name?"

"Glen. G-L-E-N."

A few screens and a couple of minutes later, Tessa said, "He's living in an apartment complex in Lancaster."

"I'm not going to even ask how you found his address."

"All I need is some vital information—like a name, a vicinity, and possibly an area code. If this is the right Glen Storm, he'll be easy to find, unless of course he isn't home. We can drive into Lancaster after the tea garden closes, then I can drop you off at Sarah Jane's for your dinner date. If you're serious about doing it. You have all day to think about it."

And think about it Daisy did.

The apartment building looked like a motel, an old-fashioned motel. There were five apartments on the lower level and five apartments directly above those. The brick building could use a face-lift. Peeling paint marred the white pillars that rose from the ground to the roof.

Tessa gave Daisy an are-you-sure-you-want-to-do-this look.

Daisy just nodded, and they took the stairs up to the second floor. The stairway was open and led to the walkway in front of the apartments. They found apartment 9.

Daisy glanced at the dirty window in the door, at the paint peeling around the doorframe, at the button for the doorbell that had turned green. She pressed it but heard nothing when she did.

"I doubt if it works," Tessa said. "You're going to have to knock. My guess is these are one-bedroom apartments. If he's home, he'll hear you knock."

"What makes you such an expert?"

"Before you came back to town, I had looked at apartments all over Lancaster and Willow Creek. I was able to size them up pretty accurately from the outside. The apartment I have now above the tea garden is the most spacious I've ever had. You and Iris are the best landladies."

"Before I get into you being the best kitchen manager and friend, I think I'd better knock." She rapped on the door with her knuckles. Turning to Tessa, she said, "That door doesn't sound too thick."

A slight breeze lifted Daisy's hair from her cheek. Even though the sun wasn't as intense this time of day, the temperature was still near ninety. She could feel moisture forming on her forehead.

Her anxiety tightened her chest when she heard footfalls approaching the door. Not knowing what to expect, she stepped back.

When the door opened, she decided Glen Storm was hot too. He wore a navy tank, faded red shorts, and flip-flops on his feet. The tattoos up and down both arms had so much ink they almost looked like long sleeves.

"Mr. Storm?" Daisy asked, stammering, even though she knew it was him.

"Yeah, that's me. You from some church or something? Because I'm long past being saved," he growled.

"No, not from a church," Daisy responded quickly. "I'm Daisy Swanson and this is Tessa Miller. I own Daisy's Tea Garden."

When he scowled, his thick brows drew together. "So you're selling something?"

"No, sir, we're not. I knew Barry and I know Otis. They were customers of mine. I'm just trying to gather a little information to help out a friend who the police have on their suspect list."

Glen Storm crossed his arms and leaned against the

doorframe, eying them speculatively. "Since I'm an ex-con, the police have me on that list too. If you think you're going to help a friend by asking me questions, you're wrong. I don't know nothing."

Tessa stepped in now. "Daisy has been involved in a couple of other murder investigations. She's good at putting clues together."

He closed one eye to study Daisy. "Better than the cops?"

"No, I'm not better than the police detectives, but I've found out information in the past that can help them."

"She's confronted murderers too and walked away unscathed," Tessa bragged.

Daisy almost groaned. Tessa was laying it on thick and Daisy wasn't sure that was the right way to go.

"What kind of questions are you asking?" Glen Storm looked a bit intrigued.

"Can you tell me when you last saw Barry?"

The ex-con sighed. "Same question that detective asked. I saw him two days before he was murdered."

"Had you reconnected with him? Otis led me to believe that you and Barry weren't in contact when you were in prison." This was all very sticky territory, and she didn't know how Barry's father would react.

His stance seemed to become even more defensive, but he answered her. "After I got out of prison, I went to see Barry. He didn't want to see me. Not until last week. He called me. We met up face to face at McDonald's, but he didn't want to share a cup of coffee."

"What did he want?" Daisy asked.

"He just wanted to tell me face to face that he wasn't going to be like me. He was going to marry Mariah and he'd never do to her what I had done to Carol.

That was Barry's mother. I'd hoped after he got that off his chest, we could have a real conversation, but Barry just walked out."

There was a hurt look in Glen's eyes that Daisy recognized. It was disappointment that a son or daughter didn't want to connect . . . didn't want to get to know their parent as an adult.

Daisy felt sweat inching down between her shoulder blades, but she went on anyway. "So Barry never told you anything about his business arrangement with Otis?"

At that, a shadow crossed Glen's face and he seemed reluctant to answer. He looked out over the parking lot, then back at Daisy. "Barry made enemies. One of the days I stopped at Pirated Treasures to try and make contact, I heard a customer threaten my son."

"Did you catch a name or find out who it was?"

"Nope. But I know what the item was that the supplier had brought in. It was a brass bugle. The supplier said he wouldn't accept two hundred dollars when it was worth at least five hundred. He told Barry if he didn't pay up for what it was worth, he'd have the police check on him, telling them that Barry was committing fraud."

Was Glen Storm telling the truth or trying to misdirect them? "I don't think there's anything illegal about Barry lowballing someone who brings in an object to him for sale. Why would the police possibly care about that?"

Glen shrugged. "I don't know. Maybe it wasn't just about the sale of the brass bugle. Maybe it was about something else. I never got the chance to find out."

Barry's father unfolded his arms and retreated into the doorway of his apartment. "That's all I know. I have things to do. You ladies have a good day." With that, he shut the apartment door.

As Tessa and Daisy returned to the parking lot, Tessa repeated, "Things to do? Really?"

Tessa apparently knew her car would feel like an oven even though they had only been at the door to Glen's apartment for a short amount of time. She advised, "Wait to get in. It's hot."

Daisy stood at the open passenger door watching Tessa over the hood of the car. Her friend switched on the ignition and turned on the air-conditioning full blast.

Then she climbed back out and returned to Daisy's eye contact over the hood.

"What are you thinking?" Daisy asked Tessa.

"I'm thinking I don't know if we can believe him."

"Because he's an ex-con?"

"Not just that. It's just a vibe. I think he would lie to save his skin."

"Maybe. But I saw real grief in his eyes when he talked about his son. And at the funeral, it really did seem that he blamed Otis for Barry's death."

"Pure deflection. Maybe he feels guilty because he couldn't take care of Barry."

Daisy sighed. "You mean, like if Jazzi or Vi got into trouble—legal trouble or criminal trouble—I'd blame myself."

"Parents are like that."

"Just for theory's sake, let's stipulate that Glen is innocent. If he is, where do we go from here?"

"If he's guilty, where do we go from here?" Tessa returned.

"If I could have any of my questions answered right now, there is a main one. Just what if that bugle really was a replica rather than the real thing? What if *Barry* was in the right, and the person supplying it was trying to cheat him?"

"I could turn that around. What if Barry was trying to cheat his customer?"

"I guess we'll never know. But that customer of Barry's could have had a motive to kill him too. I'll have to ask Otis about him. Maybe he'll remember the bugle."

Tessa checked her watch. "If you want to be on time for your date with Jonas, we'd better roll."

Daisy grimaced. "I suppose I'll be telling Jonas about all this, but I think I'll wait till after dinner, and after Iris and Russ leave. I don't want them to become embroiled in this too."

"I bet I know what Jonas is going to say."

"The thing about Jonas is . . . sometimes he's unpredictable. I never know how he'll react. But I'll tell you tomorrow if we're still speaking."

Tessa rolled her eyes and climbed back into the driver's seat. Daisy hustled in beside her, letting the air blow on her face. The temperature outside was hot, but the murder investigation could be heating up too.

Chapter Twelve

Jonas Groft and Daisy's aunt Iris and Russ must have just arrived at Sarah Jane's Diner because they were standing outside when Tessa dropped off Daisy. Daisy gave Tessa a wave and hurried over to the group standing under the huge hex sign of birds on the front wall. There was a hex sign with hearts on the other side of the door.

Jonas asked Daisy, "Did something happen to your car? Is that why Tessa dropped you off?"

"No, nothing's wrong with my car. After we eat, maybe you can take me back to the tea garden so I can pick it up. I'll tell you about our errand later."

"You don't want to talk about it in front of your aunt Iris and Russ?"

"It's probably better if we don't." That definitely clued in Jonas on the fact that the errand had something to do with the murder investigation. He studied her for a moment as if he was going to say something, but her aunt beckoned to her from the door. "Come on. We don't want Sarah Jane to close up before feeding us."

Russ gave Daisy a tolerant smile and straightened

his titanium black glasses. His hair was gray with a high receding hairline. He was a retired teacher and good company for her aunt. They had been dating casually since May and seemed to be becoming good friends.

Inside the restaurant, Daisy spotted Sarah Jane coming through the kitchen doorway to the sales counter. The owner of the restaurant as well as the usual hostess, she had strawberry-blond curls that fell over her forehead and around her ears to her jaw. She insisted she had to get them cut once a month to keep them from flying everywhere. Overweight, she claimed those extra pounds stayed on because she over-saw every dish on the menu and cooked some of them herself. She was high energy and Daisy knew she was the main force behind the idea of a thrift store in Willow Creek. Generous with coupons for her elderly customers, Sarah Jane knew many of them were on a fixed income budget.

Sarah Jane's blue gingham apron with its pinafore ruffles was her usual protection against spills and mishaps. Today she wore fuchsia sneakers with rainbow laces. Just looking at her made Daisy smile.

Sarah Jane said, "My favorite foursome."

"I bet you say that to all your foursomes," Russ teased.

"Can't fool *you*, can I? Come on. I'll show you to a booth. I know you usually like one of the back ones."

Customers preferred the booths because the diner was quieter back there and conversation could be carried on more easily.

Once they were seated and a waitress had brought them menus, Aunt Iris said with delight, "Pork chops stuffed with apple bread filling are on the menu. I'm so glad we came tonight."

"Jazzi was going to warm up leftovers for her and Vi

tonight. Maybe I'll take them shoofly pie. I'm trying to keep Vi's spirits up any way I can."

Iris set down her menu. "I'll have to stop in and see Vi. I can bring my knitting along and stay a while and keep her company. Maybe tomorrow evening?"

"I'm sure she'd like that. Mom has visited her briefly, but I wasn't there."

"I don't think Vi would like Rose fussing over her for very long. You know how your mother is," Iris reminded Daisy with a frown.

Unfortunately, Daisy knew exactly what her aunt Iris meant. Her mother probably asked Vi every question under the sun that made her uncomfortable. Are you sure you want to marry Foster? What happens if you have a miscarriage? Isn't Foster going to give you a proper engagement ring instead of his high school ring? Then she'd probably start on the garage apartment, commenting that it was too small for a growing family. Daisy knew there must be some reason for her mother's critical attitude, but she'd never known exactly what it was. And her aunt Iris didn't seem to want to enlighten her. Since Daisy's mother, as well as her older sister Camellia, were close, Daisy had depended on her aunt Iris and her dad for affection and encouragement. Running Gallagher's Garden Corner had been her parents' focus since they'd opened it. Working hard and long hours had always been part of their life from March until after Christmas. Daisy understood the time demands of owning a business since she and her aunt had opened the tea garden.

A few minutes later, Daisy's reverie ended as they all decided to order the pork chops with sides of pickled beets and mashed potatoes. After they spoke about new shops moving in to the vicinity—a hat shop, a yogurt bar, and a bike shop—their meals arrived, steaming hot and smelling heavenly.

After they'd all dug in and were silent for a few minutes, Iris asked, "Have you heard from that gentleman and his daughter that you were helping? Keith, wasn't it? And Mandy?"

Daisy didn't keep secrets from her aunt, and she'd told her all about the situation. "I saw Keith after church yesterday. He and Mandy are settling into their new place, and Mandy seems quite happy at day care. Karina said so too."

Conversation continued throughout dessert as all enjoyed slices of peanut butter pie. A short time later, Iris and Russ left to continue their date night.

After they'd gone, Jonas said to Daisy, "Okay, fess up. Where did you and Tessa go?"

"You make it sound as if I were someplace I shouldn't be."

His lips quirked at the corner. "Weren't you?"

She bumped Jonas's shoulder with hers. "You're beginning to know me too well."

"It's hard to shake off detective skills," he mentioned offhandedly.

After taking a deep breath, she said in a burst of words, "Tessa and I went to see Glen Storm."

Jonas just stared at her. But the question he asked wasn't what she expected. "Aren't you afraid of *anything*?"

"Of course I am. But Tessa was with me and we made a pact before we went that we would stay outside his door and not go inside his place. We didn't even know if he'd be home."

Jonas's jaw was a little set as he frowned. "But he was."

Daisy filled him in on everything Glen had told

them. She noticed Sarah Jane was at the table next to them, talking to a customer.

"I want to dive into Otis's invoices again," Daisy said. "I thought I saw real grief in Glen Storm's eyes. I also want to figure out if Otis inadvertently does know what Barry was involved in."

The customer Sarah Jane had been speaking to had left. Sarah Jane leaned down to Daisy. "I overheard you talking about Otis and his nephew. Barry often came in here and picked up meals for his uncle. But he also came in to have dinner with another man about his age and a woman too. It often looked like a business meeting. They had a printout with them. You know. One of those spreadsheets from the computer."

"Did you ever hear them talking about it?" Jonas asked.

"No, not really. As soon as I'd approach or my waitress would approach, they'd clam up. They always wanted the farthest booth back in the corner. I just figured they had private things to talk about. Lots of people want a back booth."

"By any chance do you know the name of the woman who was with them?"

Sarah Jane shook her head and that sent her curls tumbling. "Not offhand. If I heard it, I'd know. It was one of those old-fashioned names . . . like Grace or Olivia."

"How about Mariah?"

Sarah Jane snapped her fingers. "That's it."

One of the waitresses called to Sarah Jane.

"I'm needed. I'll talk to you folks later. Have a good night."

"Are you thinking the other man was Ian?" Jonas

put his arm along the back of the booth and around Daisy.

"I am thinking that's who it was. It almost sounds as if the three of them met and were here in some type of business together."

"Or some type of scheme."

"There's that detective in you thinking the worst again."

"I'm thinking the worst because something got Barry killed."

Unsure if she was being wise or not, the following day Daisy called Detective Rappaport. He'd been the detective on the cases that she'd been involved in over the past year. At first, he'd been hard-nosed, suspicious, and unaccepting of any help she could possibly give. But by the time they'd crossed paths at the third murder case, they'd come to an understanding. Rappaport appreciated her deductive skills and her passion to get to the truth. He'd begun stopping in at the tea garden now and then, even though he claimed to not like hot tea. He did like her scones.

Watching over the tea garden from the hall outside her office, Daisy saw her servers and customers were getting along like clockwork. She had Morris Rappaport on speed dial. She touched his name and the call went through. It was his private cell number and she didn't know if he'd answer or not.

"Hello, Mrs. Swanson. To what do I owe this pleasure?"

"I haven't seen you for a while. Why don't you come to the tea garden for a scone or peach cobbler and iced tea? We just brewed a new one I think you'd like. It's a pineapple green tea that makes you think of Hawaii. Didn't you say you wanted to go there someday?"

"You're laying it on a little thick. And I suspect there's more to this invitation than me sampling your iced tea."

"Why, Detective, you wound me."

"I doubt it. Do I have to remind you that I am *not* on this case?"

"What case?" she asked in all innocence.

He actually chuckled. "I stopped in last week but you weren't there. I particularly liked that cucumber salad. Maybe I'll have some of that along with peach cobbler. I am watching my diet—eating more vegetables. I have a few forms to finish up here. I'll be there in about an hour."

Detective Rappaport was precise when he questioned a suspect . . . and when he set a time for an appointment. Almost exactly an hour later, Daisy showed him to the spillover tearoom.

In deference to the weather, he wore a pale blue lightweight sports coat and khakis. Before he sat down, he looked at her antique teapots and cup and saucer sets on the shelves on the wall.

He motioned to them. "Do people actually buy and use those things?"

"That depends. I use the cups and mugs that are bone china with glazes that are intact. But as far as the shapes and beauty of teapots, yes. Lots of people actually use them. Have you heard of the song 'Tea for Two'?"

He sat in a chair under the shelves, his back to the wall. "Yeah. I thought maybe they originated during the decade that old song was written. My mom liked forties music."

"Sharing tea with a friend is a calming experience.

I think it has to do with just taking time out of your day to talk and to share. It doesn't matter the type of tea or if you use sugar or honey or milk. It's just the experience of sipping it that counts."

"I must have missed something in my upbringing."

"So you want to try the new tea with peach cobbler and cucumber salad?" She wasn't sure all that went together very well, but this was Morris Rappaport, not her usual customer.

"Sure. I'll just sit here and cool off."

It wasn't long until Daisy returned with a tray. She'd poured a glass of iced tea for herself too.

"Before we get started on whatever I'm *not* doing here," the detective said, "I have a question for you."

Having no idea what his question might be, she just nodded. "Go ahead."

"Is it true that your aunt Iris is dating a retired teacher? Somebody I know saw her on a buggy ride with him. A buggy ride. Can you imagine?"

It was difficult for Daisy to suppress a smile. The detective was from Pittsburgh, not Amish country. He was just learning how to enjoy the food and other attributes of a more rural lifestyle. "Yes, it's true that she's dating Russ Windom. But if you're interested too, you can ask her out. As far as I know, nothing serious has developed yet."

The detective's face reddened. After a few swallows of his tea, he picked up a fork to eat the cucumber salad. "Why did you ask me here?"

"Has Zeke Willet brought you up to date on the Barry Storm murder?"

He waved his fork at her. "If he has, you know I can't talk about it."

She resisted the urge to roll her eyes. Instead, she

filled him in on everything she had seen so far—from Keith's role in the investigation, to what she'd found in Otis's files, to what Sarah Jane had told her last evening about Mariah, Ian, and Barry meeting there and looking at a spreadsheet.

Rappaport was silent during her whole recitation, but he obviously was hungry. He finished the salad, pushed the dish away, and pulled the cobbler in front of him. He shrugged. "If those three were friends, if this Barry Storm and Mariah were going to get married, that spreadsheet could have been about the wedding. It could have been about anything. You know better than most that you can't jump to conclusions in an investigation."

"I'm trying not to jump to conclusions. That's why I'm sharing all this with you."

"Why aren't you talking to Zeke Willet?"

"Because Zeke Willet won't listen to me. He has an attitude like you used to."

"What attitude is that? That you're all blue eyes and blond hair and don't have any wit behind it? Certainly Zeke learned otherwise quickly."

"It isn't just that. He knows Jonas and I are dating. He and Jonas still haven't resolved their differences."

Rappaport snorted. "Differences? Don't make it sound like they can compromise on a business deal and that would be the end of it. It won't. Their history runs deep and you just have to respect that."

"Oh, I respect it. And I'll stay out of it. But if it affects what Detective Willet listens to and what he doesn't, then I'm going to have a beef with him."

The detective's mouth turned up at one corner, and he shook his head. "You don't have anything concrete.

When you do, *if* you do, you should call Detective Willet."

She must have looked more than a little disappointed.

Morris Rappaport took a bite of his cobbler, chewed, swallowed, and sighed. "That's the best thing I've eaten in a long time."

She sat there, studying him until he finished.

When he did, he wiped his mouth with his napkin, crunched it into a ball, and tossed it onto the plate. "I'll keep everything you said in mind."

She knew he would. One thing she was certain about—Detective Morris Rappaport kept his word.

When Daisy walked into her bedroom that evening, she stopped in surprise. It looked as if Jazzi had emptied out Vi's closet and laid all of her clothes across Daisy's bed. She'd heard Jazzi running up and down the stairs but hadn't known the reason. She'd been putting supper dishes away and waiting for Jonas's arrival. They were going to have a glass of wine on the patio.

"What's going on?" she asked her two daughters. Suddenly she spotted a black tail sticking out from under a shirt. Pepper liked to burrow under blankets . . . or in this case, clothes. She heard a *murrp* from Marjoram, who was in pounce position on the bench at the bed, watching her sister.

Vi was in bed reclining on pillows while Jazzi held up a dress for her examination.

Jazzi explained, "I heard some of the women at the tea garden today talking about the thrift store opening. They said they'd like to have a nice supply of clothes to start. This is donation week. I know Vi and I have things that don't fit and aren't in style anymore."

"She's trying to keep me from being bored," Vi acknowledged with a grin at her sister. "Aunt Iris is too. She's coming over later. I'd have to sort through everything anyhow in order to take it over to the apartment. The closet over there isn't as big as I have now. Do you think they'd take shoes too?"

"I'm not sure about that," Daisy said. "Not as far as worn shoes go. I do know Sporty Digs was going to donate ten pairs of men's shoe boots. You know the kind they use for work? And the Rainbow Flamingo is going to donate twenty pairs of sneakers for women in a variety of sizes."

"Are you going to go to the Rainbow Flamingo to look for a dress for the wedding?" Vi asked.

Daisy knew she had to take care of that soon. "I think I'll start there. Heidi usually has trends in fashions that I like." Heidi Korn often stopped in at the tea garden. Daisy always tried to buy locally if she could.

"I'm glad I have my dress," Jazzi said. "I wouldn't want to have to find something the last minute. Mom, you really should go on your next lunch hour. If the dress would need any alterations, you need time to let Heidi do them."

"I know," Daisy agreed. "But I'd like Aunt Iris to go with me, and we can't both leave over the lunch hour."

"Then go after work. The Rainbow Flamingo is open till seven."

"That would probably be better. I'll ask your Aunt Iris when she gets here when she's free. I'll be taking off Thursday morning to take you to the doctor."

"Foster said he'd take me," Vi said, "but I think I'd

rather have you drive me. He's uncomfortable there and just as anxious about this as I am. You'd be better support."

Thank goodness, her daughter felt that way. She didn't know what she'd do if for some reason Vi didn't want her involved with this baby. "I'll be glad to take you. Pam is coming in again to cover for me."

"If Aunt Iris can't go with you, Tessa could," Jazzi suggested. "I don't think she's dating anyone, so she's probably free."

Tessa's last relationship had ended in tragedy. Daisy didn't think her friend was over it yet, and dating was the last thing on her mind. "That's a great plan B."

"Mom, do you think the thrift store will have maternity clothes?" Vi asked.

"I suppose they might."

"I hate to waste any money on clothes I'll only wear a short time. I'm so glad I picked a wedding dress with an empire waist so my bump won't show at the wedding. But I'm either going to have to go up a size or buy maternity clothes soon. I can hardly zip my jeans, and I can't wear any of my crop tops."

"I know you and Foster have a budget and the thrift store could be a good option. But I'd like to buy you an outfit for the rehearsal picnic at Gavin's. If you'd like a maternity ensemble, there's a little shop on Oak Street, Baby and Me. They sell mostly baby clothes but they have maternity outfits too."

"I haven't heard of it. Is it new?" Vi asked.

"About three months old. I met the manager, Nettie Bollinger, at the last Chamber of Commerce meeting."

The doorbell rang.

Daisy told her daughters, "I'll get it. Jonas and I will be out on the patio if you need us."

"We won't need you," Jazzi said. "That way you can make out all you want."

"Jazzi—" Daisy could feel her cheeks turning red.

"We know all about the birds and the bees, Mom," Vi teased. "We'll even keep Aunt Iris busy when she gets here."

Daisy waved off her daughters' comments and left the room. She and Jonas hadn't made a physical commitment to each other yet. Jonas insisted he wasn't going anywhere, and he would stand by Daisy throughout the new changes in her life. Still, Daisy was concerned that he really didn't know the demands Vi's new baby would make on everyone.

After Jonas stepped inside, he wrapped his arms around Daisy and gave her a sound kiss. So sound, it made her dizzy.

"The girls were just teasing me about making out," she murmured.

Jonas kept his arm around her as they walked into the kitchen. "Let me guess. They promised to give us alone time."

"In a roundabout way." Daisy had already set a tray with two wineglasses and a bowl of bar mix on it. She took a bottle of wine from the refrigerator and handed it to Jonas. "Can you do the honors? I'm not good with a corkscrew."

"I think this one has a simple turn-top," he said with a laugh.

"I didn't even look. That just shows where my head is these days."

He used a knife to slit the wrapping around the top on the wine bottle. "And where is that?"

"Worried about what the doctor will tell Vi."

He made easy work of the cap and filled the two glasses. Then he lifted the tray and nodded to the patio.

Daisy had set a lantern with a flameless candle on the side table next to two patio chairs. Jonas lowered the tray to it and they sat on the flowered cushions. "I know you're hoping Vi will get a clean bill of health."

"She talked about having a baby bump tonight. I'm looking forward to the time when the baby's big enough that *I* can feel it move. I remember when I felt Violet move for the first time."

"What did it feel like?" Jonas asked softly.

Daisy could remember vividly. "The first time, it felt like the tiniest of flutters . . . like a little wave moving inside me. It was nothing like I'd ever felt before, so I knew it was the baby. I can't wait to hold my grand-child."

Jonas reached out and took her hand. "Tell me something, Daisy. If you had the chance, would you want another baby?"

She paused a moment, not knowing how her answer might affect them. "I never honestly thought having a baby was still in my future. What about you? Do you want children?" If he did, and she couldn't have them, then what?

Jonas held his wineglass and stared into its depths, swirling it absently. "When I was a detective, I didn't want kids. I saw too much sordid stuff. The other side of that was how my job would affect a family. Anything could have happened to me at any time. When you deal with homicides, let's just say that characters you meet often don't care about who they hurt."

"I can see that, and I can see why you didn't want kids. What about now?"

Setting down the wineglass, his gaze sought hers in the glow of light. "Now, anything's a possibility. If not a baby, well, there are a lot of kids out there who need someone who cares."

Adoption. She'd done it once. Would she do it again?

She squeezed Jonas's hand. He was right. Anything was a possibility.

Chapter Thirteen

When Daisy exited the tea garden the following evening, she breathed a sigh of relief. Although they had had enough hands on deck, she'd still felt that she was a beat behind in everything she needed to do. Maybe that was because of Vi's absence. If Vi didn't come back to the tea garden to help—and Daisy didn't think she should—then she might have to hire someone else who would be a full-time employee until after the new year began. Then after the new year, the position would drop back to part time or maybe even not at all.

Who would want that kind of job?

One never knew. Maybe someone who merely needed money for the holidays. Her mind was targeting putting together an ad when she approached her work van. She'd brought that today because on the way home she was going to pick up a few crates of peaches. They would be wonderful for fruit cups, muffins, or more cobbler. She'd decide which to make after she saw the condition of the peaches. In her garage, they would stay fine until morning.

Her work van had been older when she'd bought it,

but it had been in excellent condition. The tea
garden's logo as well as DAISY'S TEA GARDEN had been
painted on both sides and the phone number on the
back as well as under the logo. As she approached
the van, she pulled her key from her purse, ready to
insert it in the lock. However, she found the door
wasn't locked. That was odd. Had she forgotten to lock
it in her rush to get into the tea garden this morning?
Anything was possible.

There was nothing of particular value in the van, so
there was no harm done. Still . . .

She made a quick trip around the van examining
the tires, and generally checking it over. No problems
that she could see. Maybe Iris had gone to the van to
get something out of it and she'd forgotten to lock it.
That was the simplest explanation.

Daisy had left the passenger side window of the van
open about two inches, not that a bit of outside air
would help much on a day like this. After she opened
the door, she slung her purse over to the passenger
seat. She would let some of the heat escape before she
slid in to start the air-conditioning.

She considered again the ad she might post on her
Web site as well as in the community paper that was de-
livered once a week. If she didn't elicit any results that
way, she'd post an ad in the *Willow Creek Messenger*.
That would be more expensive, but it would be worth
it if she could hire quality help.

*Full-time work until New Year's at Daisy's Tea Garden.
Possible part-time position afterward. Seeking a
dependable person to serve tea and bus tables. Possible
other duties depending on individual. Call the number
listed below for salary and interview appointment.*

She hoped that would be enough to start. Maybe she should ask Foster about posting the ad on a bulletin board at the university too. Lots of options.

While she'd been standing outside the van, she hadn't looked inside. Now, however, what she saw halfway across the running board made her freeze. Not only freeze in action, but shiver in the heat and humidity. Those shivers scraped up her arms and down her back.

She couldn't believe what she was seeing. What she was seeing was a snake and *not* just a garter snake. It was reddish with bands of reddish brown. Was it a copperhead? If so, it was poisonous!

She almost ran around to the other side to open the door and retrieve her purse, which contained her phone. What if there was a snake on the other side? What if there were four or five snakes? How had it gotten into her van?

Her breaths came in short pants and she knew she had to get a grip. She had to get help. Everyone else had gone home. She could go back into the tea garden, or . . .

She made up her mind in a second. She ran.

Jonas would probably be in his workshop. She didn't head to Market Street but ran behind the businesses that led to Woods. Some had gravel parking lots in their backs, but some had grass, others were paved with concrete. The soles of her shoes slipped on a stone but she scrambled to keep her balance and kept running.

When she reached the rear entrance of Woods, she tried the door and found it locked. She pounded on it, hoping and praying that Jonas was still there.

Seconds later, he opened the solid wood door with the words, "What's the racket?"

But then he saw Daisy. She imagined her face was red from running. She could feel the sweat falling in rivulets from her temple to her chin.

He held her by her shoulders. "What's the matter? What's happened?"

It took a moment for her to catch her breath. Then she pointed to her parking lot. "A snake . . . a copperhead . . . in my van."

"Are you sure?"

"I'm sure it's a snake!"

"Come into the air-conditioning," he ordered.

"But the snake—"

"He won't go anywhere very fast." Jonas went to his safe. A moment later, Daisy spotted what he'd taken out. "You have a gun?"

"I have a concealed carry permit. Stay here."

Because of her total surprise, she did stay stock-still for about thirty seconds. Then she took off after Jonas, who was running. She reached her van only a little behind him. Was he going to shoot the snake?

He held his gun in one hand and his phone in the other. He brought up his contacts and pressed a name. She couldn't see whose. "I thought I told you to stay back there," he grumbled.

"It's *my* van."

He shook his head. A moment later she heard him say, "Zeke, I'm at Daisy's Tea Garden. Someone put a snake in her van. I have my Glock. Right now the snake is basking in the sun on the running board, but if it moves—

"Yes. I understand. I'll wait until you get here if you make it fast."

Daisy watched the snake almost in fascination. It turned one way and then the other. She hated reptiles of any kind. Rachel Fisher's little brother had always known he could scare her with a frog or a tadpole or a toad. But snakes had been off-limits altogether.

The snake seemed to look around outside and didn't appear to want to go that way. He began slithering back into the footwell of the van.

She and Jonas watched it together as it slowly, very slowly, curled back into the vehicle. As soon as it had, Jonas slammed the door. Then he took Daisy into his arms. She was shaking all over.

An hour and a half later, Animal Control had removed the snake and Detective Zeke Willet was still scowling. Jonas had led Daisy to one of the outside tables after Zeke had arrived, and there they'd stayed. Now the detective pulled out a chair, tore a piece of paper from his small notebook, and laid a pen on top of it. He pushed it across to Daisy.

Summer was ripe in the air—the scent of rosemary from the herbs along the outside tables, the sweet perfume of heirloom petunias in pinks and purples and yellow, the pungent odor of potted marigolds, the heat-baked asphalt as well as dampening earth as dusk descended. She'd stopped shaking. She'd tried to keep her focus, not only on the summer smells, but on the town noises as a horse and buggy *clip-clopped* up the street. She'd phased out the men from Animal Control who were speaking to Zeke as she'd concentrated on birdsong. All the while Jonas's arm had been around her shoulders. Now, however, she couldn't ignore the detective.

He stated factually, "That was a milk snake, not a copperhead. Young milk snakes can be mistaken for copperheads, but they're not poisonous." With his no-nonsense approach, he tapped the paper before her. "I want you to write down absolutely everyone you've talked to who might have known Barry or had anything to do with his murder."

"You think one of them might have put the snake in my van?"

"Do you have other enemies I don't know about?" The detective wasn't kidding.

She felt her cheeks flame, and Jonas's arm tightened around her. He leaned close to her ear and murmured, "There's no way to trace a snake. This is the best way to go about it."

Daisy threw up her hands in frustration. "I suppose the people I've talked to could have done it."

"Copperheads, as well as milk snakes, are native to this area. But not everyone can handle a snake." Zeke's voice was sarcastic but with no humor.

Sitting up straight, Daisy felt her energy and her backbone returning. "Maybe not just anyone can handle a snake. However, anyone can *hire* somebody who knows how to handle a snake."

"That's true," Zeke admitted.

Did she see a spark of respect for her in his eyes? Possible, but doubtful.

She picked up the pen and gripped it tightly. "I know you want Keith's name on this list."

Zeke remained silent.

She quickly added Otis, Ian, Mariah, Penelope and Clovis, and Glen Storm. She pushed the paper over to the detective.

"This is a start." He stood. After he pushed the paper into a pocket, he leaned forward on his hands on the table. "Stay out of this. I'm not going to tell you again. A bullet or an arrow or a knife blade isn't as easy to remove as a snake."

She was wise enough to keep quiet. The onlookers from the street as well as shopkeepers who had come to see what was happening when they heard the police car and the Animal Control van had dispersed. When she turned her head to scan the street, she spotted somebody she knew coming toward them. Somebody she'd rather not see right now—Trevor Lundquist.

He was wearing shorts and a green, Willow Creek T-shirt. He gave her a tentative smile. "I just waited until everybody left. Since you and I have a relationship, I thought you might talk to me."

"Relationship?" Jonas asked with a quirked brow.

Trevor's brown hair was cut for summer, shorter than he usually styled it. "Daisy knows what I mean. I help her and she helps me. It's been a while, but we did that on the three murders she investigated."

"I'm not investigating," Daisy assured him. That was going to be her line with everyone except Jonas.

"Hmmm," Trevor said thoughtfully. "Then what was all this commotion about? I heard you were asking questions about Barry Storm."

"From who?"

Trevor gave her a sly smile and cocked his head. "You were at Sarah Jane's discussing the murder."

"Sarah Jane told you this?" Jonas sounded surprised.

"No, a customer who was in the booth in front of you. Not only little pitchers have big ears."

Daisy didn't know whether to laugh or cry. Of course, Trevor was correct. In a town this small, gossip was a part of the entertainment.

"What happened here?" he asked more seriously. "You look shaken. Did somebody threaten you?"

"In a manner of speaking," Daisy answered truthfully.

"I saw the Animal Control van," he explained. "I doubt that this many people would have lined up to catch sight of a dog unless it was rabid."

She might as well tell him. He'd find out anyway. Trevor could be bothersome but he was a good journalist, and he had helped her in the past.

"Not a rabid dog—a snake."

Trevor let out a whistle. "You must have really disturbed somebody's equilibrium."

"I don't know how. The only two people I talked to who weren't enthusiastic about answering questions were Ian Busby . . . and Glen Storm, Barry's dad."

Trevor shook his head. "Who is Ian?"

"He was a friend of Barry's."

"Ah, I see. Maybe not a friendly friend."

Jonas gave Daisy a tap on the shoulder. "We should go. I can drive you in my SUV if you don't want to take the van."

"So this snake was in your work van?" Trevor asked.

"You're not going to print any of this, are you?" Daisy asked.

His steady gaze told her he was thinking about it. "I'll tell you what. Why don't we do the same thing as our previous deals. I won't print anything until the murder is solved. Then you can give me the whole scoop, at least from your perspective."

She thought of Zeke Willet. "I'd have to have information cleared with the police."

"We have a first amendment so you can tell me anything that happened to you. Are you going back to being a goody two-shoes?"

"What do you mean going back to it?" Jonas asked. "She still is."

"Not from what I hear. I heard she can heft a pretty mean garden tool."

Daisy sighed and made a cut sign like a movie producer would after a scene was shot. "After Barry's murder is solved, I'll talk to you. I promise. But Detective Willet is on this case, and he doesn't want anybody poking into it but him, and whoever he authorizes."

"You were never afraid of Detective Rappaport."

"I'm not afraid of Zeke Willet," she maintained.

Trevor swiveled his head between her and Jonas. "I smell another story there, but I'll let that go for now. Jonas came from Philadelphia and Zeke Willet came from Philadelphia. Same police force."

When neither Daisy nor Jonas commented, Trevor pushed back his chair and stood. "I'll give it a rest for now. Will you be attending the town council meeting tomorrow night?"

Daisy nodded. "There is supposedly news about businesses moving into the Sage Street area."

Trevor nodded. "That's why I'm covering it. The council has been tight-lipped about it." He took a few steps away, then turned back around. "For what's it worth, I think you should be careful. A snake is mean stuff."

Yes, it was. If that snake had been meant as a warning, she would take it as such. It was time to concentrate on her daughter and her wedding, not a murder investigation that she possibly couldn't solve.

Daisy and Vi exited the medical center on the east side of town on Thursday morning. Not only was Vi's gynecologist there, but a dentist had moved in along with an eye doctor, an optician, and most importantly an urgent care center. Willow Creek badly needed one of those. No, it wasn't a hospital, but the facility did have X-ray machines. There was a second floor too, with an elevator for handicapped patients. Some of those offices were empty, but a general practitioner occupied one. The Chamber of Commerce was working on enticing other doctors to move in. Medical care was essential for any community. With Willow Creek slowly growing, the residents needed the services.

Daisy said to Vi, "Wait here in the shade until I turn the air on. I don't want you to overheat in the car."

"Mom, you're not going to treat me like spun glass, are you?"

"No, I'm going to treat you like a daughter who's pregnant."

"I'll call Foster while you're cooling off the car."

Once they were inside the PT Cruiser, Daisy made an observation that she had made before. "You can't lift heavy trays and you probably shouldn't be on your feet all day."

"I know. Dr. Geisler said I can resume normal activities for a pregnant woman. If I have any symptoms again, I should call her right away. But she doesn't expect anything else to happen. I asked her about a midwife and she gave me a list of those she works with." After a pause, Vi said, "Mom, Foster and I need the money from me working too."

"I know you do. And I have an idea. Let's stop in at Pirated Treasures."

"Why?"

"Because it's quite possible that Otis can use help with his books."

Ten minutes later Daisy parked in front of Pirated

Treasures. The sign on the door said OPEN, so she was hoping Otis would be there.

"Have you ever been inside before?" she asked Vi.

"No. We went thrift store shopping in Lancaster. I never thought of coming here."

"Many people don't. Otis doesn't have a Web site."

"Do you think I could do that for him? Foster's the expert. But I *have* created Web sites at school."

"Let's just see how Otis is today."

After they went inside, they found Otis at the front of the store. He had a statue in his hand and was squinting at it. It was about a foot tall of an old man holding a shovel.

"Hi, Otis," Daisy said cheerily. "I brought my daughter in to take a look around."

"I could use young eyes in here." He squinted at the statue again. "I think I have a mate to this fellow somewhere in here—a woman who looks like a grandma with a basket in her hand. But I can't find her. I can't even read the number on the bottom of this one to check on the computer."

Daisy nudged Vi. "Vi, this is Otis. Otis this is Vi."

"Hello there, girl. You have your mom's pretty blue eyes."

Vi's eyes were brown, but she didn't comment about that. Instead Vi asked, "Was the other statue you're looking for as tall as the man?"

Otis thought about it. "She might have been a little shorter. If I remember right, she had grapes in her basket."

"I can look around and see if can find her, or if you want me to check the computer for you, I could do that. I have a year's training in business management, and I have good eyesight."

Otis studied her more carefully, but Daisy wasn't sure how much he could see. Vi had worn a summer sundress decorated with flowers with her strappy sandals.

"Your mom said you're pregnant. Is that true?"

"It is. I'm going to be married in ten days. But I already had a little trouble with the pregnancy, so carrying heavy trays at the tea garden is out of the question. I need to work, so I thought if I took on book work for small businesses, that would help. I can do that up until when I have the baby as well as afterward."

"I surely do need somebody here. The problem is you don't know nothing about antiques, do you?"

"I can learn."

Otis rubbed his chin thoughtfully. "I'd be able to hire you, and maybe somebody who knows antiques too. I didn't realize it, but Barry had a life insurance policy and named me as beneficiary. The thing is, that won't be settled until after Barry's murder is solved. It's another reason for your mom to ask a bunch of questions to find out who hurt him."

"She could get into trouble doing that," Vi warned.

"I don't want her getting into any trouble, but I do want to know who would hurt Barry. He had funny ways about him sometimes, but down deep I think he was a good boy. Having that life insurance policy kind of proves that."

"Do the police know about the policy?" Daisy asked.

"Yep, they do. They're the ones who told me about it. I guess when they went through his papers, they found the information about it."

"Does that mean they suspect you?"

Otis shrugged, his suspenders rising up and down with his shoulders. "Don't know and don't care."

Daisy wondered if that was because Otis felt all alone in the world.

"That one detective said something nice about you, though," Otis revealed.

"Detective Willet?"

"Oh, no. He's got a bug under his britches. No, the other detective . . . Rappa—something."

"Detective Rappaport?" Daisy filled in.

"Yeah, that's the one. Detective Willet asked if you'd been around anymore. I just said you brought me soup. That Detective Rappa—whatever—said Detective Willet should lay off you, that you were a kind woman just trying to do what was right."

Daisy felt her cheeks flush. "That was nice of him to say."

"I know it's true. You've been kind to me."

While they had been talking, Vi had migrated around the shop. She came back to them with a smile on her face. "Is this what you're looking for?"

It was a statue that was the obvious complement to the one Otis had been holding. "Well, I'll be. You did it that fast and you didn't even know what you was looking for."

"You described her to me. That's all it took."

He put the statue he was holding on the shelf, took the other one from her hands, and set that one beside it. "Do you mind getting dusty?"

"No, sir."

He waved his hand over the contents of the shop. "You could help me put all this in order . . . no lifting anything heavy, of course. Why don't you come back here to my office with me and show me what you can do on the computer."

Daisy supposed this impromptu interview could land Vi a job. Some days life could go right. She just hoped it kept going right for Vi and Foster . . . and for Otis too.

Chapter Fourteen

The town council meeting that night was held in the social hall attached to the fire company. Jonas walked beside Daisy from the parking lot to the entrance.

"I'm surprised at the number of cars," Daisy said.

"Revitalizing Sage Street, especially since Barry's murder, is on the mind of a majority of Willow Creek's residents. No one is exactly sure what the council has in mind."

"It's an open meeting. Anyone can state their opinion."

The town council meetings were held once a month. Daisy had to admit she didn't often attend, not unless something was on the docket that she cared about.

After entering the building, she and Jonas walked down the aisle along the folding chairs. To her surprise, Daisy spotted Rachel and Levi Fisher. That was unusual. Even though they were New Order Amish, they tried to stay separate from anything that spoke of governing or law enforcement. Their district set their own rules and standards. Getting involved with *Englischers*, as they called non-Amish folks, wasn't something many of them wanted to do.

She and Jonas headed toward the couple and took two seats beside them. The chairs were filling up fast.

Daisy leaned over to Rachel. "Are you interested in the redevelopment of Sage Street?"

Rachel wrapped one of the strings from her *kapp* around her forefinger and murmured, "Not necessarily. But it's hard to see family farmland bought up by development companies."

"Do you see more of that happening?"

Daisy knew the Amish split up their farms for each generation, giving them a piece of land to build a house until eventually they couldn't split the property anymore. If development companies bought up *Englischers'* land, there was less farmland available when a son wanted to buy a property to make a life for his family. It was a way of life that Daisy didn't want to see fade away, maybe because Amish family unity was so strong. They took care of each other. The Amish didn't buy insurance, and when there were medical emergencies, they dipped into a community fund to pay the expenses. It was a way of life many of the residents of Lancaster County still didn't understand. Since Daisy had been around it all her life, she did.

Levi leaned across Rachel and said to Daisy, "We hope this is just about Sage Street, nay about anything else. But we'd like to make certain sure."

When the mayor, Gil Freemont—an insurance salesman—took his place at the podium, the room actually quieted. That meant these were interested residents of Willow Creek who intended to have a say in whatever happened in the town. Gil, in his fifties with salt-and-pepper, thick, military-cut hair and bearing, was respected in the community. He'd served his country, and most town residents respected that service. After Gil gave a few opening remarks, he passed the mike to a member of the town council. Daniel Copeland was a good-looking man in his midthirties. He had rusty brown hair, a patrician nose, and a firm jaw. Daisy knew he was the assistant manager of the Willow Creek Community Bank. In deference to the heat, he'd worn a striped, short-sleeved dress shirt with charcoal slacks. Daisy didn't know much about him except his occupation.

He took hold of the mike as if he knew how to use it and smiled broadly at the group. "I know gentrification can be a bad word among some because it symbolizes taking down the old to put up the new." His smile vanished. "But on Sage Street, where a murder recently occurred, we need to take notice of what is becoming of our town. We need to clean it up before decay harms us all. There was a rumor recently that a homeless man had been living in his van on Sage Street. We can't have that."

Daisy's brows raised and she glanced at Jonas. He was listening intently.

"We, on the council, put our heads together and decided the best thing to do would be to build a shelter. For safety reasons, it should be well on the outskirts of town."

Daisy's hand shot up before she could prevent it.

Mr. Copeland studied her for a moment and then nodded. "We were going to take questions at the end, but they could mount up if we do that. If there's something I can answer easily now, let's do it."

Daisy stood, wondering where she got the nerve. That wasn't so hard to figure out. She felt deeply about

Keith and Mandy and what they had been through. She also knew she had to put her thoughts into positive terms for them to carry any resonance. "I think it's a fine idea to build a shelter. I wondered if just the town council is going to vote on that or if all the residents will have a say."

Mr. Copeland looked from one member of the town council to another and then the mayor.

Gil admitted, "That hasn't been decided yet. We will, of course, have to have a fund-raising event if we make the decision to build a shelter."

"May I make a suggestion?" She hated the deference in her voice, but the council was still a boys' club of sorts.

Gil glanced at Copeland and Copeland again nodded. "Go ahead."

"Just something to think about. Men and women who are homeless are homeless for a reason. They have to have basic needs filled first and then they need other help—like job training or at least suggestions of work opportunities to put them back on their feet. A shelter involves more than a shelter. To avoid future issues, counseling and maybe even opportunities for drug rehabilitation need to be provided. This is a mammoth project, not simply a fund-raising event to build a shelter and forget about it."

The town council members gazed at each other as if they hadn't thought about these points.

Amelia Wiseman from the Covered Bridge Bed and Breakfast raised her hand.

Copeland frowned. "We didn't intend to have this discussion now."

Amelia didn't wait for permission, but answered back, "What better time than now?"

The town council member to Copeland's left, Lawrence Bishop, leaned toward Copeland and whispered something to him.

Copeland looked as if he'd lost his patience, but he nodded to Amelia.

She proceeded with, "If you put the shelter outside town, you realize, don't you, that you will have to put a cafeteria in it. If, however, the shelter was *in* town, maybe there could be some kind of program for meals that could include church outreach."

Daisy murmured to Jonas, "That is such a good point."

Bishop, in his late forties and a science teacher, confessed, "These are all good points. And you're right, we haven't thought this through completely."

The other town council members scowled at him, even Gil. But it looked as if he was being honest, and Daisy knew that's what they needed—honesty with no politics surrounding this idea and no spin.

More hands were raised now, and the mayor conceded, "All right. I can see we're going to need another meeting to discuss this. My suggestion is that we form a committee—town folk, business owners, professionals, and everyday people. We can look into available properties, speak to ministers and the pastor of Holy Family, and then bring our findings back to this meeting in a month. Will that suit everyone?"

There was murmuring and the nodding of heads. Gil pointed to a legal pad on the table. He turned it around, pulled a pen from his pocket, and laid it on the pad. "Sign up here after our meeting. If you want a say in this, then volunteering is the right way to go. It's a bigger project than anyone anticipated."

This time he passed the microphone to Bishop.

Lawrence waited until the murmuring stopped, then he said seriously, "And I have good news to report. A building on the same side of Sage Street as Pirated Treasures has been sold to a proprietor who makes stained glass. That shop will be a draw for tourists and for anyone who would like a stained-glass window in their home. Even more of a draw, a storefront across the street from Pirated Treasures will soon house a chocolatier. We hope in future months to draw even more businesses to that area. We might want to think of a theme for the street, if not in words, then in appearances. For instance, each storefront could be painted a different color or all of them could be painted white with black trim. Another idea proposed would be giving each shop a sign for their door or a hook with a sign along the street stating their wares."

Daisy raised her hand again.

Bishop nodded. "Mrs. Swanson?"

He probably knew her because Vi had been a student at the high school and Jazzi was now. "If we want to encourage tourists and even residents of Willow Creek to shop in these stores, maybe we should think of a way to pretty-up the areas, even Market Street. Other towns, like Gettysburg, have hanging baskets on light fixtures. Brightly colored pots with herbs growing in them along the storefronts wouldn't take much care."

"Your parents could help with that, I suppose," Lawrence said. "Gallagher's Garden Corner sells pots like that with plants, correct?"

"That's not why I suggested it," Daisy said. "There are plenty of Amish farmers who sell flowers and shrubs. We should include them in whatever plans we make."

When Daisy resumed her seat, Rachel elbowed her

and then gave her a smile. Daisy's parents had gotten started in the nursery business because of Rachel's parents' family farm. The Eshes had allowed them to use some of their land. Since Daisy's parents had been in business over thirty years now, they had suppliers to fill their needs. But many Amish farmers also did that.

More residents were making suggestions on how to pretty-up the town when Jonas bumped Daisy's shoulder. "Zeke Willet's in the back. I don't know how long he's been there."

Daisy considered a plan, coalescing her thoughts. "I know he doesn't want me to investigate anything, but would it really hurt if we drove to Gettysburg to see the flowers and maybe stop in at a memorabilia shop or two?"

"Is that a question or an invitation to go along?" Jonas asked with a slight smile.

"Are you free Sunday?" Daisy inquired.

"Sure am," he answered.

The meeting went on for another half hour or so with town residents interacting with council members. Finally, the mayor adjourned the meeting.

Daisy and Jonas stood. Jonas moved his shoulder around a few times. Daisy knew that it sometimes pained him and even stiffened, especially if he was in one position for too long. It was the result of a shooting and one of the reasons he'd quit the Philadelphia police department.

"Are you going to join the committee?" she asked.

"I think I will. I might be able to help with security issues if a representative from the police department doesn't sign up."

They'd headed for the table and the line of people adding their names to the volunteer list when Zeke approached Daisy from the side. He tapped her arm. "Mrs. Swanson, can I have a word with you?"

She almost rolled her eyes. Here they went again. "Sure."

His scowl said he recognized the frustrated patience in her voice.

She followed the detective to an empty corner of the room. To her relief, Jonas accompanied her. However, Willet expressed his annoyance. He said to Jonas, "I don't need you here."

Jonas didn't react. Rather, he said in a calm voice, "Daisy might. If you want her alone, I guess you'll have to take her down to the station."

Daisy shot him a look. That was the last thing she wanted. But Jonas apparently was calling his former friend's bluff.

Willet pointedly faced Daisy. "I want to know why you had a meeting with Detective Rappaport. I talked to him about that snake and he revealed you had shared information with him. Nothing I could use. Nevertheless, if you have something to say, you should call *me*, not sneak behind my back."

Apparently, Jonas couldn't help himself from stepping in. "Daisy doesn't sneak. Rappaport came to the tea garden. We both have a comfortable rapport with him."

Zeke practically snorted.

Daisy's hackles went up because she didn't need his disdain. Pinning him with her gaze, she asked, "Would you welcome a call from me?"

He didn't flinch. "I might, if you have real information, not something you're going to put in my way to divert my attention from Keith Rebert. You have to remember, I can't dismiss the fact that his fingerprints are on that marble rolling pin."

"He explained that," Daisy protested. "Otis explained that . . . to *our* satisfaction anyway. Apparently, you don't listen to reason."

Jonas placed a hand on her shoulder. It did calm her but didn't ease her annoyance.

"I listen to reason when the evidence lines up. If you have any information about the case, you call *me*." With that Willet strode away and left the cafeteria.

Daisy had reached a boiling point. Her face felt hot. She didn't believe in violence settling anything, but she would have liked to have poked Zeke Willet in the nose.

Jonas easily saw her aggravation and he touched her cheek. "Hot to the touch. We might have to buy you an ice cream cone to cool you off."

Jonas was trying to add levity to the situation and she appreciated that. The rest of their night didn't have to be marred by Zeke Willet.

With a sigh, Jonas admitted, "Zeke didn't used to be like this. He once had an easygoing nature. He knew how to joke. He knew how to interrogate witnesses without antagonizing them. This Zeke Willet is one I don't know."

If Brenda's death had affected Zeke Willet the way it seemed it had, what was the underlying cause? Whatever it was, it was the same cause that had destroyed Jonas and Zeke's friendship. Zeke had said once that he believed Jonas was responsible for Brenda's death. Was that the only reason? One of these days, Zeke would spill that resentment more fully and the true reason for his attitude would come out. But that might not be any time soon.

* * *

On Friday, Daisy and her staff were getting ready for a special tea service for the following afternoon. They would be hosting a children's summer fling tea. Mostly girls and their moms had signed up. Karina would be bringing Quinn and had encouraged Keith to bring Mandy. Daisy, Iris, and Tessa had planned the menu and were looking forward to serving happy face sandwiches, brownies with sprinkles, and tiny vanilla cupcakes with edible glitter dust on them. Tomorrow they'd prepare a strawberry and pineapple salad in mini parfaits. They'd also serve homemade ice cream in miniature china bowls. The homemade ice cream came from King's Bakery and Ice Cream stand at the farmers' market.

Daisy had enlisted the help of a crafter from Intercourse who fashioned dolls from clothespins and pretty flowered material. She even decorated their dresses and hats. Each child who came to the tea would receive one to take home.

Iris, in her best calligraphy, had made place cards for each guest and the parent who brought her. At a Halloween costume sale last October, Daisy had bought Disney princess outfits as well as a variety of lace and crocheted shawls that she'd scooped up at a secondhand store in Lancaster. Her market basket of hats that she'd been collecting for a while ranged from sun bonnets to sequined visors to feathered headbands. Something for everyone, she hoped. On the tickets she provided when parents signed up, she had suggested that the moms dress up too and not forget their hats or fascinators. It was going to be a fun day.

Daisy was at the counter editing the menu that Iris had created when Mariah Goldblum entered the tea garden. Whenever the bell jingled, Daisy looked up to see who was entering. It behooved her to know her customers well.

Mariah glanced around the main tearoom, which was filled with tables of four. Catching Daisy's eye, she pointed to the spillover tearoom with raised brows. Only two tables were occupied in there.

Daisy nodded that Mariah could sit in there. It was quieter, and on a day like this, had a more calming atmosphere with its bay window and sun-glistened diamond-cut glass.

As Cora Sue passed by the counter on her way to take Mariah's order, Daisy hurried around the counter and stopped her. "I'll handle Miss Goldblum."

Cora Sue threw her a questioning look, but Daisy didn't explain. Cora Sue shrugged and simply responded, "I'll make sure we have the fruit ready for tomorrow's fruit cups. Just give a holler if you want me to fetch anything."

Daisy sent Cora Sue a smile and crossed to the spillover tearoom. Taking a menu from the antique serving table, Daisy carried it to Mariah. "Hello there," she said. "It's nice to see you again."

Mariah brushed her dark brown hair away from her face with splayed fingers. "It's hot out there."

"Yes, it is. Not many customers have chosen to sit outside today." Daisy pointed to the menu. "I can ice any of the teas for you. The one we have on tap, so to speak, is an orange-blossom green tea."

"That sounds good. I think I'll have some of your rum-raisin rice pudding along with the tea and six snickerdoodles to go."

"All of it will be coming right up."

Mariah was looking around at the shelves with their teapots and cozies . . . at the handmade pot holders and placemats. Daisy sold some of the creations Rachel and her daughters made. All of the businesses in town tried to cross-promote any way they could. Helping one another helped them all.

Daisy gathered Mariah's order from the kitchen and the refrigerated case. She'd assembled all of it on a glass-covered round tray. Underneath the glass was a painting of hydrangeas.

She stopped at Mariah's table, removing everything from the tray and setting it before her customer. Then she took a small pitcher from the tray and set it beside the iced tea. "This is sugar syrup in case you'd like sweetener. Sugar granules don't dissolve very well in cold tea. This will add that sweetness if you desire it."

"What a lovely idea. Is it hard to make?"

"Oh, no. It depends on how big a batch you want to provide. I use one cup of water to a half cup of sugar at home. I heat it on the stove or in the microwave until the sugar dissolves. Then you can keep it in the refrigerator."

Mariah poured a little into her tea and stirred it with an iced teaspoon. She took a sip. "That's delightful. Do you sell the orange-blossom green tea?"

"Yes, we do. If you'd like some, just stop at the counter over there before you leave."

"Is that where I pay my bill?"

"This service is on me. I can only imagine how difficult the past two weeks have been for you."

When tears came to Mariah's eyes, Daisy knew she'd had deep feelings for Barry. "I miss him," she said, her voice breaking.

"I imagine that you do. I think losing a loved one is the most difficult thing we have to go through in this life."

Mariah ducked her head. "People say time heals all wounds, but I don't think that's true. I'll always have a hole in my heart."

That was exactly what grief felt like, a hole that could never be filled up.

Mariah went on. "Barry was going to marry me and turn his life around."

Taking a stab at what that meant, Daisy asked, "Were you going to marry and move away from Willow Creek?"

Mariah vehemently shook her head. "Oh, no. Barry was going to convince Otis to make him a partner instead of an employee. That way he'd have more control over the business and be able to rev it up. He had big plans. He was even thinking of opening another store, maybe in Lancaster or York. At least, he wanted to do some traveling to craft fairs and set up tables there. He thought he knew how to increase business."

Daisy wondered if that's how he'd planned to make money, by underpaying suppliers and overcharging customers. But she didn't say it. Instead she said, "I spoke with Ian."

Mariah's eyes widened. "Did you? Was he helpful?"

"Not really. He acted as if I was interrogating him. I told him I just wanted to help Keith since he was the police's number one suspect."

"I had heard that. But I didn't know if it was still true. Maybe it's like the TV shows and the police focus on one person to try to make charges fit."

"That's what I'm trying to prevent. Keith has a future to find and a little girl to raise."

"I don't know what kind of future I'm going to have now. I work at one of the outlet stores in Lancaster . . . Rockvale Plaza."

Daisy knew it well. Tourists often drove to Lancaster just for the outlet stores. "Is it a women's boutique?"

"No, it's a shoe store. I can't see them promoting me when there are employees who have been there much longer."

"If you have sales experience, you can probably find another sales job somewhere where you can move up."

"Maybe. Or maybe I should move out of the area. I have friends in Philly. I could probably get work at one of the malls."

"Do you think you'd enjoy big city life after living here?"

"No reason I wouldn't. There are much more exciting things to do in the city."

"Do you think Ian will stay here?"

Mariah looked wary. "As I said, I haven't talked with Ian. I just saw him briefly at the funeral. I doubt if he'll stay with his parents for very long. He's a loner. That's why he liked living in that cabin out on the farm. It's one of the reasons we broke up. We were just very different. I didn't want to hurt him, but Barry and I were so much more alike. We could see the future so clearly. Are *you* married?" Mariah suddenly asked.

"Not anymore. My husband died over three years ago."

"Then you do understand. Some days when I think of Barry being gone, I just want to stay in bed. I don't want to go to work. I don't even want to look at my smartphone."

"I know that feeling," Daisy empathized. "But it's important that you don't give in to it. Even if you just get out and come for tea, that might lift your spirits."

"I might have to do this more often," Mariah said with a smile.

"We're open seven days a week. My staff rotates. I opened the tea garden with my aunt because we both believe a cup of tea and a goodie can calm or lift spirits anytime."

"I'm glad I came today," Mariah said. "Do you have any cherry tarts? They were Barry's favorite and Otis likes them too. I think I'll stop and share with him on the way home."

"Two cherry tarts to go coming right up. I'm sure if you stop to see Otis you'll lift his spirits too. You could be good for each other."

Mariah gave Daisy a wan smile.

"Say good-bye before you leave. I'll probably be over there at the counter."

As Daisy walked away from the young woman, she remembered that Ian, Mariah, and Barry had gone to school together. Was that what had bonded them as friends? Or had there been something else?

The fact that Mariah and Ian didn't turn to each other after Barry's death told Daisy their breakup hadn't been a friendly one. Did that breakup have anything to do with Barry's murder?

Chapter Fifteen

Daisy rushed from the kitchen to the spillover tearoom. After she checked her customers in the main tearoom, she was glad to see smiles on many of their faces as they peered into the yellow tearoom. Children's laughter and chatter spilled through the first floor of the tea garden. Yes, a few customers in the main serving room hurried their orders and left, not liking the noise. But Daisy had warned customers with a big sign on the door that stated CHILDREN'S TEA TODAY AT 1 P.M.

She passed the clothes rack with costume-like attire that the little girls had used to dress up. A mini trunk that she'd stored at home, which held letters from years past from everyone important in her life, had served as a jewelry box with costume jewelry—necklaces, bracelets, and earrings. The many-colored beads and rhinestones had pleased the girls as they'd selected their dress-up adornments. A lime-green plastic bin held an assortment of hats and it was almost empty.

Karina and Keith were sitting at the same table as their girls, enjoying pouring tea with them and eating mini cupcakes sprinkled with edible gold dust. Keith even sported a derby that he'd found in the hatbox while Karina's straw sunhat was adorned with a huge pink bow.

Aunt Iris had been attending to their table. She stopped now at the serving station to say to Daisy, "It's admirable the way Keith has joined in. He seems to be enjoying the iced tea and the cupcakes as much as the kids. Did you see Quinn hug him when he and Mandy came in?"

"I did. I think Keith and Karina have arranged playdates for Mandy and Quinn."

"I wonder if they've had playdates of their own," Aunt Iris suggested with a sly smile.

Daisy gave her aunt a chastising look. "I think it's hard to be chaperones to two three-year-olds and have any romantic inclinations."

"I suppose that's so," Iris admitted. "I wish I had experience in that area. The fact that I've never had any children sometimes haunts me."

That was the first time her aunt had ever expressed that regret. "You feel as if you've missed out?"

"In some ways." She gently capped Daisy's shoulder. "But I've always had you. You don't know how that kept me going sometimes, especially when you were a teenager rebelling against your mother's dictates."

"I never rebelled," Daisy protested.

"You might have kept it inside . . . you might not have let it show . . . but you rebelled. Sometimes I think that's why you married Ryan, knowing you'd move to Florida."

Daisy's face turned a little red. "I loved Ryan."

"Of course you did. I don't doubt that. But he was a chance to have a different life than you'd had here . . . away from your sister and away from your mother."

Was her aunt Iris correct? Was that really why she'd married Ryan? She murmured, "I always got along with *Ryan's* mom." His mother, deceased now too, had been a positive force in their lives. Daisy had never known Ryan's dad, who had died before she and Ryan met.

"And you always got along with me, and every other older woman in your life that I saw you interact with. So your mom's attitude was always on her, not on you."

Daisy couldn't believe they were having this conversation here, but it seemed to be an important one. "I never openly defied her."

"No, you didn't. Rather you argued with your sister, and you came to see me to escape your mother's criticism."

"Do you know why she was always so critical of me and not of Cammie?"

"I have my ideas, but that conversation is better saved for another place and time."

As Daisy glanced at the bay windows and tables near it, she caught sight of Foster. A little girl of about ten sat at the table he was serving. She had adorable dimples and short, dark brown hair that was mostly covered by a picture hat that was way too large for her. When she leaned toward her mother to talk to her, the hat fell off and plopped onto the floor. Without any hesitation, Foster scooped it up. He said something to the little girl that made her laugh, then he plopped the hat on her head and arranged it so the flower adornment danced across the front. He seemed to have a back-and-forth with the child, and they both laughed.

Daisy nodded in the direction of that table. "I think Foster will make a good father."

Iris looked in the same direction as Daisy. "He might if the weight of family responsibility doesn't get the better of him."

"You know, don't you, that Vi and Foster will ask you to babysit as often as you want. I suspect their child will look at you as a great-grandmother as much as my mom."

Aunt Iris frowned. "Something else to make your mother annoyed with me."

Her aunt sounded sad about that.

Daisy knew Iris and her mother had never had a placid relationship. She also knew that she and Cammie had argued many times because of their mom. What had happened in her mom and her aunt Iris's relationship to cause a competitive rift? Maybe someday she'd find out, when her aunt Iris was ready to tell her.

Daisy had returned to the kitchen and then hurried back to the children. She wielded a tray with ice-cream cups as she noticed Gavin come in. Maybe he was checking in with Foster. On the other hand, maybe he simply wanted a glass of iced tea.

After serving the ice cream, she left the children in the capable hands of Aunt Iris, Foster, Cora Sue, and Pam. Rachel's two daughters were helping her out with service in the main tearoom during the hours of the children's tea.

Daisy crossed to Gavin, who was seated at one of the tables for two.

Gavin grinned at her. "Busy as ever."

"Did you come to see Foster . . . or is this a relax-ation time?"

"Maybe both. He told me about the children's tea and I was curious as to how he would handle it."

"He's doing a great job. I think he'll learn daddy skills quickly. My guess is that he's already learned them from you."

Gavin ducked his head and his cheeks had taken on color when he raised his gaze to hers. "Thank you once again. I don't know if I deserve that. Maybe Foster learned those skills after his mother died. He basically took over for me for about a year."

"Everyone has to deal with grief one way or another."

"Yes, but I did it in a stupid way by befriending Jack Daniels. That isn't an example I want any of my children to emulate."

Daisy looked over her shoulder, and seeing that all was well, she pulled out a chair and sat at the table with Gavin. "Foster knows that, and I'm sure Ben and Emily do too."

"Just a reminder," Gavin said, "your family is invited to the rehearsal picnic as well as Jonas, if you want to bring him."

"I'll ask him. The picnic is a wonderful idea. It might relax everyone."

"Relax? I don't think any of us are going to relax until after the baby's born."

"That's certainly true."

Gavin's expression changed to one of concern. "How is Vi?"

"With her life changing, I think she's anxious. But she's looking forward to the wedding. Physically she's feeling good. Did Foster tell you she found a job?"

"He did. I was surprised you're letting her work at Pirated Treasures where that murder happened."

Daisy wondered what Gavin had heard and what Foster had told him. "I don't think there's any chance of anything like that happening there again. Renovation has started on two of the storefronts on the street and there are more workers and people around now, gawking if nothing else. I think Otis's business will pick up because of that. Vi is taking care of the book work for him and helping him sort items in the shop."

"You're not afraid that whoever came after Barry will come after Otis?"

"Truthfully, I never thought of that. But I do believe whatever Barry was involved in, Otis had nothing to do with. He's also having a new security system with cameras put in at the store. I think the new businesses that are moving into the area will do the same."

"New businesses?"

Daisy told him about the chocolatier and the stained-glass crafter.

"It sounds like the area really will perk up."

"Did you hear about the homeless shelter the town council wants to build?"

"One of my foremen told me there was a heated discussion about that. I hear you offered a few comments."

Daisy laughed. "I don't know what got into me that night. I guess I feel like I can state my mind more than I used to."

Gavin eyed her with a smile. "My guess is that you were raised to be a proper Lancaster County girl with orders to only speak when you were spoken to, listen to your elders, and always follow the rules."

She knew Gavin was teasing. "What happened to me?" she asked with fake horror.

He laughed. "My guess is you grew up, and when

your husband died, you knew you had to speak up for yourself and your daughters."

Daisy was enjoying this conversation with Gavin, but a group of four women had just walked in and she wanted to make sure her servers weren't overwhelmed. "I have to get back to work," she said apologetically. "What would you like to order? Whatever it is, it's on the house."

"You don't have to do that."

"It's the least I can do for the man who carried all that furniture up to the garage apartment. Vi can't wait to move in there with Foster. I think she'd do it now, but she thinks I wouldn't approve."

"Would you?" Gavin asked with a raised brow.

"She's pregnant. I think we already know the story on that one. Probably her main reason for not moving in yet is that she doesn't want her grandmother's disapproval."

"That would happen?"

"You'll meet my mom at the rehearsal picnic and the wedding reception. You can make your own judgment."

Gavin checked the sales board hanging above the register. "I see you still have cherry tarts. I'd like one of those and peach iced tea."

"Coming up." Daisy headed for the kitchen.

She'd relieve Foster so he could talk to his dad if he wanted to. With classes, work, and preparing for the wedding, Foster didn't have much time to spend with his father anymore, and she knew Gavin missed his son. Foster and Vi were adults, soon with their own lives and their own family. She and Gavin both had to accept that.

* * *

On Sunday morning, Daisy and Jazzi went to an early church service, then Jazzi helped Vi and Foster put the finishing touches on their apartment. By the time Jonas picked up Daisy, clouds had taken over the sky, making rain a good possibility. But at least the temperature had dropped to the low eighties.

Daisy and Jonas followed Route 30 to Gettysburg, which was a town known for its battles in the Civil War. The battlefield and its monuments were about an hour and a half away. Besides catering to tourists, though, Gettysburg was, in fact, a college town. Gift shops, galleries, and theaters dotted the area while the restaurants and cafés invited college kids as well as tourists into their eateries. However, since history was a mainstay of the town, visitors could find antiques shops and memorabilia stores with artifacts on the main streets.

Deciding to drive about a bit to check out the hanging baskets and storefronts, Jonas aimed for Lincoln Square where the major routes coming into town joined. In Daisy's estimation, Lincoln Square was really a circle.

As they went halfway around the circle and proceeded up Chambersburg Street, Daisy glanced at the James Gettys Hotel, which had opened in the early 1800s. It had seen many reincarnations as an army hospital during the Battle of Gettysburg, apartments and now a hotel. On the ground floor was one of Daisy's favorite art galleries. The hanging baskets along the street with their fuchsia waterfall begonias were gorgeous.

After they had gone a few blocks, Daisy said, "We

should probably head for Cannonball Memorabilia and Collectibles."

"Do you still have that photo of Barry on your phone?" Jonas asked Daisy as he took a side street and then another to take them to their destination.

Otis had let her take a photo of a photo. When she'd told him what she and Jonas wanted to do, he'd thanked her for the time she'd put in trying to find information to solve Barry's murder. He'd found an old photo of Barry and Ian and she'd snapped a photo of that one too.

"How many memorabilia stores are you willing to visit today?" Jonas asked.

"Maybe just one. Keith said this one was our best bet and I remembered the name from Otis's book work."

"I think you're a little too optimistic. What we'll probably find out is that Barry bought or sold memorabilia at the Cannonball . . . and other places."

"If he did, we'll have another puzzle piece."

"As I said . . . optimistic."

Jonas found a parking space about a block from the memorabilia shop on Baltimore Street. After he parked, Daisy sent him a smile as she unfastened her seat belt. He did the same. They climbed out of his SUV and leisurely walked toward the Cannonball.

Civil War reenactment was popular in this area. A uniform on a mannequin hung in the shop's window as well as equipment that would take tourists back in time. This particular shop, and floors above it, looked as if it had once been a historic home. In the front, corbels lined the roof. A large bay window protruded from the second floor while an awning in maroon and black covered the facade of the store.

Jonas opened the door for her, and when he did, a buzzer sounded. They stepped inside. Daisy was aware of a musty smell right away, similar to the odor in Pirated Treasures.

"Did you ever go on a ghost walk?" Jonas asked Daisy.

"No, and I don't feel the need to do it."

Jonas chuckled. "Gettysburg is supposed to be one of the most haunted towns in the nation."

"Seriously," Daisy admitted, "considering its history, I can see why."

As they walked further into the store, Daisy bypassed the display of VHS tapes of the Battle of Gettysburg and stopped to look at a photograph of Civil War CDV Union captain Charles C. Wehrun. The price on the item was $495. She didn't know if that was a bargain or not. Nearby she spotted a Civil War map of Gettysburg, the 1864 rebel invasion in Maryland and Harrisburg. That was only $85. She imagined the condition of each piece also set the price.

Next, her gaze fell on a glassed-in case where a Confederate cannon bolt had a price of $1,500. All of it was baffling to her. This was history for sale. Didn't it all belong in a museum somewhere?

Over on the left side of the store, Gettysburg memorabilia for tourists hung on racks and lay folded on shelves. There were short-sleeved and long-sleeved T-shirts, billed caps, and even socks. Kid-sized clothes and paraphernalia were stacked beside the rest.

Taking her phone from her purse, Daisy tapped it and found the photos she wanted. She went to the man at the counter who stood near the computer register.

"This is an amazing shop," she said.

Over her shoulder, Jonas seconded that comment by adding, "You have memorabilia here I've never seen anywhere before."

The man extended his hand to Daisy and then Jonas. "I'm Harry Wilson. I'm glad to hear you're impressed with the shop. First time in Gettysburg?"

"Oh, no," Daisy said. "I'm originally from Lancaster."

Jonas added, "I've been through Gettysburg before."

Harry pushed back a clump of his russet red hair that was falling almost to his eyebrows. He was about sixty with a wide nose and a sharp chin. His T-shirt read GETTYSBURG OR BUST. His jeans rode low under his paunch.

"What brings you here today?" Harry asked, obviously to see where their interests lay. After all, a sale for him could be imminent.

Jonas said honestly, "We're involved in a murder investigation that happened in Willow Creek. Maybe you heard of it?"

Harry's expression saddened as he frowned. "Oh, yes. There was a story about it in the *Gettysburg Times* . . . Hanover's *Evening Sun* too. I paid special notice because I knew the victim, Barry Storm."

"How did you know him?" Jonas asked.

"Now and then he'd bring in items for me to sell that he couldn't find a buyer for on his own."

"What was the last thing he brought you?" Daisy asked.

"I remember what it was because I hadn't seen another like it. It was a Civil War period leather cup with a pair of bone dice. He said he couldn't get enough for it at Pirated Treasures or even from the e-mail list of collectors that he'd put together. I'm not sure why. As soon as I posted the item on eBay, it sold."

"For how much?" Jonas asked.

"Three hundred fifty. Not a fortune but nice enough."

"Do you know if Barry ever put items for sale on eBay?" Daisy asked.

"No, he wouldn't do that, and I'm not sure why. Sure, Pirated Treasures had a lot of tourist trade, but most tourists don't want collectibles."

"Did Barry say whether this was a side venture for him?"

Harry nodded his head. "I got the feeling it was, but he never said."

Daisy showed Harry the photo of Barry and Ian together. "Did you ever see this man?"

Harry shook his head. "No, I never did. Barry always came in alone."

"One more question," Jonas said. "What's the most expensive item you have to sell right now?"

It took Harry a minute to squint and think about it. "I have a Confederate soldier's Civil War diary from 1863."

"How much is it going for?" Daisy asked.

"I'm asking fifty-seven hundred."

"And you have collectors who will pay that?" Daisy wondered, amazed.

"You wouldn't believe what collectors will pay. Might I ask a question?"

Daisy and Jonas both nodded.

"Do you think Barry might have been trafficking some of the stuff on the black market so that he didn't have to pay taxes or include it in his income?"

"We don't know anything for sure yet," Jonas admitted. "But you just gave us another possible puzzle piece. I suppose this black market exists on the dark web?"

"There's a market for anything on the dark web," Harry said with a nod. "I stay out of that. I run a legitimate business and that's the way I want to keep it."

After a bit more conversation back and forth, Daisy and Jonas headed for Jonas's SUV. After they settled in and fastened their seat belts, Jonas offered, "We could ask around at the other memorabilia stores, but if we found another one that took collectibles from Barry, we'll probably get the same story."

"So what are you thinking about what Barry was doing?" Daisy asked.

"I think he searched for collectibles he could double or triple his money on. You know, sort of like that pickers' reality TV program?"

"And then he sold them any way he could?"

"Anything he sold at a store like Harry's would have paperwork behind it . . . or a record. My guess is that was a last resort if he couldn't sell it anywhere else. So he might have been breaking laws. We don't know that yet."

She sighed.

"Is there any place else you'd like to go while we're in this neck of the woods?" Jonas asked.

It didn't take her long to present an idea. "Can we stop for sandwiches and take them along for a picnic, maybe at the Peace Light? There's something about that place that always touches me."

Jonas gave her one of those smiles that warmed her from head to toe. "Sure, we can."

It didn't take long to find a sub shop and then drive to the Eternal Light Peace Memorial. Northwest of

Gettysburg, it was located on Oak Hill. It had been dedicated by President Franklin D. Roosevelt during the observance of the seventy-fifth anniversary of the Battle of Gettysburg.

After Jonas parked, he asked, "Sandwiches or Peace Light first?"

Jonas had slipped the sandwiches into a cooler he kept in his SUV, so she answered, "Peace Light. I just feel I need the inspiration."

A few minutes later, they walked up to the steps that led to the memorial. A bronze urn sat on top of the tower. On the memorial itself, there were relief sculptures of two women and an American eagle.

After they'd walked up to the tower and then around it, they stood quietly for a few moments, reading the quote—AN ENDURING LIGHT TO GUIDE US IN UNITY AND FELLOWSHIP. The Peace Light was a symbol of the blue and gray uniting under one flag.

A companionable mood dropped over Jonas and Daisy. She said, "I read that the base is made of Maine granite."

"And the rest is limestone," Jonas filled in. "Did you know the gas-lit flame was once replaced by electricity?"

"I think I heard that. Eventually, it was restored in the late eighties."

"This monument and the eternal flame inspired President Kennedy's grave at Arlington."

"When I was little, my parents brought Cammie and me here almost every summer. We'd bring our bikes and ride them on the battlefield, stopping to study the monuments, climbing up to Devil's Den. It was always like a mini family vacation."

Silence descended over them again until Jonas asked, "Ready for that picnic?"

The sky had turned threatening. Smoky clouds alternated with steel-gray ones.

They decided to sit in Jonas's SUV. He lowered all the windows and a damp breeze that forecasted rain blew through. After they'd unwrapped their sandwiches, taken a few bites and swigs of soda, Jonas laid his sandwich on the console and turned toward her. "I'd like to talk to you about something."

Daisy tried to prevent her guard from going up. Jonas had wanted to end their romantic relationship once before, and *she* had thought about doing it when she found out Vi was pregnant. But now she hoped they were on an even keel. "About the investigation?"

"No . . . about us. You said you always want me to be honest with you about my feelings."

As a former detective, Jonas had been guarded when she'd met him. It had taken him a while to share his history with her, but he had. "Yes, I want you to be honest. It's the only way we know where we both stand."

"It's about Gavin," he said.

That took her totally by surprise. "Gavin?"

Jonas's brows drew together and his jaw became set. The scar on his left cheekbone was more pronounced. He looked as if he didn't really want to talk about this, but it was something that had to be done. "I know you and Gavin have many reasons to be in close contact now. You both care about Foster and Vi and their future. It's because of you and Gavin and your generosity that your kids are hopefully going to have a good start to their marriage."

"We're trying to make circumstances easier for them," Daisy said warily. Did Jonas think they shouldn't do that? He'd even built the cabinets in the kitchen at cost for the garage apartment.

His next words confused her more. "I admire you both for that."

Swiveling toward him, she asked, "Then what's this about?"

"You really don't know?"

She shook her head.

Jonas gripped the steering wheel with one hand as if he needed a ballast to have this discussion with her. "Gavin is a good man. He's a dad who's had experience parenting. You two have a lot in common."

Okay, so now she had an inkling of where they were headed. "Jonas, I'm not interested in Gavin."

"You're going to have plenty of occasions to be together . . . family occasions. Your mother might even decide she likes him."

Daisy took hold of Jonas's arm. "My mother doesn't know you. She also doesn't know Gavin. But I do know *you*, and I like what I know."

"Gavin likes you." It was a statement with no recriminations.

"And I like him," she admitted honestly. "That's a good thing in our situation."

Jonas nodded. "Yes, it is. I just want to make sure that you know I'm serious about us—you and me—separate from anything else that's going on. I want to allay your fears, safeguard you, and show you that I'm all in."

When Daisy leaned forward, he loosened his grip

on the steering wheel and caressed her cheek. She kissed him. It was a kiss that told him she was all in too.

When her cell phone played its tuba sound, she pulled away and groaned. "Someone has lousy timing."

"Check. It could be Vi."

Whenever Jonas kissed her, she forgot about everything except him. Checking the screen, however, she saw that it was Keith. She tapped on the speakerphone. "Hi, Keith. I'm with Jonas. Is everything all right?"

"I don't know. I found a trapdoor in the cabin, and I think you and Jonas should see it."

Chapter Sixteen

Daisy and Jonas stood in the kitchenette of Keith's cabin staring at the old linoleum rug on the floor. The rest of the cabin was plank flooring, but here in the kitchen preparation area, linoleum had been laid from under the sink to the other side of the small kitchenette.

"Is Mandy asleep?" Daisy asked Keith.

"Yes, she is. She's a sound sleeper, thank goodness. You can peek in if you'd like."

Daisy went into the small living room and peeked into the only bedroom. Mandy was asleep on her side, her teddy bear stuffed under her chin. The single bed was pushed against the wall, while a nightlight glowed in the receptacle. She looked like an angel. In a way, she'd been Keith's angel. He'd had to survive for her. He'd had to keep pushing . . . for her. She had probably saved him in more ways than he knew.

Keith had the door propped halfway open and Daisy left it that way. The bed pillow on the sofa indicated that that was where Keith spent his nights. She supposed the sofa was better than the floor of the van. An old wooden rocker with carvings on its back sat under a pole lamp. Blocks and puzzles were strewn around it.

Back in the kitchen area she saw that the men were studying the stained, old linoleum with its veins that had developed into cracks.

Keith said, "I scrubbed that linoleum before we moved in, but it still looked dirty. I was afraid Mandy would scratch herself on those cracks or trip over them. Lowe's had a sale on a linoleum roll that I guess they couldn't sell to anybody. It was about the measurement of this one. After Mandy fell asleep I started to pick this up. I was going to scrub the floor under it and then put the new one down in the morning. But I found this."

Crossing to the corner of the kitchen kitty-corner from the mini refrigerator, Keith lifted the edge of the linoleum. As he folded it back, he revealed what looked like a door cut into the floor. A place had been carved out for the round, black ring handle that lay flat. It didn't leave a bump under the linoleum.

Jonas squatted down and ran his fingers along the edges of the door. "No hinges," he noted.

"No hinges," Keith agreed. "The whole panel just lifts up by using the ring. When it's back in place, it sits in a groove that's depressed all along the edges. Are you ready to see the rest?"

Daisy wasn't sure she wanted to, but Keith had said he'd already been down inside so there wouldn't be any surprises. She didn't want to be a coward about it, but she didn't like cold, dark places.

As if Keith had read her mind, he gave her a wry smile. "I left a lantern glowing down there, and Jonas can probably take a flashlight along. I'll stay up here with Mandy."

"But you found something down there, didn't you?" Jonas asked.

"I did, but I'll tell you where to look. I didn't touch them. If they're evidence, I didn't want to take a chance my fingerprints would be on them."

"Wise thinking." Jonas put his fingers in the ring, tilted the door up, and then lifted it out. He propped it against the wall. As he peered down into the hole, he said, "At least we don't have to climb down a rope ladder. It's a real one."

"Any idea how old it is?" Daisy asked. If it was too old, wouldn't it be rickety and not sturdy enough for their weight?

Keith took a flashlight from the counter and shone it on the first few rungs. "I think it was repaired at some point. Some of the rungs have been replaced. You can tell they're newer than the rest. I made sure it was sturdy when I was climbing down. The last thing Mandy or I need is a broken leg. She counts on me, so I can't take chances."

Jonas looked at Daisy. "Do you want me to go first?"

She nodded, her legs already feeling a little trembly.

"I can watch out for you on this end," Keith assured her.

Before Daisy knew it, Jonas was climbing down. Keith helped her onto the ladder and she followed Jonas. It was a short ladder as ladders went, about seven feet from the floor to the opening. Once Jonas stood on the dirt floor, he held Daisy by the waist as she climbed down the last few rungs. She turned toward him, aware of the dampness, the smell of earth, of old wood. But she was close enough to Jonas to catch a whiff of his aftershave too. That reassured her. That made her feel safe. *He* made her feel safe.

His hands on her shoulders, he asked, "All right?"

"Yes," she answered breathlessly. "This isn't a place I'd want to spend much time."

He gave a little chuckle. "Let's see what's down here." He called up to Keith, "Do I have to worry about stepping on anything?"

"No."

Jonas picked up the lantern that Keith had left on the floor. It gave a good amount of light. When he lifted it, Daisy spotted a tall shelf filled with jarred goods—canned potatoes, tomatoes, onions, jarred beets, jams, and bottles of water. There was a can of salted peanuts too. To the right of the shelf, old picture frames leaned against the wall.

"Is this a storm shelter?" she asked.

"Could be. Maybe it started out as a root cellar. What am I looking for?" he called up to Keith.

"Do you see those old picture frames?"

"I do," Jonas said.

"Move the first one from the second one, then look down on the floor."

Now Jonas handed Daisy the flashlight. "Shine that down there too. We'll make sure we find what he wants us to find."

After he moved the front picture frame, he crouched down. Daisy studied rectangular badges of some kind that looked as if they'd been torn from material. There was an outer border, also rectangular, and the inside of the rectangle was red. There was a stripe on either side, the same material as the border.

"What are they?" she asked both men.

Keith answered, "They're Civil War collectibles— lieutenant of artillery shoulder straps. I've seen them in Civil War museums. They can be worth about five hundred bucks."

Jonas stood and looked around the floor again, peering at it carefully, as if he wanted to make sure there wasn't anything else down there. "And you didn't touch them?" he called up to Keith.

"No, sir. But I also didn't know what to do. That's why I called you."

"I hate to say it, but you need to call Zeke Willet."

Even from down below him, Daisy could hear Keith's troubled groan. "Are you sure about that?"

"I'm sure. I have a feeling that Barry and Ian were selling memorabilia and goods from Pirated Treasures on the side. If that's the case, and these are part of their stash that somehow got left behind, Detective Willet should know about it."

"I don't want Mandy to be scared if he comes trudging through here."

"I'll stay with her," Daisy promised. "If she's a sound sleeper, we'll just make sure we tell the detective to keep his voice down."

"Oh, I'm sure that will work," Jonas mumbled.

"You go up first," he told Daisy. "If you stay with Mandy, maybe you can avoid this altogether."

Daisy hoped that was true. She really didn't need another run-in with Zeke Willet this week. She didn't need another run-in with Zeke Willet . . . at all.

A half hour later, Daisy heard a car on the gravel driveway. It parked close to the cabin. Before she could even think about going to sit with Mandy, there was a knock at the door.

Keith opened it and invited Zeke Willet and another

patrol officer to step inside. Daisy knew the patrol officer. It was Tommy Kruger. He often stopped in at the tea garden because he had a sweet tooth for her snickerdoodles. He was standing behind Zeke and he gave her a half smile. At least she felt *he* was friendly. His attitude was very different from Zeke's.

Tommy was all business. Whereas Tommy was dressed in a blue uniform, Zeke wore a T-shirt and khakis with a tan wrinkled sport coat on top. Daisy wondered if he was hot. Mandy's room had a room air conditioner and Keith had set up a fan to blow it into the living room. He told Daisy he wanted his daughter to be comfortable.

Zeke's glance targeted each one of them and then came back to Keith. "You have a trapdoor and something to show me?" Keith led him to the kitchen where the hidden root cellar was obvious. Zeke himself pulled at the door. "What did you say you found?"

"They're shoulder straps." He demonstrated their size with his thumb and forefinger. "They're about this long and about an inch wide. I didn't touch them."

"What *did* you touch?"

"I mostly just looked around. You'll see when you get down there. There's already a lantern there."

Jonas offered his flashlight to Zeke. "You might need this to find the shoulder straps. They're between the first and second picture frames."

"So you've been down there?"

"I have. Keith called me and Daisy when he found the trapdoor."

"Why were you lifting the linoleum?" Zeke asked Keith.

"Because it's stained and cracked, and I didn't want my daughter crawling on that floor, which she sometimes does. I bought a new piece and was going to lay it down in the morning."

"For a homeless guy with no job, you seem to have some money."

Keith kept silent.

With a shrug Zeke said to Tommy, "You stay up here. I'll go down and take a look around."

Zeke had no trouble accessing the ladder and climbing down to the dirt floor. He might have spent about ten minutes down there. Daisy wasn't sure. Every few minutes she checked in Mandy's room to see if the little girl was awake, but she still slept peacefully. The sound of the air conditioner probably muted their voices.

After Zeke returned to the kitchen, he took off his latex gloves, stuffed them in his pocket, and held out the evidence bag with its shoulder straps inside. "Are these what you found?"

"They are."

"They look like something that someone would throw away."

Rebutting the detective, Keith corrected him. "If they threw them away, they'd be throwing away about five hundred dollars."

Zeke's brown brows arched. He had circles like shadows under his eyes, telling Daisy that he'd been putting in long hours and was probably fatigued. That didn't excuse any rudeness, though.

Zeke turned over the evidence bag and shook his head. "If these are worth that much, then I suspect that root cellar could have held stolen merchandise. Maybe you knew about this place. It turns out Ian Busby often visited Pirated Treasures and was almost like a second nephew to Otis Murdock. Maybe you and

Ian cooked up this scheme, and when Barry found out—" The detective let his voice trail off.

Where Keith had kept his patience before, now he turned belligerent. "Prove it. I never laid eyes on this place until Daisy told me about it."

"Daisy again. She's done an awful lot to help you."

"Yes, she has, and Mandy too. She managed to get Mandy into her doctor when she had a cold."

While they'd been talking, Zeke was taking in everything about the cabin. He spotted the cauliflower and broccoli heads on the counter and Mandy's little sneakers under the sofa. Mostly his eyes swerved to the blocks and puzzles, and he seemed mesmerized by them. Just what was he thinking about?

"Just so you know," Zeke warned Keith, "I'll talk to the couple who live in the farmhouse. They can tell me if they ever saw you around here before you started working here."

"Go ahead and interview them," Keith said. "Clovis and Penelope will tell you exactly when I arrived. They're becoming Mandy's surrogate grandparents."

"So you're getting involved with lots of people in this community. I wonder why. So they'll all defend you?"

Daisy stepped in this time because she knew sometimes Zeke Willet actually listened to her. "Maybe you don't understand the concept because you don't have children, Detective Willet, but it *does* take a village to raise a child. The more connections Keith has for him and Mandy, the better. If you don't have anything else for us, I need to get home so I can be with my daughters."

"I'm not stopping you. Why are you here to begin with? I can't believe you'd be interested in a trapdoor."

"I came along in case Keith and Jonas wanted to

examine the root cellar and someone was needed to stay with Mandy. None of us wanted her waking up and finding strangers here."

Zeke seemed to wince at the word "strangers." Taking his evidence bag with him, he went to the door. Keeping his eye on Keith, he muttered, "So you've convinced them you're a caring dad. You haven't convinced me."

He opened the door and beckoned to Tommy.

Tommy gave an apologetic shrug as if he was sorry for the detective's attitude.

Daisy was relieved when she heard the unmarked car pull away.

After closing the tea garden on Tuesday evening, Daisy and her aunt Iris headed into the Rainbow Flamingo, a boutique dress shop a couple blocks away from the tea garden.

Her aunt Iris said to her, "You're leaving this a little close, aren't you? With the wedding on Saturday, whatever you buy has to fit perfectly."

"I just haven't had time to shop. I'm hoping I can just buy something right off the rack. If Heidi doesn't have anything here, I'll have to drive into Lancaster tomorrow. Park City Mall should have something if Heidi doesn't."

"Are you wearing anything special to Gavin's barbecue?" Iris asked.

"No. I have a skort set that will work just fine."

After they stepped inside the shop, Daisy knew she had about an hour until the Rainbow Flamingo closed. Hopefully this wouldn't be that hard.

The proprietress, Heidi Korn, was adding blouses

to a rack of separates. She added the last one in her hand to the rack. "Hi, Daisy. It's been a while."

"Yes, it has. I intended to come in before now. I need a mother-of-the-bride dress."

Heidi's eyes opened wide. "I heard Vi was getting married this weekend. I'd supposed you found something in one of those wedding shops in Lancaster."

"Jazzi and Gavin's daughter, Emily, found dresses when Vi did. But I never got around to shopping for me. You've always had such pretty clothes here. I'm hoping this will be easy."

Heidi laughed. "That depends on how picky you are. What are you looking for?"

"It's an evening wedding, but not real fancy. I'd like something classic and elegant, maybe midlength."

"You're in luck because midis are in style this year. For wedding dresses too. I just had this one returned. A canceled wedding."

Daisy saw the simple, satin, off-white gown hanging on a hook near the dressing room door. It had a cinched waist and an A-line skirt that floated to midlength, and the spaghetti straps proclaimed that it was a summer fashion.

"You said it was returned?"

"Yes, a sad story. It was the fiancée of that man who was murdered on Sage Street."

"Barry Storm?"

"Yes, I think that was his name."

"So Mariah Goldblum returned this?"

"Do you know her?" Heidi asked.

"I met her. She came into the tea garden with Barry's uncle."

Heidi frowned. "A beautiful young woman, and she's so sad now."

Daisy traded a glance with her aunt. "When was her wedding supposed to be?"

"Oh, she didn't have a date yet. When she bought the dress, though, she said it would be soon. I felt so sorry for her when she returned it."

"Was she alone when she brought it back?"

Heidi gave Daisy an odd look, as if wondering why she wanted to know. Then she shrugged. "No secret, I guess. She was with a man about her age. I think she called him Ian."

So Mariah and Ian had had some contact. That fought against what both he and Mariah had told her. Why wouldn't they want their support for each other to show?

Iris nudged Daisy's arm. "Time's a wasting."

Her aunt was right. She'd have time to think about Mariah and Ian later. Now she had to find a dress.

Thankfully, it didn't take long for Daisy to find her dress. One stood out amid all the others, at least for her. It was sea green with a touch of vintage that lent it to wedding fashion. It was a trumpet-style sheath, embroidered with a floral design. What clinched it for Daisy was the touch of lace around the V neckline, capped sleeves, and hem. It was just perfect. The price tag was a little steep, but this was her daughter's wedding.

Her aunt wasn't so sure. "It's a beautiful dress, Daisy, but where else could you wear it?"

"With a shawl or a shrug, I could possibly wear it on New Year's Eve."

"That's if you go anywhere on New Year's Eve. Jonas needs to take you out dancing somewhere."

"I'm not sure Jonas is the night club and dancing type. I'm not sure I am. But it's okay, Aunt Iris. The tea garden's doing well, especially this summer. Our cookbook has even been selling online."

"You spent so much to make this work for Vi and Foster. I'm not criticizing, by the way."

"Mom thinks they should have moved in with us," Daisy said. Her mother had told her that many times since Daisy had made the decision.

"I suppose that's what Rose would have done, but you and Rose have your own way of doing things. You're looking to the future for when Vi and Foster move out, and you'll have an income property. I think that's smart."

Daisy smiled at her aunt. "Would you tell me if it wasn't?"

"You know I would, but ultimately your life is *your* choice."

Yes, it was. Her mother seemed to understand Cammie's life choices. Why not Daisy's?

"Is Camellia able to get away for the wedding?" Apparently, her aunt's mind had run on the same track as Daisy's.

"I'm hoping she can. I think Vi would miss her if she's not there."

"I think Vi's going to be concentrating on Foster."

Daisy found herself looking forward to the wedding as Heidi slipped the dress into a plastic garment bag and handed it over to Daisy. "I hope the wedding goes off without a hitch."

That was Daisy's prayer too.

Outside the dress shop, they crossed Carriage

Avenue, walked a block, and stood at the curb. They waited for a horse and buggy to clatter down the street, followed by a brown pickup truck traveling just as slow.

"It will be dusk soon," Iris noted. "It's happening earlier and earlier each night."

"Before we know it, it will be Labor Day and school will be starting."

"Is Vi's job with Otis working out?"

"It seems to be. She's still helping him with inventory and recording figures on the computer. I think she's trying to convince him to see an eye doctor. If cataracts are the problem, he can have them taken care of."

As they jaywalked across Market Street to the front of the tea garden, they both stood and examined it. Though it was Victorian in design, it wasn't overly ornate. The wide porch with its rocking chairs was welcoming. They started for the driveway that would lead them to the back parking area. Employees and visitors who needed handicap access parked there.

As they rounded the corner that led to the back of the Victorian, Daisy said, "I think I'll take the work van home tonight. Foster said he'd load up the centerpieces for the tables. Tessa offered to keep them in her apartment until we're ready to decorate."

Iris's sedan was first in the lineup of parked vehicles, then Daisy's PT Cruiser. Next was Daisy's work van.

She stopped cold when she saw it. "Oh, my gosh. Who could have done that?"

"Call Jonas," Aunt Iris told her.

Daisy handed Iris her dress and pulled her phone from her purse. She tapped on Jonas's icon but the call went to voice mail. She bit her lower lip. "I think he said he was driving to Smoketown tonight to look at reclaimed wood. He probably left his phone in his car."

Daisy thought a moment, then she said, "You know what? I'm going to call Zeke Willet."

Iris frowned, but Daisy didn't care. Zeke had told her that, if she had any more information, she should contact him personally. So that's exactly what she was going to do.

Chapter Seventeen

Daisy and Iris had stepped aside when Zeke had arrived. He'd pulled up in an unmarked car, gotten out, and glared at Daisy. On the phone she'd told him about the graffiti on her van, but he hadn't had much to say about it. He'd arrived in ten minutes.

Now he asked, "Did you touch anything?"

"No," Daisy answered. "I know better than to do that."

He gave her a sharp glance, then took out his phone. She thought he might call someone, but instead he took photos of the van. The spray paint on the side, in sloppy lettering, ordered STOP ASKING QUESTIONS. The paint was bright orange.

Next the detective took a latex glove from his pocket. Slipping it on, he moved closer to the lettering. He tried to flick a corner of the paint with one gloved finger.

Turning to Daisy, he shook his head. "I thought if it was latex paint, you might be able to wash it off. But it looks like enamel. Somebody wanted to make this expensive for you. You'll probably have to have the van repainted and your logo put on all over again."

Daisy must have looked crestfallen.

He started to say, "This is what happens when—"

She cut him off. "Spare me the lecture. The problem is . . . I need to use the van to transport things this week for my daughter's wedding."

"My guess is, whoever did this stood a foot away and just sprayed the paint. No telltale evidence left behind."

Iris put her arm around Daisy's shoulders. "Jonas has an SUV and we can all use our cars. We'll make do."

"It will inconvenience everyone."

Zeke frowned. "If you take this to a body shop, they'll tell you how long painting it will take. If you're going to have the van repainted anyway, you could just spray paint over the orange with white paint. It would look messy but nobody would see the orange letters."

"Call Jonas again," Iris suggested. "Maybe he knows someone who can paint it quickly."

"Paint takes a certain amount of time to dry. Even Jonas can't fix that," Daisy answered automatically. Yet she called him anyway.

Jonas answered his phone from his SUV. Daisy summed up what had happened, telling him Zeke had just left without being very helpful.

"Zeke is right."

"About?"

"About not finding fingerprints. On the other hand, I wouldn't take any chances. You should take your van to your usual mechanic and have him go over it with a fine-toothed comb. Make sure the brake linings are intact."

"You don't think someone would actually cut my brake linings?"

"Daisy, they obviously want you to stop asking

questions. They put a *snake* in your van. So far those have been minor inconveniences."

"This isn't minor. It's going to be expensive. I don't have insurance that covers vandalism. There's no way I can do this myself, is there?"

There was a long silence. "Some vehicle owners try to paint their own cars, but I really don't advise it. You have weather to contend with and dust. You need a place to put the vehicle, an electric or air-powered sander, an air compressor with a spray gun, a buffer, paint thinner, face masks, and safety glasses."

Daisy sighed and she knew Jonas heard it.

"A dust extractor too," he added, "because that would keep the area clean. That's just the beginning, Daisy. You need to prime it, put on three coats of top coats and maybe two coats of lacquer. I really don't think this is something you want to tackle on your own, especially now."

Especially now. Her busiest time of work, Violet's pregnancy, and . . . the wedding. Jonas was right. "Do you know someone who does this kind of work for a reasonable fee?"

"First of all, do you trust your mechanic?"

"Yes, I do. My dad has had his car and trucks serviced there as long as he's lived here."

"All right. I suggest you get at least two paint estimates. There is a body shop I used when I first arrived here. My car was parked along the street and somebody sideswiped it. The owner of the body shop repaired and painted it for me. It's late but he sometimes works evenings in his shop. I'll call him and see if he can take a look at it. In the meantime, pick someone from the yellow pages and call them. After both estimates come in, then you can decide what you want to do."

"Jonas, this is the worst possible time."

"I know that. But unless you want to use your van as it is, it's going to be out of commission until a body shop can take it, and then a week for the paint."

Daisy suspected as much when Jonas had listed all the coats of paint and the work involved. "I can drive it home and put it in my garage, but I don't want to even drive it to the mechanic like this."

Jonas was silent for a few moments. "I'm almost in Willow Creek. I'll rig up a tarp on the side of the van. Duct tape is a useful thing. It's not going to look great, but it will be better than the paint."

"That's a wonderful idea. *You're* wonderful. I just hope the mechanic can get me in soon. I'll call him first thing in the morning to see if he can come here to look it over."

"I'll want to look at the van too. To start, I want to make sure it's not leaking brake fluid or that there isn't a severe cut in the lining. If either are present, we'll call Zeke again. Are you going to wait there till I arrive with the tarp and duct tape?"

"Yes. I'll call Jazzi and tell her I have a problem with the van but not what it is. I don't want her and Vi to worry."

"I should be there in about fifteen minutes. I'm glad your aunt Iris is with you."

"I'm glad too. Jonas, thank you."

"I didn't do anything yet."

"But you will. I know I can count on you. That means a lot."

"See you shortly," he said gruffly, and then ended the call.

Daisy was grateful that Jonas Groft was part of her life.

* * *

Tonight was the night. Violet was marrying Foster.

Daisy caught a glimpse of Foster and Gavin at the doorway on the right side of the nave of Willow Creek Community Church. They were both dressed in black tuxes, crisp white shirts, and bow ties. She gave a little wave and then shooed them back in. She didn't want Foster to catch a glimpse of Vi or even Vi to catch a glimpse of Foster. When Violet's grandfather walked her down the aisle, Gavin would walk Foster toward her.

She had to admit that last evening at the barbecue at Gavin's house everyone had seemed relaxed. The casual atmosphere had helped family just enjoy the lawn party and talk about mundane things. Anything but the wedding. The rehearsal at the church had gone well, and even Vi had seemed to be looking forward to her big day. Now it was here.

The gauze bows on the pews and the candleholders along the side aisles of the church added to the festive but holy ambience. The lily and yellow rose arrangements on the altar spread a lovely fragrance.

Daisy turned to Iris, who was standing beside her. "I'm going to see if Vi needs any help." Vi was in the dressing room, making sure her hair was perfect with her veil in place.

As Daisy walked toward the rear of the church, she spotted Jazzi. Her younger daughter looked much older than sixteen in a rose-colored bridesmaid dress that matched Gavin's daughter's. It had short sleeves and a scooped neck. The bodice was a stretch lace while the A-line skirt and sash were fashioned of chiffon. It was young and pretty, like she was, and she could probably wear it for a formal occasion. With her high-heeled white sandals and her hair up on top of her head in a flattering bun, Jazzi should have had a smile on her face. Instead, as she spoke to Portia and her husband, Jazzi's expression was tentative.

The Hardings had decided to stay at the Covered Bridge B and B rather than with Daisy. Colton did *not* look delighted to be here. Daisy hoped that expression would change once he spent more time with Jazzi. As Daisy moved to greet them, her aunt Iris waved at Daisy's mother and dad and Cammie. Daisy concentrated on Jazzi.

After a smile for her daughter, Daisy asked Portia, "How was your drive?" As soon as the question left her mouth, she realized maybe she should have addressed Colton.

Portia's husband looked straight-laced with his short, conservatively styled, sandy-brown hair. He held his shoulders straight as if he was in a military inspection lineup. He was only slightly taller than his wife at about five-foot-nine.

Colton was the one who answered Daisy's question. "Traffic was heavy, but that's what happens on a Saturday in the summer, especially in your area of Pennsylvania. We don't have as many tourists in Allentown."

Portia, who looked very pretty tonight in a champagne-colored dress, sent him a pointed look.

He shrugged. "What?"

"The Covered Bridge Bed and Breakfast is really a beautiful place," Portia said. "This is a getaway weekend for us."

Oh, really? Daisy thought. She'd expected the couple might want to sightsee with Jazzi and let Colton get to know her better. Maybe this was the reason Jazzi was quiet.

"I hope you enjoy your time here. There's an Amish farm that you can tour in Strasburg and little shops with handcrafted items."

"We're looking forward to the reception," Portia said. "I told Colton that the tearoom belongs to you."

"My aunt and I run the tearoom," she explained.

"But you own it, don't you?" he pressed.

What if she said she didn't? Would he respect her less?

Jazzi spoke up this time. "Mom and Aunt Iris own it and run it. They're very good at business. They rent out the apartment above it to our kitchen manager." She addressed Portia. "Did you ever see the Daisy's Tea Garden cookbook? I help collate it each year."

Colton's expression grew surprised. "You help collate it?"

"I'm good at the computer. I don't just do social media even though teenagers get a bad rap about that."

Daisy knew where this conversation was going, but she didn't get the feeling it was going anyplace good. So she tapped Jazzi on the shoulder. "We'd better go into the dressing room and calm down Vi."

"I have to check my makeup," Jazzi agreed. She put her hand on her birth mother's arm. "I'll see you later?"

Portia didn't look at Colton this time. "You bet. Just take one step at a time down that aisle and you'll be fine."

Jazzi gave Portia a genuine smile and a thumbs-up.

As Daisy and Jazzi crossed to the dressing room, Daisy asked, "Are you worried about tripping going down the aisle?"

"Yeah, I was. My shoes are a bit slippery. I didn't want to bother you with it."

"Jazzi, of course you can bother me with it. I think we had tape we used with some of the arrangements. It's probably in the flower box."

"What good is tape going to do?" Jazzi looked confused.

"It's an old trick. You just tear off a piece and put it on the sole of the shoe. It will keep your shoe from slipping."

"That's a great idea."

"You know, speaking of the flowers, I'd better make sure Mom's corsage is perfect or I'll never hear the end of it. Tell Vi I'll be in in a minute."

As Jazzi continued on to the dressing room, Daisy crossed to her father, mother, and sister. The corsages looked lovely on their outfits. Knowing her mother's dress was the palest pink, she'd chosen a corsage of pink roses for her. For Camellia she'd chosen a corsage of variegated day lilies and tiny carnations.

Camellia laughed when she touched hers. "Mom's is sedate and mine looks like a fiesta."

"That's you," Rose teased, "a fiesta."

Her dark hair in a bob, Camellia was wearing a sundress with a riot of colors, slashes of red and blue and green and yellow. The corsage complemented it well.

Camellia went on, "I'm looking forward to the reception at the tea garden. I haven't had a tea service there yet. This will be interesting."

"And I hope joyful," Daisy added. "I'm going to join Vi in the dressing room. Jonas will escort me up the aisle after you. As soon as the 'Butterfly Waltz' begins, Jazzi, Emily, and Vi will start toward the front."

Foster had his list of friends for two functions. The first was the music. The piano and a violin would be played by friends. Another friend from school would be making a video of the wedding and taking photographs. It was an economical way to save memories, and it made sense to Daisy.

Fifteen minutes later, the ceremony began. Vi looked absolutely beautiful in a midcalf wedding dress fashioned of lace and chiffon. The piped empire waistline fell softly into the skirt of lace-covered chiffon. Tiny lace appliqués danced around the hem of the dress. As Vi walked to the altar, and her grandfather gave Foster her hand, Daisy kept herself from crying by studying the back closure of the dress with its small covered buttons and loops. It was so pretty. Vi absolutely glowed as she faced Foster and he faced her.

Beside Jonas, Daisy held her emotions in check until Vi and Foster shared the vows they'd written themselves. The words dove straight into Daisy's heart.

"You're my best friend, my confidant, and you will be my home," Vi promised.

Foster seemed a little awkward, and his voice turned husky as he vowed, "I'll love you and respect you each day, and give you all the love I have to give."

Jonas must have realized what was going on inside Daisy's heart. He wrapped his arm around her waist and pulled her a little closer. She could have laid her head on his shoulder and cried as memories of her own marriage, hope for Vi and Foster's future, and longing to have real true love again swirled around her heart. She noticed Aunt Iris blowing her nose, and her mom doing the same. Even her dad had a tear in his eye.

Gavin's jaw was clenched as he listened to his son's vows, and Daisy imagined he was remembering his wife too. As she glanced at Jonas, she thought she saw everything she wanted to see on his face, but everyone was so emotional right now it was hard to tell.

Reverend Kemp spoke about Foster and Vi and to them as he gave them advice and hope. Afterward he blessed them and pronounced them husband and wife. Foster kissed Vi as if he'd forgotten there were guests in the church. His face turned red when Reverend Kemp cleared his throat.

With wide smiles, Foster and Vi turned to face their friends and family and left the church proper to Beethoven's "Ode to Joy."

The pews in the front emptied first. After Foster's brother, Ben, escorted Jazzi down the aisle and one of Foster's friends escorted Emily, Jonas walked beside Daisy, his arm entwined with hers.

Although Daisy's staff at the tea garden was overseeing the setup for everything for the reception, she wanted to arrive as early as she could. Vi and Foster had decided to visit each table at the tea garden instead of having a reception line in the back of the church. Foster beckoned Daisy and Gavin to accompany him and Vi back into the church for photographs. Daisy was about to head that way when she spotted Keith, Mandy, Karina, and Quinn. Mandy ran over to her and wrapped her little arms around Daisy's legs. Daisy couldn't help but stoop down, scoop her up, and hold her for a few minutes.

As Karina gave a thumbs-up sign, Keith crossed to Daisy to fetch Mandy.

Daisy asked Keith, "How did Mandy do?"

"Not too restless. She kept pointing to all the flowers and to Vi and saying, 'Pretty, pretty, pretty.'"

Mandy repeated after her dad, "Pretty, pretty, pretty."

Keith and Daisy laughed, then Daisy handed Mandy over to her dad. She was wearing a pink dress with ruffles around the skirt hem. "You look pretty tonight too. It's soon going to be your bedtime."

"We'll stop in at the tea garden for a little while," Keith said. "Hopefully Mandy and Quinn will keep each other occupied."

"I think they'll both like the cake and icing," Daisy quipped, then headed into the church.

She didn't get very far. Suddenly her mother and Camellia were by her side.

"I'm glad you're going to be in the photos too," Daisy said to her sister.

"Camellia and I would like to ask you a question," her mother returned with a frown.

That tone in her mother's voice made Daisy brace herself.

Camellia put her hand on her mother's shoulder as if restraining her. Then she said sweetly, "We were just wondering why you invited that man and his daughter to Vi's wedding. They're not friends or relatives."

"How would you know?" Daisy returned swiftly. She wasn't going to take any flack from her mother or sister tonight.

Camellia began, "Mom said—"

Rose interrupted her. "That man is homeless, and customers at the nursery were telling me the police interrogated him about the murder on Sage Street. You're not involved in that, are you?"

Daisy put her hand to her temple, closed her eyes,

and counted to ten. She'd just reached ten when her father came up beside her. Without preamble he pointedly said to his wife, "I told you Keith is no longer homeless. He and his daughter live in a cabin on a farm and he's employed there."

Daisy didn't want to lose her temper on this beautiful evening. "Let's not discuss this now," she suggested.

Foster was motioning them inside. To escape her mom and sister, she said, "I have to grab Aunt Iris. We want her in the pictures too."

After leaning close to her dad, kissing his cheek and saying "Thank you" in a very low voice, Daisy found her aunt. The photographs would never reveal the tension that always bubbled up within her family. But that was the point of happy photos, wasn't it? To remember the good times and cherish them.

Daisy was in the process of gathering her shawl and purse where she'd left them on the window ledge in the nave of the church. Vi and Foster were going to take a short drive before arriving at the tea garden to give all their guests a chance to settle in. Jonas, as well as Russ, were bringing around their vehicles when Daisy glanced to the other side of the nave. She saw her mother and dad talking with Reverend Kemp. He was also invited to the reception.

Suddenly a shadow loomed over Daisy's shoulder and she gasped.

"Whoa there," the man said, his hand on her shoulder. When she looked up, she saw Trevor Lundquist.

"What are you doing here?" she asked.

"I wanted to see what type of event you'd put on for

the reception. I thought I'd write it up in the *Messenger*. But you have to invite me first."

Daisy and Trevor had made deals in the past, and she didn't quite know who would come out on top. "You're going to write up the event at the tea garden without me taking out an ad?"

"That's not the way it works and you know it. I report on anything in Willow Creek that's interesting. Have you ever done a reception at the tea garden before?"

"No," she said slowly, drawing out the word.

"If I write it up, you could have more receptions there, don't you think?"

Trevor always looked put together and tonight was no exception. His stylish brown hair stopped at the collar of his beige linen suit jacket. He wasn't wearing a tie with his dark brown shirt, but his loafers were polished.

"What do you want, Trevor?" Of course, she really didn't have to ask.

"I still want an exclusive when you solve the case."

She had to get to the reception. "I'm not involved in the case. Really. Zeke Willet is the detective and he won't tell me anything."

"Maybe not, but I remember that snake." He waved his hand outside. "And I heard about the damage to your van."

Right now, the van was parked in the tea garden's back lot until the body shop could paint it. The tarp covered the side panel and the graffiti. "I'm not going to ask how you learned about that. You're invited to the reception, but I can't promise you I'm going to have anything to tell you once Detective Willet solves the case."

Trevor winked at her. "Oh, I think you will. My bet is always on you, Daisy Swanson."

Before she could protest, Trevor had left the church.

Chapter Eighteen

The reception took off from the moment Vi and Foster entered the tea garden, and all their guests clapped and cheered. At the announcement made by Jonas, that Mr. and Mrs. Foster Cranshaw had arrived, Daisy could see tears in her mother's eyes, Aunt Iris's eyes, Tessa's eyes, and even Cora Sue's and Karina's.

Vi and Foster, as well as the guests, were happy with the food, from the cold creamed strawberry soup, to the Cordon Bleu chicken bites and crab-stuffed mushrooms, to the sandwich course consisting of egg salad triangles, chicken salad on rye, and pimento and cucumber on pumpernickel. The tiered dessert trays held chocolate mousse cups, a chocolate brownie draped in white chocolate ganache, mini lemon tea cakes, and whoopie pies that were chocolate with peanut butter filling. Foster had pretty much determined the dessert course.

Most of the guests requested iced tea, but a few had hot tea. Daisy's serving staff had all been invited to the wedding and reception. She'd enlisted the help of Rachel's daughters and one of Ruth Zook's teenagers. In addition, Foster had given Daisy the name of a friend of his at Millersville who would be interested in a part-time position. Daisy had called her to see if she could help with the reception. Jada Green was doing a fine job of serving. Daisy couldn't help but keep her eye on everyone to make sure service went smoothly.

After the cake was served, Vi's smile was wide as she ate a bite of the strawberry and white cake layers topped with cream cheese frosting. It had turned out exactly as she'd envisioned it. Foster's brother, Ben, as well as his sister, Emily, seemed to have a good relationship with Vi as well as with their brother.

Jazzi gave a toast after Foster's father had given his. She said, "I've always wanted a brother, and now I have one."

Everyone laughed.

Jazzi continued, "I just want to say how thankful I am to Vi. She's led the way for me in so many ways. I respect and admire her, and I wish her and Foster every happiness they can dream up."

Jazzi seated herself to a round of applause.

Daisy was aware of Colton's gaze on her daughter as if he was trying to figure her out . . . or maybe try to see if she was like his wife in any way.

Daisy had spoken to the mayor and received a permit to have music outside on the patio until ten p.m. Eva, Tessa, and Cora Sue had strung fairy lights all around the umbrellas. A small patch of patio had been left for dancing to Vi's and Foster's favorite songs. Their playlist, connected to a Bluetooth speaker, blared onto the patio. After the bride and groom's first dance, Daisy had danced with Foster, and Vi with Gavin.

Afterward Gavin danced with Daisy. "We pulled it off," he said with a grin.

She smiled back at him. "Yes, we did. Now we just have to hold our breaths until a healthy baby is born."

He groaned. "You had to remind me."

"Oh, I think you'll have a lot of reminders."

He laughed.

As soon as the song ended, she went to Jonas and held out her hand to him. "Dance with me?"

He looked surprised. "I don't dance."

"How about sway back and forth to an old classic?"

"*That* I can remember doing in high school." He took her into his arms, but not in the traditional ballroom position that she and Gavin had danced in. He wound his arms around her waist and she wound hers around his neck. Swaying to the music with Jonas was better than dancing with anyone else.

Daisy noticed that her parents were dancing too. That was nice to see. Marshall Thompson had asked her aunt to dance, and they looked as if they knew what they were doing.

After Jazzi readied baskets of rose petals for guests to access, Vi and Foster left under a shower of petals. Afterward Jonas said, "I'll go inside and see how cleanup is going. Eva and Cora Sue said they'd help so you could get out of here sooner."

Daisy was about to go inside with Jonas when her mother stopped her. She was looking attractive tonight, wearing makeup, her usual bright pink lipstick, and dangling earrings. Her cheeks were rosy either from blush or the outdoor heat. Her mom tugged on her arm and they walked away from the chatter and music so they could be heard.

To Daisy's dismay, her mother ended up near her work van. "Your dad and I are leaving shortly. We just wanted you to know. It's a shame you limited the number of guests. I had so many more friends who would have liked to come."

"As we knew from the beginning, Vi and Foster wanted to keep the list small, so it was a more intimate gathering," Daisy reminded her.

"I was glad to see Vi didn't look pregnant in that gown."

Daisy bit her tongue. Whether Vi looked pregnant or not, they would have celebrated this event for the milestone it was . . . and for the future it represented.

Rose glanced around, maybe to see if anyone was nearby who could hear. She started to say, "Vi told me that Iris and you and Jazzi were sending them on a short honeymoon. I wish you had told me—" She suddenly stopped. "Why is that tarp across your work van? And with duct tape?" Her mother started moving toward it.

Daisy really hadn't seen the harm in leaving the van in the parking lot with the graffiti covered until the body shop could take it on Monday. It was a shame her mother couldn't leave well enough alone.

To Daisy's dismay, her mother lifted the bottom corner of the tarp. A strip of duct tape tore free. Rose peered underneath and gasped. "Daisy, what is this?"

Daisy tried to downplay it. "There was some vandalism."

"Vandalism. This is more than vandalism. I can read the words. 'Stop asking questions.'" Her mother looked horrified.

"Mom, really. I'm taking care of it. The body shop is picking up the van Monday. A mechanic checked it over and I'll have a new paint job."

"I'm not worried about your paint job. Your life has been in danger before. This is what happens by befriending a homeless man. Goodness knows what his past is like."

Although Daisy had enjoyed every minute of planning the wedding, she was tired down to her bones. This time her mother's criticism felt like it trapped her into a vise, and for a change she forgot to weigh her words. "Mom, what you don't seem to understand is that my life is *my* life. Merely once in a while, I'd like support from you instead of always being criticized. Why do you think I confide in Aunt Iris?"

Her mother looked shocked. Then her face reddened even more, and her voice became shrill. "If Iris wanted your safety too, she'd be criticizing you rather than aiding and abetting you." With that salvo, her mother walked away.

Upset over what had just happened, Daisy couldn't return to the reception. She knew eventually she and her mom would have to have a sit-down, hash it out, and figure out what would happen going forward. She also knew neither of them could do that tonight.

She'd wanted nothing to mar the wedding day, but she'd done this. If she'd just held her tongue.

Tears welled up with all her emotions. She needed a little space and air. Walking away from the fairy lights on the umbrellas, she headed to the door at Tessa's apartment. When she reached it, the motion detector light switched on. She'd forgotten about that. It seemed there was nowhere she could go right now to get away from people, lights, music, and even her own thoughts. She had a key to Tessa's apartment, and she knew the security code. The problem was she'd left her purse in her office in the tea garden.

Determined to escape the light and the motion detectors, she crossed the narrow parking lot and sat on the ground in the dark. However, a moment later, Jonas called her name. She couldn't hide from *him*, not if she didn't want him to hide from her. She didn't have to call to him. He'd taken out his phone and was using the flashlight app.

"What are you doing out here?" he asked before he'd even reached her.

She couldn't answer. Her throat was too thick. Her thoughts were too jumbled. Everything in the past few months seemed to come crashing down on her.

Noticing her sitting on the ground, apparently not knowing what to say, he murmured, "You're going to get that pretty dress all dirty."

That was the least of her problems, but she couldn't articulate it. Seeming to forget about his suit, he took off his jacket and laid that on the ground beside him. Then he sat down next to her and put his arm around her. "You're worrying me. What's wrong?"

She held up her hand, trying to tell him to give her a moment. But when he squeezed her tighter, her tears flowed more freely.

He waited for a few heartbeats, then he commented, "I know Vi's okay. She and Foster looked happy when they left."

After a glance at her, he went on. "I saw Jazzi and Portia talking. Granted, Colton was standing a few feet away, but Jazzi seemed okay."

Daisy swallowed hard three times and took in a couple of bracing breaths. "I know everyone's leaving. I have to get back to the reception."

Jonas gently put his hand on the side of her face and nudged her around to him. "Not before you tell me what's wrong."

"My mom and I . . . had words."

"I saw your mom and dad leave."

"Did she look upset?"

"I'm not sure that I know what your mom looks like when she's upset. She was speaking to your sister, and they left with your dad."

"She and Camellia always band together. No surprise there."

His voice was exceedingly gentle as he asked, "Are you going to tell me what happened?"

"I'm embarrassed. I caused Mom heartache and I didn't intend to."

"I know you, Daisy. You wouldn't say anything that was hurtful."

"I did," Daisy insisted. "She came at me again about Keith. She saw the words on the van. She gave me her version of what I was supposed to do, and I just popped. I told her her critical attitude is one of the reasons I always confide in Aunt Iris."

Jonas made a low sound and Daisy couldn't tell if it was disapproval or surprise. "Are you going to talk to her again tonight?"

"No, I can't. I might say something else that I shouldn't say. I've always bitten my tongue before. I've always tried to keep the peace."

"You know, you tell your daughters to stand up for themselves. Why is it so wrong if *you* do it?"

Wasn't *that* a very good question? "I guess it's wrong when I do it because I've never done it with her before. I tell Dad what I think, but not my mom."

"Are you going to be able to sleep tonight if you don't talk to her?"

"I don't know. I'm so tired I already feel half comatose."

She looked up at the night sky, the thousands of

stars, the beautiful half-moon. Life was never simple. "Maybe I make life more complicated than it should be. Maybe I should have stayed out of the situation with Keith and Mandy."

"You *are* tired. You step in because you care. There's nothing wrong with that."

She leaned into Jonas, relishing the strength of his shoulders, the tightness of his arms, the caring in his voice. "This is going to take time to fix."

"Start small," Jonas advised. "Don't try to fix everything at once."

She needed a good night's sleep tonight so she could think straight. Tomorrow morning, she was going to make breakfast for Vi and Foster, and she and Jazzi would see them off. Afterward, maybe she and her daughter should go for a very long hike.

After work on Monday, Daisy took leftover pancakes from the refrigerator. She studied Marjoram and Pepper, who were finishing their dinners. "I'm considering pancakes for supper. What do you think?"

Marjoram gave her a narrow-eyed glare and returned to eating. After all, she'd rather have her chicken primavera than Daisy's pancakes.

Pepper, however, swung around toward Daisy and meowed. She seemed to be asking, "Pancakes? Seriously?"

For the first time in a long time Daisy felt . . . adrift. Yes, Vi had gone on her honeymoon with Foster. They'd be back in a few days. However, Vi wouldn't be living here anymore. Jazzi had been picked up by a friend and was spending the night with Stacy. She was taking advantage of the last days of summer before school started.

And Daisy's rift with her mother . . . She still wasn't sure how to handle that, but she knew she had to. She knew her mother and dad were super busy at the nursery. They were open later and they didn't have much time to themselves this time of year. Maybe Daisy could suggest a time or let her mother choose the day when they could meet for lunch or dinner . . . or anything.

Marjoram and Pepper were her companions for tonight and she appreciated that. Better to count her blessings than dwell on life changes.

Daisy set the microwave to warm her pancakes. She'd stored leftover bacon in the fridge in tinfoil. Now she pulled that out too, took out two pieces, and laid it on the dish with the pancakes. Then she pulled syrup from the cupboard and poured it over all of it. She'd forgo the butter.

As a dietician, she knew this meal was the last thing she should have. Too many carbs and not enough fiber. But tonight she was beyond a salad or yogurt or anything else that could be good for her.

Sitting at the island, she considered breakfast yesterday with Vi, Jazzi, Jonas, and Foster. It had been congenial, warm, and everything a mom could want. Nevertheless, she'd had an empty feeling in her chest when Vi and Foster had left. This was different than when Vi had left for college. This was a total life change for them all.

She was eating her last bite of pancake when her doorbell chimed. Out of habit she took out her phone and checked the security system screen. It was Keith and Mandy!

She tapped the mic icon and said to Keith, "I'll be there in a minute."

Hurriedly putting her dish in the sink, she went to the front door and opened it. Mandy, dressed in a lime-green tank and shorts, launched herself at Daisy. Daisy caught her and picked her up. "It's good to see you." She tickled the little girl's tummy.

"I hope you don't mind our barging in," Keith said. "Otis was cleaning out Barry's apartment and he had two boxes of Barry's clothes. Apparently, you told him you'd take care of them for him by sending them to the thrift shop."

"I did tell him that. Sarah Jane is using her storeroom at the diner to go through all the clothes before she sends them to the thrift shop."

"Should I just bring them in, or would you like them somewhere else?"

"Just bring them in. I'll look through them myself to make sure nothing is too worn to give Sarah Jane. How is Otis?"

"He's still pretty sad and lonely. Today he told me he missed Vi being there."

"She'll be glad to hear that. Though, once she gets his books up to date, she might have to take on another business to keep her busy."

"I wish Otis would see the eye doctor. If he has cataracts that need to be removed, his vision could be corrected. But Vi and I told him we'd make him an appointment if he wants either of us to. He's thinking about it."

Marjoram jumped down from the bench in front of the window. She came over to Daisy, wrapping around her legs. Mandy bent over, as if she was trying to touch the cat.

"Marjoram might let you pet her if you're really gentle." She set Mandy on her feet.

"I'll get those boxes," Keith said.

After he brought both boxes inside, Mandy was sitting on the sofa with Marjoram next to her. Every once in a while, she petted the cat's back.

"I hate to just stop in and run," Keith said, "but Mandy needs a bath tonight, and I want to get her to bed. It's easier to coax her up in the morning if she's had enough sleep."

"I remember those days," Daisy agreed.

Before Mandy and Keith left, she gave the little girl a hug and a kiss. Then Keith lifted her into his arms, said good-bye, and left with a "See you soon."

Daisy felt aimless after Keith left. She pulled one of the boxes over to the sofa and sat there, ready to go through it. Boxes always fascinated the cats. Marjoram and Pepper hopped onto the sofa on either side of her, as if they wanted to peer into the box too.

"I doubt very much if there's anything in here you want to play with."

Marjoram meowed as if in protest. When Pepper sidled up to Daisy and rubbed against her arm, Daisy got the message. "Oh, I understand now. You want the box. We'll see. If I can combine everything into one box, I'll give it to you."

She had two pairs of golden eyes staring at her. "I promise," she said, raising her hand. These cats were good. They could make her feel guilty . . . just as her daughters could.

But apparently they didn't just want to help. They wanted to examine the clothes too. Daisy felt odd going through Barry's clothes. She only imagined how Otis must have felt. The first box mostly consisted of

T-shirts and casual shirts. A couple of the T-shirts were too worn to give away and she set them on one side of the sofa. Marjoram immediately went over and kneaded them.

"I don't know, you might have to negotiate with Pepper about that."

Marjoram seemed to shrug, tucked her paws under her as if to say, "You'll have to move me from here if you want these shirts."

Sarah Jane had told Daisy that the one thing she should do was to go through the pockets of any clothes that were donated. Vi and Jazzi had done that with the clothes they'd given and they'd found lots of things . . . from a mirror to change to coupons.

Daisy discovered a couple of receipts in the pocket of a pair of Barry's shorts, but they were from the convenience store and the fast-food restaurant. The fast-food restaurant must have been popular with Barry because she found several more receipts from there.

After she went to the foyer to pull the second box over to the sofa, she found Pepper settling in the first box. She just shook her head. "I'm so glad the two of you are easily pleased." Pepper eyed her over the box flap. Her look said she didn't want that line when she wanted tuna instead of chicken.

The second box was bigger and it was easy to see that Otis had packed Barry's winter clothes in there. She found sweatshirts and sweaters that didn't look worn. They went on a pile on the sofa since Pepper was in the box.

She went through the pockets of one of the pairs of jeans and found coins and an empty money clip. The jeans were more torn than they should have been . . . as if they'd had that new ragged look when they'd been bought. Otis had left a belt in a second pair of jeans. She pulled that out and set it with the pile on the sofa.

The third pair of jeans were black and looked fairly new. When she sorted through the pockets, she found a wad of paper. Pulling it out, she could see it was an 8½ x 11 sheet that had been folded into fourths. It was printed from a Web site called Gettysburg in Your Hand. The printout looked like a screen shot. On it there was a list of Gettysburg memorabilia. The list included a Civil War cavalry stirrup and its provenance, a Civil War 1820 large cent, a shadow box simply entitled *Civil War Battlefield Relics*. It went on with a limited-edition Civil War signed print—*The Road to Gettysburg*—as well as a Confederate spherical case shot shell.

The list was interesting. Were these items Barry wanted to buy, or possibly items he wanted to sell? She could check the inventory at Pirated Treasures. Vi had given her a flash drive in case she needed it while Vi was away.

In a matter of minutes, Daisy had retrieved her laptop from her bedroom, fired it up, and loaded the flash drive. An inventory list came up. Daisy scrolled through it carefully. None of the items were the same as those on Barry's list.

Time to turn in another direction. She phoned Jonas. "I know you said you were going out for a beer and to watch a game with a friend tonight."

There was a loud cheer from Jonas's end and Daisy could hear a TV in the background.

"I'm at Bases," he said. "Let me go outside." Bases was a sports bar where fans could enjoy games.

"I don't want to interrupt you."

"I was drinking a beer and watching a game, Daisy. No big deal. Usually I don't have deep conversations about the secrets of the universe when I go out to watch a game."

At that she smiled. "Are you saying women try to do that when they go out?"

"That's my guess. What do you need?"

Daisy told him what she'd been doing and what she'd found.

"I think I know what's coming," he said wryly.

"Can you trace the Web site to the administrator? If we find out who set up the Web site, or even who it belongs to, we might have someone else to question."

"You might be jiggling the nerves of a murderer," Jonas warned her.

"Not if we just find out who set up the Web site."

"I might have to call in a favor from a friend for this. It's beyond my tech skills. But I'll get an answer for you . . . one way or another."

"I hope you can catch up with what happened in the game."

Jonas laughed. "I'm sure that won't be hard to do with constant replays. Instead of catching up with the game, I think I'd rather be kissing you. Date tomorrow night?"

"Absolutely."

"I'll see you then," he said in a husky but sexy voice.

"See you then," she said, smiling. After talking with Jonas, she didn't feel so alone.

Chapter Nineteen

Daisy was closing out the register on Tuesday evening when her phone signaled that a text had come in. She finished what she was doing, glad everything balanced, then plucked her phone from her pocket in her apron. The text was from Jonas. **There's someplace we should go. Can you run an errand after you close up?**

Jazzi peeked over Daisy's shoulder at her phone. Before Daisy could scold her for intruding on her privacy, Jazzi said, "Good. Jonas wants to go somewhere. Can you drop me off at Cassandra's? She has a pool and an extra suit and wants to know if I can go swimming there tonight. Stacy will be there and Cassandra's parents will too. I'm hot, Mom. Night swimming would be great."

After a situation in April, Jazzi had had to win back Daisy's trust. But she'd done a good job of it. Jazzi's request took her back to a time when she and Rachel had gone swimming in the Esh family's pond after dusk—Rachel in her long dress and Daisy in her shorts and top. The Amish didn't believe in air-conditioning. It was a luxury they didn't need and they stayed away from the electrical grid except for business concerns. Those days when Daisy had helped Rachel in their garden, picking tomatoes and squash, cucumbers and peppers, summer had seemed too hot for words. She'd minded it but Rachel hadn't seemed to. Still, after they'd finished for the day, after they'd enjoyed chicken and dumplings, shoofly pie, and cool glasses of sweet tea, Rachel's mom and dad had consented to their going swimming in the pond. That part of her life had slipped by without her appreciating it fully.

"Let me text Jonas back and I'll see what he has in mind," she told Jazzi.

> Where are we going and what time do you want to go?
>
> I can be at the tea garden in fifteen minutes.
>
> Can we drop off Jazzi at a friend's?
>
> No problem. See you soon.

A half hour later Jonas and Daisy dropped off Jazzi at her friend's and Daisy still didn't know where she and Jonas were going.

After Jazzi waved and went through her friend's front door, Daisy asked, "What's up? I figured this errand had to do with the investigation or you would have said something."

"I didn't think you'd want Jazzi involved."

"You're right, I don't."

"I discovered the administrator of that Web site is Ian Busby."

"I expected it to be Barry, but I guess Ian isn't a surprise."

"I think we should visit him or his parents. If we find

anything out, I'll call Zeke. Or maybe you can call Zeke."

"We'll flip a coin," Daisy said sarcastically.

Neither of them wanted to talk to the detective, but if it took that to get this murder solved, then that's what they'd have to do.

They spoke about their day as Jonas drove. He kept his eyes on the road and both hands on the wheel . . . except for those times when he reached over and took Daisy's hand. She liked the physical connection.

When they arrived in the retirement development, Daisy guided Jonas to the Busbys' home. The double garage door was down. No cars were parked in the driveway.

"This could be a wasted trip," Jonas said.

"Maybe, but I figure when three people live in a house, at least one of them should be home."

"Is that optimistic logic?"

She laughed.

In the driveway, Jonas shut off the ignition. "If we think the way you do—that somebody might be home—maybe you should go to the front door and I'll go to the back."

"That sounds like a good idea. One of his parents could be gardening in the backyard."

They exited the vehicle and Daisy went up the walk to the front door. Jonas rounded the corner of the house and headed for the backyard.

Daisy rang the doorbell and waited a good two minutes, but nobody answered. So she rang again.

Maybe Jonas was right and nobody was home. However, just then her phone signaled a text. Plucking it from her skirt pocket, it read, I'm on the back porch with Ian.

So either Ian had been in the backyard or he'd tried to leave by the back door. If so, that meant he didn't want to talk to them.

She hurried around the side of the house and there she found the two men sitting on the small porch with their feet propped on the first step.

"You said you wanted to wait until she was here to ask me questions," Ian said in a disgusted voice. "Let's get them over with."

Jonas glanced at Daisy but then back at Ian. Looking him straight in the eye, he warned, "I can either treat you like a hostile witness or as a friendly one. That's up to you."

"You aren't a lawyer," Ian mumbled, his foot tapping nervously on the step.

"No, just a detective who's used to questioning criminals."

"I'm not a criminal!" Ian protested.

Daisy supposed she was the good cop, so she stepped in. "Ian, we don't want to believe you would hurt Barry."

"I *wouldn't*. I *didn't*."

"Then just talk to us, okay?" Daisy said gently.

After Ian plucked at the material of his denim cut-offs, he agreed. "All right. Ask."

"Why did you quit your job at the Platt farm and leave in the middle of the night?"

Ian scowled. "It wasn't the middle of the night. It was hardly midnight."

"Why did you quit?" Daisy pressed. "I really don't want to believe you killed Barry, but you have to give me a reason to believe that."

"You don't understand." Ian seemed deflated, but yet unwilling to cooperate.

If he didn't want to talk, there was nothing they could do except keep him on their suspect list.

However, Daisy could see Jonas wasn't ready to give up. "I found out that you're the administrator on the Gettysburg in Your Hand Web site."

"So what?" Now Ian sounded like a belligerent sixteen-year-old.

"Did you set up the Web site to sell stolen merchandise?" Jonas pushed.

Since they didn't have any information about it, Daisy supposed Jonas was taking a wild guess, but it was an educated guess.

"We didn't steal anything," Ian maintained. "Not one thing. All of it was merchandise we found or collected and nobody can prove otherwise. Mariah writes up descriptions and prices the items to sell. She can tell you all about it. Maybe you should go talk to her."

"Maybe we should," Daisy agreed. "If this business was on the up-and-up, why did you store items in the root cellar of the cabin?"

That took Ian by surprise. His eyes widened, his mouth opened, then he shrugged. "It seemed a safe place. Some of that stuff was worth a lot. Nobody knew about that trapdoor. How did you find it?"

"Keith Rebert is living there now with his daughter. He was going to replace the linoleum so she'd have a clean surface to play on," Jonas said.

"But how did you know we kept stuff down there?"

"Because you left something behind."

Daisy could see Ian wanted to know what that something was, but he didn't ask and Jonas didn't say.

* * *

In the car again after their little talk with Ian, Jonas asked, "Are you game to talk to another witness—Mariah Goldblum?"

"Why not? Vi's on her honeymoon. Jazzi is swimming. I'm on an investigation date with you."

The corner of his mouth quirked up. "Is that what we're calling this?"

"Sure. There are romantic dates, and then there are investigation dates."

"I see. Does an investigation date also end with a glass of wine at your place?"

"It could," she responded coyly, and realized she was actually flirting.

Jonas reached across to her and ran his knuckles over her cheek. The gesture melted Daisy until, completely disconcerted, she said, "We have to look up Mariah's address." Jonas gave a nod as she moved away to search on her phone.

After she looked up Mariah's address, Jonas tapped it into his GPS. They were on their way.

Daisy didn't travel in the east end of town as much as she did in the west end. There were more individual homes on East Market Street, some from when the town was first established in the late 1800s. For the most part, the grass had been carefully mowed, the hedges seasonally trimmed, and annual flowers planted in the gardens around the house or down the driveway to the road. The medical center was out this way, though Jonas turned off Market Street onto Booker Road to follow the GPS directions.

As they drove past single-family homes, from

brick to clapboard to stone, he asked, "What are you thinking?"

"I'm trying *not* to think."

His brow wrinkled as he kept his foot steady on the accelerator. "That probably means too many thoughts are running through your mind at once."

"And you don't have that problem?" she joked.

"Oh, I do. But even as a patrol cop I learned to compartmentalize. I had to."

"And as a detective?"

"That was a bit different. As a detective, I tried to keep a wall between my personal life and my professional life. But investigating a case, I had to keep my mind on that so ideas could just run rampant and then connect. I have a feeling that's what you do."

Daisy didn't often ask probing questions about Jonas's past. Rather she gave him the opportunity to tell her what he could when he could.

Painful experience didn't usually lead to easy sharing. But now she asked, "How did you keep your professional life separate from your personal life when Brenda was your partner?"

He slowed a bit as they passed a horse and buggy that was traveling in the side lane. Then he sped up again. "That's where I made the mistake," he confessed. "I thought I could keep them separate. But that night when we were ambushed, my senses were half on our surroundings and half with my feelings about what Brenda had told me. She was happy about being pregnant and she wanted me to be happy too. I couldn't be. My dad had been a cop and he'd given his life to it. I never wanted a child that I brought into the world to go through that. Brenda couldn't understand how difficult it would be if I were a dad *and* a detective. My thoughts would never be all on one or the other. Some men could do that, but I didn't think I could."

"What about Brenda? Wouldn't she have remained in law enforcement?"

"We didn't get that far. But from the little we discussed, I think she would have quit in an instant to be a mom. That's why she'd had her IUD removed without telling me. She wanted to be a mom badly."

"With or without you?"

Jonas slowed as his GPS voice told him to turn left in a quarter of a mile onto Axle Road. A row of older ranch-style houses dotted the landscape for at least a half mile.

Finally Jonas answered, "She knew I wouldn't walk away, not from a responsibility like that."

Jonas turned right this time onto Carpenter Road. They passed a two-story edifice that was run down and boarded up. The address they were looking for was next to it—a trailer with a screened room that had been added to the front. A short wall of bricks seemed to identify the property lines while a gravel driveway led to the trailer.

After Jonas switched off the ignition, he studied the domicile. "It looks old but well kept."

Jonas and Daisy exited his SUV at the same time and met on the paving stones that led to the front entrance. At the door to the screened-in room, Jonas nodded to the air conditioner in the window. "It would be hot as blazes in there without that. My guess is it wouldn't be on unless somebody was at home." Jonas nodded toward the driveway. "That probably circles around back. Her car could be parked back there."

In his spirit and soul, Jonas was still a detective. He

couldn't help but notice details. He couldn't help but watch for danger.

They walked up the cement block steps to the porch, and went to the door of the trailer. Daisy knocked.

The sun had gone down and in the darkening porch Daisy leaned closer to Jonas. "I don't know if I'd want to live out here all alone."

The door opened and Mariah stood there, looking surprised. "Daisy, what are you doing here?" Mariah's gaze went to Jonas.

"Hi, Mariah. This is Jonas Groft. He's the owner of Woods . . . down the street from the tea garden."

Mariah nodded. "I've been in the store once or twice. Nice stuff in there. But I sure can't afford it."

Jonas said sympathetically, "Handcrafted furniture is commanding a higher price these days. I guess people want something unique."

"Or they're like me and they pick up furniture at yard sales. Do you want to come in? It's not real cool in here, but cooler than out there."

Daisy and then Jonas climbed the steps into the trailer. In Florida, where Daisy had lived for years, trailers were second homes to snowbirds who traveled south and stayed for the winter. There were whole communities of them. Because of that, she was familiar with the layout of this trailer. The door opened into a small kitchen. Daisy caught sight of a table with four chairs that, refinished, could be quite pretty. She'd done that with her chairs. A small sitting area was to the left and a hall led to maybe two bedrooms and a bath. Mariah had decorated with checkered valances that hung over the windows. The tan loveseat was covered with a flowered throw.

"How can I help you?" Mariah asked once Jonas

and Daisy were inside. She motioned to the chairs at the table. "Have a seat. I have lemonade."

"That sounds good," Jonas said.

Daisy knew he was laying the groundwork for them to be friendly and amiable so Mariah would answer their questions. Daisy couldn't see any reason why they'd have to play good cop–bad cop here, but one never knew.

After Mariah poured lemonade into clear glass tumblers, she joined Jonas and Daisy at the table. "Are you still asking questions about Barry?"

"Keith won't be in the clear until we figure out who did this, or else the police do. Have they questioned you again?" Daisy wanted to know.

"No, they haven't. I wouldn't have been questioned in the first place, but they found a birthday card I'd sent Barry."

Jonas took over. "We discovered that you and Barry and Ian met at Sarah Jane's now and then. You told us you didn't see Ian after you split up."

Mariah turned her glass of lemonade around and around as her face grew red. "What did you do—talk to everybody in town about the three of us?" She was definitely on the defensive.

"No," Jonas answered. "But people remember things, Mariah. Sarah Jane knows her customers. She's observant. She told us the three of you had printouts. What were on those printouts?"

She pushed her hair over her brow and looked defiant. "Is that really any of your business?"

"It is," Daisy said, "if they got Barry killed."

When Mariah didn't comment, Daisy knew that was becoming more of a possibility.

The hum of the air conditioner vibrated through

the close quarters of the kitchen as Jonas told Mariah, "We were with Ian before we came here."

Mariah's gaze popped up to Daisy's. "What did he have to say?"

"If Ian killed Barry, and you were connected in any way, you could be a coconspirator," Daisy warned. She'd picked up the lingo from Jonas and Detective Rappaport.

"I didn't know anything about Barry and Ian's side business."

"What side business was that?" Jonas asked.

"All I know is that Barry didn't sell everything he got through Pirated Treasures."

"Why not?" Daisy held Mariah's gaze.

Mariah shrugged. "I didn't ask questions. Ian had set up a Web site for Barry. Supposedly, whatever Barry earned from it was going to be our nest egg."

"Where did Barry keep the merchandise?"

Again Mariah shrugged. "I think Ian kept it for him in some kind of shed."

Jonas didn't mention the trapdoor. "You never saw it?"

Mariah shook her head. "No. I mean I didn't see it altogether. Once in a while Barry and Ian would show me a piece and I'd write up a description for them. They always said I was better with words than they were."

"How often did you do that for them?"

"Maybe only every couple of weeks."

"One more thing," Jonas added. "How long were Barry and Ian doing this?"

"For about the past year, year and a half. More so as Otis's eyesight got worse. But Barry was going to quit doing it as soon as we were married. He didn't want to sell on the side anymore. He didn't want to feel as if he was cheating Otis."

"How was he going to make up the loss of the extra income?" Jonas asked.

"He was going to ask Otis to make him a partner. He figured once we were married, the two of us could convince Otis, then Barry could expand any way he liked. He really did have all sorts of ideas."

Daisy leaned forward and captured all of Mariah's attention. "Mariah, something got Barry killed. Do you have any idea what that was?"

Mariah shook her head. "Honestly, I don't."

It seemed as if Mariah had loved Barry. It seemed as if they had been planning a future. Someone had wanted to prevent that future from happening.

Daisy realized that Jazzi wasn't home yet when she and Jonas crossed the threshold into her barn home. Pepper and Marjoram both scampered toward them, expecting attention. They'd been alone for a while, and even though there was still dry food in their dishes and plenty of water, Daisy could tell they'd been lonely. Marjoram's meows were all about missing her or Jazzi. Pepper rubbed around Jonas's ankles until he bent and lifted her into his arms. By now, he knew she liked to be scratched under her chin.

"I have a feeling you're going to demand attention the rest of the evening," Jonas said conversationally.

"Or a sardine," Daisy said wryly. "I have a few in a sealed bowl in the refrigerator. If it's not sealed tight that smell goes into all the other food."

As if she understood the word "sardine," Pepper

wriggled in Jonas's arms, asking to be let down. He didn't argue with her but lowered her to the floor. As Daisy walked into the kitchen, both felines ran after her.

Jonas had settled at the island with a glass of sweet tea and Marjoram and Pepper had finished their portions of the sardines when Jazzi came in the front door.

Her daughter crossed to the kitchen and didn't hesitate to join them. Her hair was wet from her swim but she'd clipped it into a knot at her nape.

After she said hi to Jonas, she told her mom, "I had a shower at Cassandra's, so I shouldn't smell like chlorine." She poured herself a glass of the sweet tea. Pulling out a stool, she sat next to Jonas. When she looked pensive, Daisy suspected she had something to say.

Jonas raised his brows at Daisy, but she just shrugged. She never knew what was coming next, not really.

After a few swallows of iced tea, Jazzi hopped up again and went to the cookie jar. She brought it over to the table and removed the lid. "Oatmeal raisin," she told Jonas. "At least they're partially good for us."

Chuckling, he pulled out a cookie too.

Daisy waited.

Jazzi munched on the edge of her cookie, not as if she was really hungry. Then she set it on the island in front of her. "Mom, you know Cassandra."

"I do. Not as well as Stacy. But she seems as if she'd be a good friend."

Jazzi nodded. "She is. I've gotten to know her better over the summer."

Daisy knew Jazzi was headed somewhere. "Did you enjoy your swim?"

"Yeah, it was great. But what was even better was that Cassandra and I talked."

"About?"

"You know her mom's divorced, right?"

"I heard that." Maybe Jazzi and Cassandra had empathized about not having dads around.

"She was upset because her dad remarried. She doesn't like her stepmom."

"Maybe she needs time to get to know her," Daisy suggested.

"That's what I told her. But I think she was set to dislike her from the beginning. You know, she didn't want anybody taking her mom's place."

"I can see that."

Wisely Jonas munched on his cookie and listened.

Jazzi took another swallow of her tea, tucked a few strands of her hair into the knot at her nape, then looked up at Daisy. "I think Colton has his mind set against me. I think he thinks I'm going to ruin his family."

Daisy was stymied on how to respond to that one, but Jonas said, "Jazzi, you can't know that."

"No, I can't. But I was thinking. What if Portia invited me to her house for a weekend? I relate to kids really well. If Colton could see me with Portia and his own kids and understand I don't want to ruin anything, maybe he could get to know me and I could get to know him."

Daisy hurt for Jazzi. She knew her daughter wanted a connection with her birth mother that had already started growing. But Portia's husband could be a barrier to that. Could Jazzi's idea work?

"What are you thinking, Jazzi? How would you go about this?" She tried to let her daughters problem-solve whenever she could.

"This time I might need your help. Could you call Portia and suggest it? Labor Day weekend would be perfect."

"Are you prepared for an answer you might not want to hear?"

"I am," Jazzi insisted. "I feel like I have to try. Don't you think I have to try, Mom?"

Daisy so admired her younger daughter, and she was equally grateful that Jazzi felt she could talk about this with Jonas present. Then again, he'd made her relationship with Portia possible. "I'll call Portia and see what she says. She might have to think about it."

"I'm okay with that. And if not Labor Day, maybe some other time. But I'm hoping it's a possibility."

Daisy's daughters helped her realize that anything could be a possibility. She was grateful for that too.

Chapter Twenty

Sitting in her car outside Willow Creek High School early the next evening, Daisy watched Jazzi walk in. Her daughter had a planning meeting before school started to develop a program in peer counseling. It would connect sophomores and juniors with freshmen to help them feel more welcome. Daisy knew the group was planning a breakfast for the morning of freshman orientation. Stacy's mom had told Jazzi that she'd take her home. Daisy was hoping this evening would take Jazzi's mind off everything else, especially Portia and Colton.

After her conversation with Jazzi about Jazzi visiting Portia for a weekend, Daisy had called Portia. Portia hadn't seemed that enthusiastic. She'd told Daisy she would think about it and talk with Colton. As of now, Daisy didn't have much hope that the weekend would be scheduled, and neither did Jazzi. So anything that kept Jazzi's mind on kids her own age was good.

Daisy hadn't had much time to take a breath all day. Their busy season still had a few more weeks.

As she put the car in gear and drove away from the high school, she thought about the past week—Vi and

Foster's wedding, their reception, as well as what she'd said to her mother. All of that had been on her mind. She should call her mom and find a time to talk. Yet would it do any good? Years of hurt couldn't be resolved in a conversation. If her mother ran true to form, she'd have excuses or she would deny how Daisy felt. That was the way it usually went.

Nevertheless, Daisy wanted to make peace with her mom in some way. She'd hoped she'd see Jonas tonight, but he was working on replacing inventory he'd sold. He had scheduled an appointment in Marietta to check out bargains on granite and quartz slabs. He would be able to use those on reclaimed wood islands. Daisy had seen one of them and it was beautiful.

She speculated about going home, staying cool, cuddling with her cats, and reading a good book. But she was still wired from the busy day. She might not be able to solve anything with her mom with a conversation, but she had an idea that might provide more clues to Barry's murder. She'd need Keith's help. Nothing to lose by calling.

"Hi, Daisy," he answered. "Anything wrong?"

"No, I'm just feeling a bit edgy. Did you pick up Mandy from day care?"

"No, I didn't. Karina picked her up and took her and Quinn to the park for a while. Some days Mandy just seems to need to run free after being cooped up."

"Oh, I understand that. I remember when Vi first went to school. Her teachers told me she was a model child. When she came home, she needed to release energy or she'd act out. We thought we had a Dr. Jekyll and Mr. Hyde, or maybe Dr. Jekyll and Miss Hyde, but you get the idea."

Keith laughed. "Yes, I do. When I pick up Mandy,

we go for a walk before we settle down to dinner. Karina's going to bring dinner along with the girls."

"Oh, I don't want to interrupt anything."

"What do you have in mind? I'm sure they'll be at the park for an hour, maybe even an hour and a half. I haven't gotten a swing for the yard yet, and Mandy loves to swing."

"This shouldn't take much time," Daisy assured him. "I just thought that maybe we should have another look at the root cellar."

"Do you think the detective missed something?"

"You never know. I'd like to look at the shelves more closely and find out if what's in those jars is actually what it's supposed to be. I didn't really go through the picture frames well, but there were a lot of them. What if something else fell down between them?"

"Is Jonas coming with you?"

"No, he had an appointment tonight. We're not going to do anything dangerous. Are you free now? If you are, I'll drive out to your place. We should be done before Karina arrives."

"That sounds good. And you can join us for dinner if you don't have other commitments."

An evening with Keith, Karina, and their girls sounded like just what she needed.

When Daisy arrived at Keith's cabin, he let her inside. "Anytime Mandy's not here, I don't turn on the air conditioner in her room, so I doubt if you'll want to sit inside. I have an idea, though, before we check the root cellar."

Daisy set her purse on the small counter. "What's your idea?"

"I wonder if it's possible that Barry and Ian kept

some of their merchandise here, but not in the root cellar."

Daisy remembered what Mariah had said about a shed. "If they had any bigger pieces that would make sense."

"There's an old barn beside the one Clovis uses for livestock. I've never had a need to go inside that or a run-down shed next to it. I'm always in the main barn. It has a tool room."

Daisy frowned. "I doubt if the Platts would want us looking around the property."

"Truthfully, I don't think they'd mind. I've never seen anything unusual, but another eye might help. It just so happens Clovis and Penelope drove off about a half hour ago. They said something about Root's Country Market. Do you know anything about it?"

"Sure, it's about a half hour from here. They have auctions for livestock, plants, household goods, and a flea market. If the Platts are there, I doubt they'll be back anytime soon."

"Then it's a good time to look around," Keith said. "Let's go."

Daisy followed Keith to the shed first. There they found mostly antique tools that looked as if they hadn't been used for decades. They moved a couple around but didn't find anything of interest.

A few minutes later in the older barn, Daisy was surprised to see an old pop-up style camper. It had scratches and scrapes, and Daisy wondered if it still popped up to reveal sleeping units and a tiny kitchen and table. She and Ryan had purchased one when the girls were little. Driving it around Florida to the beaches was more economical than taking full-fledged vacations. They'd sold theirs when school and sports had taken up most of Vi's and Jazzi's time. This one looked like a pop-up for two. When Penelope and Clovis were younger, maybe they'd hitched it to their pickup truck and driven it to campgrounds.

"Let's really check this place out," Keith said. "It's the biggest area with the most places to hide things. I'll go up to the hayloft and see what's there."

While Keith did that, Daisy circled the perimeter of the barn. Tarps and a few pieces of canvas lay strewn in one corner. She picked them up one by one and smelled the mustiness and possibly mold that had grown on them while they'd lain there. There were cobwebs everywhere and dust and rain had filmed over the high windows. License plates hung on the wall along with a YIELD sign that looked authentic. For some reason, a voice inside Daisy's head directed her to take shots of the wall. She did.

Keith had come down from the hayloft by then. He pointed to a riding mower that appeared to have seen better days. "Clovis has never recommended that I use that one, so I assume it doesn't work. The same with that push mower over there. There's one in the big barn that's self-propelled. I use that where I can't mow with the John Deere tractor."

Daisy pointed to a wagon-type trailer. "They might use that with the truck."

"Possibly." Keith went to the feed bins, lifted the lids to peer inside. "There's about an inch of old grain here. It smells bad. Maybe they used these bins when they had horses. Clovis told me they used to have three, but the vet bills and the upkeep got to be too much. Neither of them ride anymore."

Daisy opened the side barn door that they had shut when they'd come in. She peered out and still didn't see Clovis and Penelope's black pickup truck. Good thing. Daisy pointed around the barn, watching the dust motes floating in the sunshine. "If Barry and Ian did keep anything in here, their merchandise is long gone."

"All right," Keith agreed. "That leaves the root cellar. Let's take another look. At least it's cooler down there than in the cabin," he said with a grin.

Daisy remembered how she'd felt a bit claustrophobic in that cellar before, but she'd asked Keith to be her sleuth buddy. She wasn't going to back out now. By the time they returned to the cabin, she'd shored up her courage.

They stood in the kitchen area staring at the linoleum. Keith asked Daisy, "Are you sure you want to do this?"

"I'm not keen on going down into a hole with no decent outlet, but I'll survive. I think we have to do this, for your sake and Otis's."

With a quick nod of assent, Keith crouched down, took the edge of the linoleum, and rolled it toward the opposite wall. After he lifted the handle and the wooden door that led to the underground cellar, he asked Daisy, "Do you want to go first or do you want me to go first?"

"I'll go," she said, "if you shine the flashlight down there."

"No problem. Once we're down, I can turn on the lantern. I left it there."

Daisy managed to gingerly step onto the first rung. Keith held her hand until she stepped down a few more rungs and could hold on to the top of the ladder. He kept the flashlight steady, lighting her way.

Once she was on the ground, she shuffled over to

the lantern and switched it on. Before, when she'd been down here, she'd been concerned about spiders or mice. She hadn't seen any evidence of either. The damp dankness surrounded her and she felt a shiver run up her spine. Yet she told herself Keith would be down here soon and they could just take a quick look around. They'd be back in the cabin before she had time to get claustrophobic or anxious.

Keith descended the ladder swiftly, still holding the flashlight. Even though the lantern glowed, he shined the flashlight around. They started searching at the right-hand corner. She carried the lantern while he used the flashlight. They circulated slowly, hoping they didn't miss anything. As time ticked by, they stepped behind the ladder and continued around the other side. She knew this was probably a waste of time. After all, if there was something to find, Zeke would have found it, right?

Except . . . Zeke hadn't spent much time down here. Scanning the shelves with the jarred goods, almost to herself she murmured, "I wonder if Zeke moved these around."

"I think Detective Willet was only interested in what we found and not anything else."

Studying the jars, Daisy could see the film of dust on top of the lids. She moved one to the right and noticed from the drag marks that someone else had done the same. The shelves were high, almost reaching to the ceiling. They were about as wide as the back wall.

"I don't want to be down here any longer than we have to be, but if we want to be thorough, we should take everything off the shelves and look behind the jars," she advised.

"We probably should," Keith agreed. "I'll remove

the jars on the left while you remove the ones on the right. We can set them against the wall so none of them break."

"Jarred goods can last a long time. Did you ever ask Penelope who put them here?"

"No, I didn't. I assumed whoever lived here before Ian did it."

Daisy knew you couldn't assume anything. She remembered what she'd seen in the shed and the barn. She looked again at the multitude of canned beets, chow-chow, pickles, even meat. There were jars of jam too—strawberry, raspberry, and peach. Those jars were smaller than the others. Could all of this have been prepared in that small kitchen in the cabin? What if . . . ?

She didn't get a chance to finish the thought.

Keith said, "Look! I wonder why this back wall is brick."

Daisy hadn't noticed that before because the lantern was on the ground and Keith had kept his flashlight low too. But now they peered at the wall as they finished taking the jars off the shelves. Daisy froze when she looked in back of the fourth shelf from the bottom. "Look."

Keith bent to peer at the back. Daisy had found a low arched door hardly big enough to crawl through.

Keith said, "That's it. I'm moving the shelves." He did so without much trouble because they hadn't sunk into the ground floor. Daisy wondered if that meant they'd been moved often. As she studied the floor more carefully, she spotted faint tracks.

An old-fashioned wooden latch kept the door closed. A hole drilled into the wooden bar was empty. For a padlock?

Daisy lifted the bar and swung the door inside. For some reason when she opened that door, an odd feeling encompassed her, as if she was stepping back in time.

She glanced back at Keith. Had he really not explored down here on his own? What if she went through that door first and he closed it behind her?

Fear trembled through her and a terrible doubt assaulted her. Could Keith be Barry's killer?

When she studied his face, she saw that he appeared to be as amazed as she felt. She took the risk of crawling through the opening. Inside, she could just stand up. The inner room was smaller than the outer space—a hole in the ground about four by six feet. However, unlike the root cellar, it was bricked up the whole way around to the ceiling. Daisy's history lessons about Lancaster County and the Underground Railroad came back to her.

"This must have been one of the stations on the Underground Railroad." She continued looking around the hidden room with its brick walls.

"I don't know much about it," Keith said, "though I know it was prevalent in this area along the Susquehanna River."

"Exactly. It was also known as the Freedom Line or the Freedom Train. Some historians estimate that fifty thousand to a hundred thousand fugitive slaves used the chain of stations to find a new life. Anyone who helped them find freedom through providing safe houses could be imprisoned or fined because of the Fugitive Slave Law. The law was tested in the town of Christiana, not far from here."

"The country was so divided," Keith murmured, studying the confining room.

"Abolitionists denied the law, believing it was contrary to basic human rights. They saved the slaves from the Southern bounty hunters called the Gap Gang," Daisy added.

"I can tell you were a scholar," Keith offered with a smile.

"I had to prove I had smarts as well as blond hair," Daisy quipped. "But I was reminded of this area's history last year when Jazzi did a project on the subject."

Running his hand over the wall, Keith asked, "So you think this room dates back to around the 1850s?"

Daisy nodded. "Probably so."

"How many people could have hidden in here— eight, nine, ten? Anyone running for their life wouldn't care about the space they had to stay in until they could head for freedom."

They were both thinking about that when Daisy heard a noise in the root cellar and froze. She tapped Keith's arm and nodded her head that way. He listened too. Maybe it was a rodent of some kind that had gotten down there. Maybe it was her nerves and no noise at all.

Keith looked puzzled until, all of a sudden, Penelope Platt pushed through the opening. She obviously wasn't there out of curiosity because . . . she was holding a shotgun!

Keith backed away from her, his hands raised.

"You couldn't mind your own business, could you?" the older woman asked.

Fear tightened Daisy's throat as panic squeezed her chest. She'd never had a panic attack before, and she doubted that this was a good time to have her first. However, she was truly scared because she had no idea what Penelope had in mind.

Daisy was still carrying the lantern. As she backed up, so did Keith. Penelope held the gun as if she knew how to use it.

They were all inside the inner room now. Penelope snapped, "Just why did you come down here? Did you think you were going to find gold?"

Daisy's voice seemed buried in her chest. She was glad when Keith answered, "Not gold. Something to help the police find the murderer. It looks like we found her."

Daisy cleared her throat since that seemed to be all she could accomplish. The last thing she wanted to do was to upset Penelope further. Who knew what crazy thoughts were running through the older woman's head? Maybe this didn't have anything to do with Barry at all.

Daisy knew she had to straighten up and get a grip. She suspected what Penelope was going to do one way or another. Daisy thought about her parents and her sister, her daughters, and Jonas. She never thought trying to help the police would end up this way. But when she saw that camper and those license plates in the barn, she should have suspected that the Platts were involved.

If she was going to die down here, she wanted answers to her questions. "Barry and Ian hid their merchandise in here, didn't they?" she guessed.

"I suppose they were the brains behind this organization," Keith taunted.

That was one way to get answers, but Daisy didn't know if it was the *best* way.

"You want answers before I kill you, is that it?"

Daisy's mind searched for anything that she could do . . . anything that would help them. She took a step behind Keith into the corner as if she were afraid of Penelope's gun. Keith threw her a sideways glance and she hoped he realized she was up to something.

"So the shotgun makes you a little weak-kneed, does it?" Penelope asked as if she were glad of that idea.

Daisy just nodded.

"I found out what Barry was doing," Penelope muttered. "One day when Ian was gone from the cabin, I checked the root cellar. Of course, I knew about it. I know about every hole and bend on this farm."

"What made you suspicious?" Keith inquired as if his mind were functioning normally.

"Barry was out here all the time, so I knew he and Ian were up to something. Two men that age don't hang around unless something is here. They must have brought the merchandise in in the dead of night because I never saw it. If I hadn't gone snooping, they would have gotten away with what they were doing."

"And what were they doing?" Daisy asked, her voice so strained she didn't know if Penelope could hear her.

The older woman must have deciphered Daisy's question because she answered, "Barry was stealing from his uncle, then he sold the merchandise online for cash or to black market buyers. It depended if it was valuable enough. I lived around here long enough to know exactly what's valuable and what isn't. I must say Barry had a good eye. I think Ian just provided the manpower."

Daisy lowered the lantern by her foot and the solidness of it gave her hope. She had her phone in her pocket, but she doubted if she'd have a signal down here. Maybe there was no signal to call out, but she *could* record their conversation. If they ever did get out of here, she'd have proof of whatever Penelope told her. Now she just had to find the RECORD icon.

The important thing was to keep Penelope interacting with them as long as possible. Apparently on the same wavelength, Keith asked the older woman, "So how did you get involved?"

"After I found the antiques and memorabilia, I waited until Barry was here with Ian. Then I just marched over here and told them I wanted a cut. Clovis and I can hardly make ends meet. The boys had a little conference, then they told me they could give me a ten percent cut. Ten percent. They were on *my* property, using *my* storage area. I wanted fifteen percent. They agreed."

If Daisy didn't do something now, she wouldn't be able to record any of this. Suddenly she let out a gasp and sunk to the ground near the lantern. "I'm feeling faint," she breathed. "Not enough air."

"Don't matter if you can breathe or not. Pretty soon you won't be breathing at all."

Penelope pointed the gun at Daisy. "You might as well stay on the floor, darlin'. You're going to be down there dead anyway." The next second, Penelope returned her attention to Keith. Daisy managed to look down and find the RECORD icon on her phone. Pressing it, she bent over as if to put her head between her knees.

"I'm going to see if she's all right," Keith told Penelope, to warn her he was going to move. Then he crouched down beside Daisy.

Daisy murmured, "Just keep asking her questions."

"What was *that?*" Penelope asked.

"She said she thinks she's going to be sick," Keith explained. Keith rubbed Daisy's shoulders as if he was helping her, and then he straightened again. "So you and your husband planned to kill Barry?"

"Clovis knew nothing about any of this. He's clueless. I've been stowing the money away in a hidey-hole of my own. But I might take Clovis along tonight to enjoy it with me."

All Penelope had to do was to switch those license plates on her truck and camper, and she and Clovis would have time to get away. Did Clovis really know nothing about this?

Daisy raised her head as if she was feeling better. She kept her voice weak as she asked, "So you planned to kill Barry?"

Penelope vehemently shook her head. "No planning there. Barry was going to stop his side of the business because he didn't want to steal from his uncle anymore. He met with his dad or something. He called me to Pirated Treasures that night to tell me. After that, he decided he wanted to be a partner with his uncle and go straight. He wanted to get married and not turn out like his dad. I couldn't let him do that. That rolling pin was just sitting there. I'm strong. A farmer's wife has to be strong. I got so mad I just picked it up and whacked him. I wiped off the handle where I held it. It was a bonus that your fingerprints were on it," she said, pointing the gun practically in Keith's face.

Then she took a step back. When she did, Daisy didn't like the look on her face. "I could shoot the two of you, but I don't like blood. It will be so much easier just to lock you in here and let you die."

Keith lunged for her, but Penelope whacked him on the side of the head with her gun, scooted out, and closed them inside.

The silence was cold and horrifying. The dankness of the room was claustrophobic. Daisy again pictured her daughters, Jonas and Foster, her mom and dad, Camellia and Iris. She thought about dying here with Keith.

Before she did, she'd record a message for them and tell them all how much she loved them.

Chapter Twenty-One

The silence inside the inner room was almost as suffocating as the damp, closed-in space. Daisy shivered from fear and trembled from the thought that she and Keith might never be found. She was sure Penelope would be putting the shelf and jars right back where they'd been . . . in front of the hidden door. And she'd surely roll the linoleum back over the trapdoor upstairs.

"Keith," she said, going to him.

He shook his head and she heard him groan. But he said, "I'm okay. She pushed me more than hit me."

Climbing to his knees, Keith tried with all his might to open the small door. It budged a fraction of an inch but no more. Penelope must have secured it somehow.

Sitting on the dirt floor, her head propped on her palms, Daisy felt Keith's hand on her shoulder. "Daisy, come on. We're going to get out of this. We have to. I can't leave Mandy alone, and you can't leave your family."

Daisy had been involved in life and death situations before, but she'd never run out of hope. What was wrong this time? That was the problem . . . *this* time.

Why did she keep putting herself into these situations? And this time, she'd been stressed out before she'd come down into this cellar. Maybe this situation had just been one too many stresses.

"I have to fix things with my mom," she said, suddenly getting to her feet.

"Fix what?"

"I made her feel bad because she'd made me feel bad. It wasn't fair."

"You're always the perfect daughter?"

"I've always tried to be."

"Daisy, if Mandy told me she hated me—and she might do that when she's a teenager—I'd still love her. Don't think the worst thoughts down here. We have to think the best. We need a plan." He checked his watch, which lit up in the dark. "Karina should be bringing Mandy home soon. My worst fear is that Penelope will try to stop her."

"I don't think Penelope is going to bother with Karina. My guess is she'll take all the money she made, hitch up that camper with Clovis, and make for the highway. I have a photo of license plates they might use. That won't do us any good if we can't get out of here. Even if Karina comes in upstairs with Mandy, we can't yell loud enough for her to hear us."

"Yelling might not do it, but we'll have to think of something else." He shone the flashlight around the small space and laid it down. Frantically, he yanked on the door handle again.

Daisy felt each beat of her heart as her mind raced. At least she was thinking now instead of fearing. She suddenly realized she had her phone. No, they didn't have a cell signal, but her battery was charged and she had ringtones. If she turned up the volume on her phone and played the tuba ringtone, Karina could maybe hear it from upstairs. Was that even possible?

She told Keith her plan.

"What if the tuba doesn't work?" he asked.

"We'll go through all the ringtones. Karina should hear something. But if she hears the tuba, she'll recognize it as mine."

Daisy hesitated, then added in a lower voice, "If she goes with Mandy into her bedroom and turns on the air conditioner, she might not hear anything."

"Eventually she'll come into the kitchen. Eventually your family's going to be looking for you," Keith offered hopefully. "We'll get out of this, Daisy. But for now we can't waste the phone's charge. We'll have to listen for Karina's car."

"If we can't hear the car, we might feel the vibrations or at least their footsteps up above."

So they waited.

Time passed as slowly as time does when desperation and hope float in the air. Daisy tried to clear her mind of black thoughts and settle hopeful ones in their place. She and Keith attempted to keep conversation going for a while as they talked about the homeless shelter. Keith expressed interest in getting involved. Daisy hoped that meant he'd make Willow Creek his permanent home.

Suddenly Daisy heard something, though she didn't know what it was. Maybe she didn't hear it. Maybe she *felt* it. She nudged Keith.

"Karina could be parking right above us," Keith almost whispered.

Daisy had been right about hearing footsteps. Not those from outside on the porch. But once Karina and

Mandy were inside, their steps echoed from above even into the secret room.

"How are we able to hear them?" Daisy asked, pulling out her phone.

"Sound travels any way it can. It might not be able to make its way through ground so easily, but it can travel along wood beams or metal ones."

Daisy set up her phone to play with its tuba ringtone. Keith stayed her hand. "Thank goodness Karina wears those clogs. You can hear them anywhere. Let's wait until they're close. Mandy always wants a snack, so they should head for the kitchen cupboards first."

"Quinn's the same way," Daisy murmured. "When Karina's at the cupboard, she'll be practically above the root cellar. I still don't know if it will help us."

Listening so intently that Daisy felt she could hear every beat of her heart in her ears, she waited for a board creak, a floor groaning, a clump of a shoe . . . possibly even a child's laughter.

Keith became animated. "Those are Karina's clogs. Play your phone."

Daisy did, the volume turned up so high she and Keith both wanted to cover their ears. She tapped the icon over and over and over again until she knew she'd dream of tubas playing if she ever found sound sleep again.

Did she hear Karina's voice? Was she calling Daisy's name? Maybe it was an auditory hallucination.

"In here," Keith began yelling. He pounded on their side of the door. "In here. Behind the shelves," he shouted.

Daisy played that tuba again . . . and again . . . and again. Keith continued to pound on the door and then pound some more.

"Wait," Daisy ordered, catching his arm. "Stop."

Now it sounded as if Karina were pounding on her side of the door. Daisy made out a word—*"Help."* Was Karina going for help?

"I think she mentioned Mandy's and Quinn's names," Keith said. "My guess is, she doesn't want to bring them down into the cellar, and she doesn't want to leave them upstairs alone. She's probably calling for help."

And just who would Karina call?

Fifteen minutes later Daisy found out. When she and Keith heard noises from the other side of the door, they pounded on their side. Daisy heard metal against metal, a final clang, and then the door was pushed open.

Jonas grabbed for Daisy, wrapped his arm around her, and pulled her out into the root cellar. She wrapped her arms around his neck and held on tight.

Finally, when her shaking died down to a tremble, he lifted his head. His eyes stayed glued on hers. "Someone had put a padlock on the door. I used a crowbar to break it open."

Behind Jonas a deep male voice asked, "Who did this to you?"

Daisy recognized Zeke's voice. "Penelope Platt," Daisy explained in a long breath. "She probably left in a truck with a camper. I have photos of the license plates." She pulled her phone from her pocket and handed it to Zeke. "I recorded her confession on there too."

Zeke's eyes widened and he looked speechless.

Keith had already scrambled up the ladder. From up above, holding his daughter in his arms, he suggested, "Daisy needs fresh air. She can answer your questions up here."

Keith was right, she did need fresh air. But even more than fresh air . . .

Jonas must have been thinking the same thing she was because he took her into his arms again and held her close.

Epilogue

Labor Day weekend had made its appearance with cooler temperatures in the seventies and a breeze that could tickle a few leaves from the trees. Remnants of summer remained but fall was on the way.

Daisy knew everyone she'd invited to the house tonight was excited. She definitely had a full house. She'd included her parents, and even though this was a busy weekend for the nursery, they'd agreed to come. Feelings were still tense between her and her mother, but she hoped that time rather than confrontation could heal. She knew she and her mom would have to sit down at some point, but now simply didn't seem the right time.

Although Daisy had extended an invitation to her sister, Camellia had said she couldn't get away this weekend. Couldn't? Or wouldn't? Daisy didn't know whether to be hurt or thankful. Having Camellia here would have definitely increased the tension between Daisy and her mom.

Jonas made the last adjustment on the DVR that was hooked up to the TV. He and Gavin had set up folding chairs in Daisy's living room so everyone would have a seat. Gavin's kids seemed as excited as everyone else.

Leaning against the edge of the sofa, Daisy turned toward the dining area when her aunt approached her.

Iris pointed to the dining room table. "All the food's set up."

"You and Mom made enough for an army."

"This is a celebration," her aunt reminded her.

Yes, it certainly was.

Foster and Vi were seated on the sofa holding hands. Jazzi and Gavin's son, Ben, were beside them. Gavin's daughter, Emily, sat on a folding chair while Daisy's mom relaxed in one armchair and her father in another. Keith held Mandy on his lap while Karina held Quinn.

Jonas came to stand beside Daisy and murmured in her ear, "Do you want to sit?" There were two folding chairs left.

"No, I'm good. Everyone will probably want to watch it more than once, and I can make sure the tea is prepared and the drinks are set up."

He moved closer to her. "I'll stand here with you." When he wrapped his arm around her waist, she leaned against him.

Jonas said to Foster, "You have the remote. Whenever you're ready."

Daisy had dimmed the wagon-wheel chandelier light in the living room and everyone gazed at the TV.

Soon there was a sound like a *whoosh, whoosh, whoosh* along with the recording of the ultrasound of Vi and Foster's baby. This was the latest one and Vi and Foster had decided to make it public. At twenty-six weeks now, the couple wanted to share their happiness and excitement.

Vi couldn't contain herself. She announced, "We're having a boy!" She hopped up from the sofa and went to the TV and pointed to an outline. "There's our baby's head. Look at those little arms and feet. And"—her voice broke—"just listen to that heartbeat."

They all did. Daisy had been correct in her estimation that everyone would want to watch it all over again. They did. When she turned up the light, she saw tears in her mom's and dad's eyes. Hers were a little misty too. Vi had gone back to the sofa and Foster had his arm wrapped around her.

"Go ahead and watch it again if you want," Jonas said. "We'll make sure the potpie's warmed just right, the chicken soup's ready to dip, and the fry pies are warmed a little."

There was much more food than Jonas had mentioned, including hot slaw with sweet and sour creamy dressing, pork chops with cranberry sauce, and shoofly pie to accompany the fruit fry pies.

Iris had already slipped from her chair and was at the table making sure the dishes and serving plates were arranged just so. While Daisy joined her aunt, Jazzi took Mandy and Quinn into Daisy's bedroom to play with blocks and art supplies so they wouldn't be bored.

Keith came over to the table too. "This looks wonderful."

Daisy glanced around the table at all the food. "I'm sure we'll have plenty of leftovers. Would you like to take some home to share with Clovis? I'll make sure Otis gets desserts and chicken soup."

"That would be wonderful. Clovis is really down in the dumps," Keith explained. "He had no idea what Penelope was doing, and I feel so sorry for him. Fortunately, when she asked him to go with her, he was smart and chose not to. Since he told the police where she might be headed—a campground in West Virginia where they'd often stayed when they were younger—they aren't charging him with anything. I've had many long talks with him and he really had no idea what was packed in that root cellar. He'd even forgotten the cellar existed. He'll be the first to admit his memory isn't what it used to be."

"Are you going to keep living there?" Iris asked.

"I think I will. He needs somebody on the property. But I don't know how long that will be because I think he's considering selling."

"Where would he go?" Jonas asked.

"He said he has a brother and sister-in-law in Ohio. He's thinking about moving closer to them."

"Penelope was arraigned pretty quickly," Iris said.

Jonas added, "Since she confessed and Daisy had her dead to rights on her phone with a confession, she'll be spending the rest of her life in prison with all the charges against her."

They were all thoughtful for a moment, but then Keith said, "I have some good news. Otis is hiring me to manage his store." He motioned toward the sofa. "I'll be working with Violet, and if things go well, I might become the partner that Otis never had."

Daisy went around the table and gave Keith a hug. "That's wonderful. I'm so glad you drove through Willow Creek and decided to stay."

Daisy happened to glance over Keith's shoulder and

saw her mom watching her. Instead of a frown, her mom nodded and gave her a little smile as if she understood now why Daisy and Jonas had wanted to help Keith and his daughter.

Jonas must have noticed too because when he stepped into the kitchen area with Daisy to make sure the water was ready in the tea urn, he asked, "Is that approval on your mom's face?"

"It could be. Wouldn't that be something?"

Jonas nodded and circled his arms around her in spite of the company. "You know I always disliked that tuba sound on your phone because it seemed like such an intrusion. Now it's my favorite sound. It saved your life."

"Are you admitting I have a few quirks that bother you?"

His wry smile said he owed her honesty. "A few, like your penchant for helping people. That always lands you in trouble. But I suppose I have a few quirks too."

She lowered her voice. "I don't think you want me to name them here."

His green eyes twinkled. "That many, huh? How about just one."

"Sometimes you put ketchup on your potpie."

His expression was so disconcerted that she laughed out loud . . . and then so did he. Maybe times were changing . . . for everyone.

She was sure of it when even with as many guests circulating in the living room, he tugged her to the most private corner of the kitchen . . . and kissed her.

ORIGINAL RECIPES

Sour Cream Cucumber Salad

4 cups sliced cucumbers
½ cup sliced sweet onions or scallions
8 ounces sour cream
2 tablespoons white vinegar
1 tablespoon granulated sugar
⅛ teaspoon sea salt
⅛ teaspoon black pepper
2 teaspoons dill

Stir cucumbers and onions together. In a separate bowl, whisk together sour cream, white vinegar, sugar, salt, and pepper. Sprinkle in dill and stir. Fold into cucumbers and onion mixture.

Refrigerate until serving.

Makes 6 side servings.

CHICKEN SOUP

1 split chicken breast (with bones)
6 cups of water
1 can of chicken broth (14.5 ounces)
4 Wyler's chicken bouillon cubes
½ cup chopped onion
1 cup sliced carrots
½ cup celery
1 cup corn
½ teaspoon salt
⅛ teaspoon pepper
1 bay leaf
½ cup peas
1 cup fine egg noodles

In a soup pot, add chicken, water, chicken broth, bouillon cubes, onion, carrots, celery, corn, salt, and pepper. Add bay leaf. Bring to a boil, cover, and lower temperature to low/simmer. Cook 1½ hours until chicken pulls freely from bone. Remove chicken from pot. Debone and cut into small pieces. Return chicken to pot and stir into broth. Bring to a boil and add peas and noodles. Boil another 8 minutes or until noodles are desired tenderness.

Serve with your favorite sandwich or garden salad.

Serves 6 to 8.

CHERRY TARTS

Shells
4 ounces softened cream cheese
½ cup softened butter
¼ cup shaved almonds
1 tablespoon orange zest (from orange rind)
1½ cups flour

Cream butter and cream cheese with mixer. Pour in almonds and orange zest. Add flour ¼ cup at a time. Divide dough into 6 balls. Roll each ball to form a crust large enough to cover bottom and sides of each tart pan. I use 6 tart pans (4 inches wide).

Surprise Layer
8 ounces softened cream cheese
1 egg
½ cup granulated sugar
1 teaspoon vanilla
1 tablespoon lemon juice

Mix ingredients together with mixer until smooth. Pour into each tart shell.

Filling
1 can (21 ounces) Lucky Leaf Premium Cherry Fruit Filling and Topping
1 teaspoon almond extract

In a bowl, mix almond extract with pie filling. Spoon cherry filling on top of cream cheese filling in each tart pan.

Bake all six tart pans at 350 degrees for 40 minutes.

Grab These Cozy Mysteries
from
Kensington Books

Follow P.I. Savannah Reid
with
G.A. McKevett